The Good Life Part 2:

The Re-up

The Good Life Part 2:

The Re-up

Dorian Sykes

www.urbanbooks.net

Urban Books, LLC
300 Farmingdale Road, N.Y.-Route 109
Farmingdale, NY 11735

The Good Life Part 2: The Re-up

ISBN 13: 978-1-64556-166-8
ISBN 10: 1-64556-166-6

First Trade Paperback Printing April 2021
Printed in the United States of America

10 9 8 7 6 5 4 3 2 1

Distributed by Kensington Publishing Corp.
Submit Orders to:
Customer Service
400 Hahn Road
Westminster, MD 21157-4627
Phone: 1-800-733-3000
Fax: 1-800-659-2436

Recap

The butterflies in Wink's stomach returned at the sight of the man coming his way. It was the first time he'd seen him in person, but his light skin and kufi looked just like the pictures he'd seen. Wink slowly stood up to greet the man he'd longed to meet all his life. His father hadn't aged a day. His skin was clear, as were his eyes. His chest bulged from under a khaki shirt. The oil he was wearing masked the smell of the prison they were meeting in.

Wayne Sr. pulled back a million-dollar smile and opened his arms. Wink gave him a brief hug, which seemed to last forever. For that short moment, Wink felt something he had never before felt in his life except when hugging his mom: love.

"Thanks for coming," said Wayne Sr. as he stood back and checked Wink out.

"I had to," said Wink. He cleared his throat to hide that he was getting emotional.

"Let's have a seat." His father waved to the chairs in front of them.

"Can I get you anything out of the vending machine?" asked Wink. He was so nervous his hands were shaking and the hairs on his body stood up.

"No, I'm okay." Wayne Sr. held his hand up. "I'll eat something when I get back to the block. That stuff's bad for you anyway." He grimaced.

There was an awkward moment of silence until Wayne Sr. noticed the gold-nugget bracelet dangling from Wink's wrist.

"Ah, man. That bracelet brings back so many old memories. Who gave it to you, your mom?" He leaned forward to inspect the diamonds. "The stones are still shining."

"Nah, Gary gave it to me. He said that you'd want me to have it."

The bright smile disappeared from Wayne Sr.'s face at the sound of Gary's name. He clenched his jaws, and Wink saw a flash of hate in his eyes.

"*Alhumdullah*," said Wayne Sr. Then he took a deep breath, obviously trying to calm himself. "So, you're eighteen now?"

"Yeah. I'll be nineteen in a couple more months."

"Wayne, I know why you came all this way, and I'm willing to answer all the questions you may have. I owe you that much."

"I mean, really I just wanted to see you. For years, all my life, I wanted to come visit you, but it was always a touchy subject around the house."

"Well, I'm glad you came. I can tell by the mink and gators that you're hustlin'. I'm not gon' tell you a bunch of reasons why you shouldn't. Just look around at where I've been for the past eighteen years."

"I'm not going to hustle forever," Wink lied.

"At least you know that much. Man, I can't believe how much you've grown. You look just like Hope. By the way, how is she doing?"

"She's doing good. She and Gary are about to get married soon."

"What?" yelled Wayne Sr. That flash of hate appeared back in his eyes, but this time it stayed.

Wink didn't understand why his dad was so bent out of shape. He hadn't been with his mom in nearly twenty years.

"You mean to tell me she's still fooling with that nigga?" He didn't wait for Wink to answer. "Don't you know he's the reason I'm serving two life sentences? The reason I've never been a part of your life? He's the reason!"

Wink frowned out of sheer confusion. He had not a clue what his dad was talking about.

"I can't believe this. How could Hope do this to me?" Wink's dad had tears in his eyes.

"What are you talking about?" asked Wink.

"What, your mom didn't tell you? Gary testified against me and gave me all this time. He's the reason I'm sitting in here with two life sentences."

The news hit Wink like a ton of bricks. It was all starting to make sense why Gary only got five years and his dad got all day. "Does my mom know?"

"Of course she knows. She was at my trial, pregnant with you, when Gary took the stand on me. All these years, you mean to tell me, she's been dealing with that rat while I'm here with life?"

Wink didn't know what to say. There wasn't anything that he could say. He knew there was a reason he hated Gary when he was coming up.

"And you say that they're getting married, huh?"

"They were getting married. That nigga ain't marrying nothing except a casket," Wink promised his father. He couldn't wait to get back to Detroit so he could push Gary's shit back. His mom would just have to be mad with him, because it was already etched in stone: Gary had to die!

Chapter One

Trey and Willie were parked right outside the UBQ Bar over on Harper and Van Dyke. It was the new happening spot for the ballers and their groupies to play high-post and try to outshine the next nigga who was rumored to be getting money. Trey was determined to be dubbed the richest nigga on the east side of Detroit, and he was well on his way. He was a master at promotion, and the masses were eating up his self-proclaimed success. His name was starting to ring in the streets. His license plate read TMONEY on his new red Benz 500SEL, and that was what everyone began calling him. Every head turned as people passed the Benz parked at the curb. T-Money was loving every second of it. He and Willie were getting their heads right with some good-good before they stepped up in the spot.

"I keep tellin' you, Will, you need to get on my squad. That li'l-boy shit Wink got you out here doin' is beneath you. Look at that old-ass Caddy of yours parked over there." T-Money looked across the street at Willie's brown El Dogg. "My young'un is out here pushin' them shits. You s'posed to be in a Benz or BMW."

Willie just listened as he had for the past couple of weeks. Every time he and Trey got together, he was shooting lugs at Wink's operation, really fishing for information because he didn't know what Wink was on. Trey, aka T-Money, figured that since he had dropped a new Benz, he was doing better than Wink. Wink was still was pushing that antique, as Trey called it, and for T-Money, the only reason to be riding around in something like that was a lack of funds.

"I'm tryin'a send some work down to Mississippi with ya cousin Ball. What's up?"

"He already getting on. He straight," said Willie.

"I know the business. I know Wink the one hittin' him off with them li'l tows and fews. But I'm talkin' 'bout sending that nigga a workload. Mo' work than a temp service."

Willie thought about it. Ball was asking to expand throughout the South, and Wink was on some slow roll, "let me set everything up" type shit. He could see Willie's wheels turning, and the greed in his heart showed itself in his eyes. So he threw fuel on the fire.

"You can keep fuckin' with Wink with whatever y'all doin'. All I'm saying is let me send some work down too. Wink don't own Mississippi. Shit, we all took those trips, remember?" Trey was referring to the past when all three of them used to drive down to Mississippi to set up shop. They began the operation down there and were a tight crew until it all went south and Wink got greedy.

Trey continued, "Off every brick you take down there, I'ma give you ten grand."

"Ten thousand," repeated Willie. That was $8,000 more than what Wink was giving him.

"It's all on you, my nigga. Think about it and get at me. But right now, I'm 'bout to slide up in here." Trey's eyes followed this petite chocolate li'l something into the bar. He reached for the door handle, and together they emerged from the Benz, looking like new money, T-Money of course being the boss. He was Gucci from head to toe, starting with the Gucci bucket hat, down to his Gucci gym shoes. His jewelry was on blast: iced-out gold Rolex President with a matching bracelet and chain.

To finish off the ensemble, he had gold rings on each finger, his prized ring being the two-fingered number on his right hand that read MS for Money Squad. Trey wanted there to be no mistake who the man was when he stepped up on the scene.

Willie fell in step with Trey and watched as he turned into T-Money. People shouted him out like he was their best friend or one of the Chamberlain brothers. T-Money smiled and hit rocks with the best of them as he inched his way through the bar. It was like he was campaigning for the Hustla of the Year award the way he was politicking up in there, making sure to say a little something to every patron in the place. He touched every corner of the UBQ before heading to his VIP booth.

T-Money's li'l squad of niggas was already posted up in the booth. Lee-Mac, Live, Dilla, and JT were all posted up with bottles of Moët in front of them. Empty shot glasses littered the table. T-Money stood in front of them. He didn't need to say a word. The moment he appeared, they scrambled to make sure he had room to slide into the middle of his squad. Once seated, he stretched his arms out like he was a king.

"Everybody! I want y'all to meet my nigga. He's more like a brother to me. This is Will$, with a dollar sign on the end."

Willie pulled back a wide, closed grin. He liked that name. It fit, he thought.

"Hopefully, Will$ is gon' be joining our Money Squad Family so we can do what we do best, which is get this money. I want y'all to make him feel welcome and all that good shit, and like I said, hopefully he'll join our family."

Willie nodded to them all as T-Money introduced them by name. He recognized Dilla and JT already as being the two li'l niggas Wink had sitting in the spot on Linwood. Trey had doubled back and swooped up their young asses, as now they were part of his Money Squad Family shit he kept promoting like it was a rap album. Lee-Mac was a li'l light-skinned, scrawny nigga with a little-ass head and beady eyes. Willie looked his peculiar-lookin' ass over and tried to figure out where the name came from. Live, on the other hand, was a wide-back black mothafucka. He couldn't have been more than 16, but his name was ringing in the streets like a seasoned vet for busting his gun. That was why they called him Live. They each had on gold rope dookie chains with iced-out MS charms dangling. He continued to entertain and be the center of attention. His li'l Money Squad Family laughed at and listened to his every word, and all the while the hustlas of the city were taking note. A new king was on the rise, and his name was T-Money.

By the end of the night, Willie, new name Will$, was convinced that Money Squad Family was the place for him. He agreed to start sending kilos down to Mississippi for T-Money.

They all staggered out of the UBQ pissy drunk, T-Money with his arm wrapped around Will$'s neck. He was all in his ear while his squad stood guard with their hands underneath their shirts clutching the handles of the brand-new Glocks T-Money bought for them.

T-Money walked Will$ over to his car. "Tomorrow, come see me so we can go over the details. I want to get things going as soon as possible. We 'bout to get this money, my nigga, on a whole 'nother level. But I need you with me."

"I'm with you."

"A'ight then, tomorrow," said T-Money.

He opened Will$'s door for him and waited until he pulled away from the curb before joining his squad in front of the bar. He wasn't finished flodging for the night. Club let-out time was the best time to pose for the camera, and in this case the camera was anyone who would look and hopefully remember his name.

Will$ stretched back in his El Dogg and counted the money he would make if he were to deal with T-Money. In a matter of months, he could be on $1 million plus, especially at $10,000 a brick. Will$ hadn't thought about Wink and the promise he made never to cross him. Willie didn't see any harm in playing both sides of the fence. Wink and Trey were both his best friends anyway, so why did he have to choose between them? They were the ones trippin', not him. They were the ones letting money change them, like the Mighty O'Jays said. Besides Wink would never find out unless Trey were to tell him, and he didn't see that ever happening. Willie smiled and pressed down on the gas. He couldn't wait until tomorrow came. It was about to be on!

Chapter Two

Willie dropped the rest of the re-up money off to Wink at his apartment. Together they sat in Wink's living room counting the dirty money and putting the bills into $10,000 stacks.

"How much you got over there?" asked Wink. He stood up from the sofa and stretched out and yawned. They'd been counting since last night, and his back started locking up on him.

"I got, uh . . ." Willie used his finger to tally up all the stacks spread across the coffee table and floor. "Four hun'd and eighty thousand."

"Yeah, it's all here. Wrap each stack up in a rubber band, and put 'em in this duffle bag. I'ma go take a shower and get ready. I gotta be at the airport by eleven." Wink looked at the clock on the wall. It was 9:45. He took a deep breath and sighed as he left Willie in the living room and headed for the bathroom.

Wink took a nice, long, hot shower. He stood under the water with his eyes closed, trying to clear his mind. He had to go meet up with Nina and put up with her shit, teasing him and playin' Ms. Boss Bitch. He had to be back for the closing on a new mansion he was buying. Not to mention, Krazy had another hearing coming up. Wink let the water run down his face a few more minutes, then reluctantly turned the nozzle off. He reached for a towel, dried off, then walked into the bedroom and dressed. That was one thing he didn't have to worry about anymore. Armeeah had set out two weeks' worth of outfits, down to his socks and boxers. She even cleaned his apartment and fixed him breakfast every morning before she went to work. It was official. They were a couple, and that was why Wink was buying a new mansion. He wanted to take their relationship to the next level.

Wink found Willie in the kitchen gladly helping himself to his breakfast. Armeeah had left Wink a plate in the microwave with cheese eggs, turkey bacon, link sausage, and French toast.

"Damn, my nigga," said Willie in between bites. He swallowed his food. "I ain't know you could cook."

"My girl made that, and it was for me." Wink snatched the last link off the saucer before Willie could inhale it too.

"My bad." Willie licked his fingers clean, then gulped down a cold glass of orange juice. "Ahh. Urppp. Damn, yeah, that was on one thousand. You need to g'on and wife baby girl. She's bad and she can cook. If that ain't wifey material . . ."

Wink took a seat on the stool beside Willie and stared off into space. "I'm not gon' lie, my dude. I been thinking about wifein' her up."

"So why don't you? I mean, I see the way you are whenever baby girl's around."

"I know, but it ain't that simple."

"Why not? You just gotta ask her."

Wink looked at the clock on the wall. It was 10:20 and time to roll out. He slid off his stool and walked the dishes over to the sink. "I'll tell you about it later, but right now we gotta get going."

The one thing keeping Wink from asking Armeeah to marry him was her cock-blocking father. He was still waiting for Armeeah to introduce them. He was nervous that Armeeah's Middle Eastern father would flip his top about Wink being black.

Willie followed Wink out into the living room while rubbing his stuffed belly. "Yeah, so when can I expect you back so we can get this thang cranked up? I got mad orders already in."

"I should be back in two days. Just fall back and chill until then."

Willie grabbed the duffle bag off the floor and set it on the sofa. "That's exactly a million," Willie advised.

"A'ight, bet that up." Wink tossed Willie two $10,000 stacks. "That's a li'l bonus."

"Shit, I'ma hit the titty bar with this and see what I can't take home tonight. Sho' is." He smiled as if he were already at the bar.

"A'ight look, go pull the car up while I put the rest of this shit up."

Wink walked Willie to the door and locked it behind him. He then took the $980,000 into his bedroom and stashed it inside his wall safe with the $500,000 he already had on ice. Wink looked at all the money for a minute before locking up the safe. It was happening, and fast. He was getting rich. Wink closed the safe, then walked out into the living room, grabbed the black leather duffle bag from the sofa, and put his arm into the strap. He clutched the bag tightly as he looked around the apartment before leaving.

Willie was parked at the curb talking on his car phone. He abruptly ended his conversation with Trey at the sight of Wink coming out of the building. "I'ma hit you back after I drop him off at the airport. One." Click. Willie shoved the phone into the console and popped the locks for Wink.

"Nigga, I know you ain't out here with the Viper lock system on. Let me find out you scared," Wink joked as he climbed into the passenger seat.

"Shit, nigga, betta safe than sorry," said Willie. He put the car in drive and pulled away from the curb. Willie was really thinking, *shit, I can't wait until your ass gets on that plane so me and Trey can hook up.*

"After we flip this next load, we gon' flip these Caddies. What you wanna jump in?" asked Wink.

"Let's do some Beemers since Trey already doin' the Benz."

"Yeah, I'm feelin' that. We can't let that nigga outshine us, feel me?"

Willie nodded and smiled at the thought because Wink had no idea Trey was now T-Money, and it was going to be a full-time job trying to outshine him and his Money Squad Family.

Willie pulled into the Sheraton directly across the street from Metro Airport out in Romulus, Michigan. He parked near the front entrance, put his hazards on, and waved the valet away.

"I'll be right back," said Wink. He grabbed the duffle bag from between his legs and reached for the door handle.

Wink casually walked inside the hotel lobby and took the elevator up to the third floor. He found the room number Nina had given him the day before. Wink turned the handle, and the door, as promised, was unlocked. The room was empty, but for some reason Wink felt as though someone were watching him. He looked behind the curtains, in the closets, and under the bed.

Once satisfied that he was alone, he did as Nina instructed and left the bag inside the whirlpool tub. He looked down at the bag knowing what was in it and became nervous. He just hoped that Nina's people got the money with no problems because that was $1 million of his own money.

Wink walked out of the hotel unnoticed by any of the hotel's personnel. He climbed back in the car and directed Willie to drive him across the street to the airport. As they pulled around the circle, Wink could see one of Franko's white Learjets parked out on the tarmac. Two middle-aged Cuban men wearing black suits and sunglasses stood outside the plane, and just like last time, there was an all-black convoy of seven tinted Suburbans.

Willie parked at the entrance and leaned up against his door to face Wink.

"I'ma see you when I touch down." Wink reached over and gave Willie some dap.

"I'll be waiting," said Willie.

Wink climbed out of the car and tapped the roof before stepping inside the terminal. Wink cut through the terminal and went out to the tarmac using the private flight section. When the two men standing outside the plane saw Wink, they ceased their conversation. Neither of the men spoke a word as Wink approached them. The shorter of the two waved his hand for Wink to board the plane.

Wink had never met the men before. Franko used a different group every time he conducted business because he wanted it to remain business and not ever get personal. It was his way of keeping everyone off-balance and uncomfortable. The only exception to the rule was Nina. Wink found her perched at the rear of the plane sipping Scotch and playing the role of Ms. Boss Bitch.

Nina smiled and patted her hand on the seat beside her. "Wink, how are you?" she asked, turning her cheek in anticipation of her greeting kiss.

Wink obliged her, then sank into his seat. Nina set her drink down and kicked her shoes off, then snuggled up under Wink like a missed lover.

Here we go, thought Wink. He wasn't in the mood for Nina's hot-and-cold teasing games, so he focused on the essence of their meeting.

"I just dropped that money off at the room. It's a—"

Nina cut him off. "I know. It's a million dollars on the nose. My people picked it up as soon as you left the room."

"For that million, I'm tryin'a see at least two twenty-five," said Wink.

"We can talk numbers later. But first things first." Nina let her hand travel down Wink's chest to his slowly rising Johnson. She stuck her hand in his boxer shorts and stroked him to life.

"You miss me?" Nina whispered.

"Yeah," lied Wink. How could he? All she did the last time was bless him with some a'ight head, and tease him for the rest of the trip.

But today was a new day, because Nina wasn't doing no faking, and Wink prayed that she wasn't just teasing him again by not wearing any panties. Nina spread her legs cock-wide open, and she took Wink's right index finger and buried it inside her. Wink's finger was buried up to the knuckle. Nina guided him to her G-spot, then closed her eyes while she took a trip to paradise.

After Nina came three times, she pulled Wink's finger out of her gleaming, wet pussy and stuck it in his mouth for him to taste her juices.

"I believe you owe me one," she said in a soft yet demanding tone.

Wink had the "ahh" face. He did owe her a head job because she had hit him off last time. "Dirty bitch." Before Wink could protest his call of duty, Nina pulled him down by his ears and put his face in the place. Wink licked and sucked Nina to another orgasm. She tried to keep him down for a second and, if God was willing, a third and fourth, but Wink gave her a dose of her own medicine. He sat up and wiped his face, leaving Nina hot and bothered. If she wanted to get that nut off badly enough, she was gon' have to break bread with that kitty cat.

Wink waited until she caught her breath and for her nerves to settle before he got back down to business. "Now that we're even, let's kick some numbers around."

Nina took a long swallow from her Scotch and fired up a Virginia Slim. She allowed the Scotch and nicotine to soothe her nerves before speaking, because she couldn't allow Wink to know that he had just given her some of the best head of her life. She had to remain in control, Ms. Boss Bitch.

"What are you expecting to get that you didn't get the last time?"

"The last time I only got a hundred kilos, which Franko fronted to me at five grand each."

Nina nodded at Wink's mathematics, and he continued, "This go-round I'm comin' up front with a million cash, so I'ma need a better deal than last time."

"I'm listening."

"Two hun'd and twenty-five kilos is what I'm thinkin'."

"I see you've been doing a lot of thinking. But I must tell you that your price does not change whether you're paying up front or I give it to you on consignment."

"Maybe I need to holla at Franko myself."

Nina laughed to cover up how she really took Wink's comment. She was the boss. "Be my guest, but he's going to tell you the same thing." Nina took a drink, then continued, "You see, Wink, this is not an arrangement where money is our only concern. When your father and Franko agreed on terms, you were brought into our family, not just a business. And what I mean is, we as family take care of each other. The price is to remain the same because our family takes care of those in prison and their families. There are a lot of us eating off the same plate, and if something were to happen to you or your dad, you too would be taken care of. All we ask is loyalty. Do you understand where I'm coming from?"

Wink nodded. He was thinking, *yeah, and if I ain't know any better, I could've sworn it sounded like you just threatened me, bitch!* Wink didn't take too kindly to a mothafucka threatening his life, or his father's for that matter. And what the hell was she talking about, family? *Bitch, please! You tongue-tied mothafuckas ain't none of my family.* What Wink failed to realize was that he was dealing with the mob, and they played for keeps. Family meant "until death do us part," which meant there would be no quitting. Wink was officially married to the mob.

Chapter Three

Meanwhile, Willie and Trey were meeting up to get started on their plan. Willie didn't want to waste any time. He only had two days until Wink got back, which was enough time to make a trip down to Mississippi and catch a flight back without Wink finding out. Willie parked his Caddy at the curb in front of Lonnie's collision shop on Mound Road and Nevada. He got out of the car and walked around the back of the small shop, where he found crackhead Lonnie and Trey. Lonnie was behind the wheel of a white cargo van showing Trey something.

Trey stepped back and smiled. "What up doe," he said, extending his hand for a play.

"Shit," Willie said while looking around the shop's yard. He met eyes with Trey's hired gun, Live. Willie nodded what's up. Live nodded back. "Fuck y'all doing out here in the cold?" asked Willie as he stuffed his hands deep inside his coat pockets.

Lonnie climbed down from the van and walked over to the back entrance of the shop, where a gigantic torpedo-style heater sat. Lonnie turned the valve on the compressor, and a streak of blue fire roared from the torpedo, instantly heating up the area. Trey flagged Lonnie over to the van before he could take his crack break. "Come show Will$ how the shit works." Trey put Willie up on game as Lonnie climbed back inside the van. "Lonnie put a stash box in the van. It can hold up to thirty bricks and two pistols."

"You see this, young blood? Now pay attention, 'cause I'm only gon' sho' you once." Lonnie had an attitude because he hadn't smoked nothing all day. He grunted as he ran down the combination to the stash box. "First, you gotta put it in neutral, then turn the AC on, pump the brakes three times, and there you have it." The entire dashboard rolled down on four hinges. Inside sat a stainless-steel compartment. It was packed to the hilt with bricks of cocaine and two Glocks.

Lonnie's eyes widened at the sight of all the coke. He instantly needed a fix. He climbed down from the van and headed for the shop to scratch his itch.

"You ready to hit the road and get this money?" Trey asked, smiling like a greedy devil.

"Yeah, but you sure this stash spot is legit? You fuckin' with Lonnie's base-head ass," said Willie.

"You know I wouldn't have you out there bogus. The shit is A1. It betta be. I paid his ass two Gs."

Willie knew better than to believe that. He was a little leery anyhow on the strength of who put the stash in the van. How many other niggas already had the same one or something similar?

Trey put his arm around Willie's neck and tried convincing him that everything was good. "Trust me, my nigga, the shit's official. You just a little nervous 'cause of the amount of work that's in there. But we good."

"Yeah, I guess that's it," said Willie as he climbed behind the wheel of the van.

Trey got in on the passenger side and continued his campaign. "My nigga, ain't no different from the last time we got on the highway. Only difference is now it's for us. We get to keep all the money this time."

Willie got to adding up his cut of the thirty bricks. All he had to do was drive the kilos down to Mississippi, and he'd automatically pocket $300,000 off the top. It was easy, Willie told himself. He had made that trip at least twenty times before.

"It's for us. The Money Squad Family," said Trey. He dug in his pocket and pulled out a gold rope chain. "Here, I got something for you." Trey put the chain over Willie's head, then looked him in the eyes and said, "You're the last family member."

Willie, aka Will$, looked down at the iced-out MS charm hanging from the eighteen-karat gold rope. It was like the one Trey was wearing.

"Let's get this money, my nigga," said Trey, holding his hand out for Willie's.

Willie smiled, then took Trey's hand. After they finished embracing, Willie looked at the two guns tucked on the side of the kilos. "Why you got two straps in there?"

Trey nodded to Live, who was standing at the hood of the van with his back turned. He was on some serious watchdog shit, and to be real, Willie didn't care for the nigga because he was too quiet, sneaky quiet.

"I'm sending Live with you to watch your back 'cause that's a lot of work we dealing with."

"Nah, I'm straight on him coming. Plus, my cousin ain't tryin'a meet nobody new."

"Who, Ball's fat ass?"

"Yeah. Trust me, Trey, I'm good. I can make the trip by myself," Willie assured him.

"A'ight," Trey reluctantly agreed. He wanted Live to go with Willie so he could meet and greet a few people in case Willie ever jumped fake on him and he wouldn't need him anymore.

"Let me get on the road while it's still light out," said Willie. He flipped the dashboard shut and started the van.

"All the paperwork is in the glove box. Call me when you get down there." Trey patted Willie on the back, then climbed down from the van. He leaned in through the passenger window and said, "I wish you'd let me send Live with you."

"Nah, I'ma let you keep yo' pit bull. Make sure that crackhead mothafucka Lonnie don't strip my car." Willie shifted the van into drive.

"Fuck strippin' it. You need to crash that old, raggedy shit," laughed Trey. He hit the hood of the van and stepped aside. Willie hit the horn twice before pulling out through the wooden privacy fence and through the alley. He was still a little nervous knowing that the dashboard was filled with enough coke to get him a natural-life sentence in somebody's prison.

Stop thinking like that, Willie told himself. He sat up straight in his seat and put his belt on, then fixed his mirrors for the long drive. He turned the radio to 98.7 and tried to relax. "Three hundred thousand dollars," he reminded himself.

Willie had been on the road for four hours, carefully watching the speed limit and driving with both hands on the wheel. The sun had long ago set, and Interstate 75 was pitch-dark with the exception of the light provided by his headlights. Willie's eyes started getting heavy. He tried cracking the windows, figuring the cool air would wake him up, but he continued to nod in and out. He started regretting not bringing Live with him to split the driving time. Willie nearly swerved off the side of the road into a ditch after nodding off again, but he caught the wheel just in time. He knew that he wouldn't make it much longer, and he had to pull over and take a rest.

Willie sat up and wiped his face and fought to keep his eyes open as he scanned the deserted interstate for somewhere to pull over and park. He spotted a Mobil truck station just up the road. He pulled into the lot and quickly found a place to park beside one of the rigs. Willie killed his lights, locked his doors, and scanned the station's parking lot before leaning his seat back. The clock on the dash read 11:46. *Couple hours and I'll be ready,* Willie told himself as he closed his eyes and fell asleep.

What was supposed to be just a catnap turned into a full night's sleep. He woke up at 7:30 the next morning to the sound of a police radio crackling. As Willie sat up in his seat and adjusted his eyes to the morning sunrays beaming in his face, he saw two Memphis sheriffs approaching the van on both sides.

"Shit," Willie whispered, realizing he had overslept and that these two crackers had him boxed in. The sheriff at the driver's side motioned for Willie to roll down the window while the other sheriff stood guard with his eyes on Willie and his hand rested on the butt of his .357 Magnum.

"How can I help you, Sheriff?" asked Willie as he rolled the window down about halfway.

"License and registration," ordered the sheriff. He rocked back and forth on his heels and spat a glob of tobacco from his mouth while he waited for Willie to retrieve his paperwork from the glove box.

"There you go, sir." He handed the sheriff the license and registration. "Can I ask why you need my license and all, sir?" Willie's stomach was turning like a mothafucka as he looked at the dashboard, knowing what it concealed.

The sheriff ignored Willie's question while he studied his credentials. He removed his mirror-tinted aviator glasses and gave Willie a stern look. "Boy, what you doin' down here in Memphis?"

"I'm on my way to visit my aunt in Tunica, Mississippi. I just stopped here to get some rest."

"You always drive a van to make a trip?"

Willie started stuttering, which was a sure sign that he was lying.

"I'ma need for you to step out of the van."

Just as the sheriff said that, Willie noticed a K-9 unit pull into the parking lot. He reluctantly climbed down from the van, and the second sheriff closely escorted him over to the squad car, where he frisked him.

"Just have a seat in there." The sheriff opened the back of his squad car for Willie.

"Am I being arrested?"

"You're being detained. Now g'on and get in."

Climbing into the back of that squad car felt like it was going to be Willie's last ride for a long time. He sat at the edge of his seat and watched as the K-9 jumped inside the van. The dog went to barking and scratching immediately at the dashboard. That damn mutt was going crazy!

"Damn!" Willie yelled in defeat. He continued to watch as the K-9 officer pulled that mutt down from the van. He was petting the son of a bitch like she had done a good job, and a good job she had done.

Two more units arrived on the scene, along with a brown sheriff van. Willie watched as the sheriffs ran a long metal rod underneath the frame of the van. Then they popped the hood and hooked some jumper cables up to the battery. Willie saw the dashboard pop open. "I think we've got it," one of the sheriffs yelled out as he raised the dashboard.

"Fuck!" yelled Willie. He couldn't even watch anymore as the sheriffs began unloading the kilos from the stash spot and placing them on the hood of one of the patrol cars. Within minutes, two Memphis DEA agents were on the scene. The sheriffs pointed them to the squad car where Willie sat with his head buried against the front seat's headrest. The taller of the two agents opened the back door, and Willie looked up at him.

"Name?" ordered the agent. He spoke with a no-nonsense tone like he didn't have all day.

Willie shook his head no, then buried his face back into the head rest. He was sick to his stomach.

The agent crouched down while his partner stood guard. "You think you're sick now, just wait until you're sittin' in federal prison serving a life sentence." The agent allowed his words to sink in for a moment, and then he continued, "That is, unless you help yourself. Where are you on your way to with all those kilos?"

"What do you mean, help myself?" asked Willie. He was willing to do anything to keep from going to jail for the rest of his life.

"You can help yourself by delivering this load to wherever it's going and helping us."

Willie thought about his cousin Ball. *Damn, I can't do that to cuz.*

"Everyone we catch like this, we give them the same opportunity, and let me tell you that the penitentiary is filled with people who wish they had made that drop. Don't wait twenty years from now to start regretting not helping yourself." The agent was watching Willie's body language, and he could tell from the look in his eyes that he was thinking about it. "You have one chance. I'm going to give you a few minutes to think about it," said the agent. He stood up and closed the door. He and his partner joined the sheriffs over at the hood of the squad car. They were all high-fiving and celebrating the bust. The crime unit was taking pictures of the kilos and two guns spread out across the hood.

Willie knew it would be the end of his young life if he didn't do as the agent said and help himself. *Damn.*

The agents walked back over to the squad car and opened the back door. Willie's time was up.

"So what's it going to be? Shall I call the county and tell 'em to set you a lunch aside, or are we taking these drugs to their owner?"

"We're gon' make the drop," said Willie in an unsure tone.

The agent slapped Willie on the shoulder, like "welcome to the team." He smiled, then said, "Trust me, you're doing the right thing for yourself. Now what's your name, son?" The agent pulled a notepad and pen from his pocket and scribbled while Willie spoke.

"Willie Hamilton." Willie felt as if he'd just sold his soul to the devil himself.

The agent contacted the DEA down in Tunica, Mississippi, and they set the drop to Willie's cousin, Ball. They would let Willie and his cousin remain free as part of a further investigation. The Feds wanted Trey and his supplier. Willie would remain free so long as he continued to assist the Feds with catching Trey. The Feds allowed Willie and Ball to sell the kilos and carry Trey's money back to him. They had five years to wrap up their investigation before the statute of limitations ran out on indicting Trey and finding out who his supplier was. Meanwhile, Willie would be their deep-cover snitch.

Chapter Four

The two days Wink spent down in Miami with Nina seemed more like two weeks. He was hoping to go down and be left alone, but Nina had other ideas. She was a needy, manipulative boss who always got her way. She wanted Wink to spend a couple of days with her just lounging around her estate and letting her get her rocks off by being in charge. After their little stint on the plane, Wink couldn't relax around her anymore.

"Wink, darling, isn't this the life?" Nina sighed as she looked at the crystal-clear water of her pool. "Come here and massage my feet."

Wink wanted to scream at her and say no, but he clenched his jaw and said nothing. He grudgingly got up from his lounge chair and rubbed her feet.

"If you play your cards right, this could be all yours." She opened her legs to give him a view of her pussy. "And if you don't play your cards right, then, well, who knows where you'll end up?"

Wink just couldn't get over Nina threatening him on the sly, and then on top of that, she really expected everything to be business as normal, or as she put it, family. She had Wink fucked up and confused with some other nigga. He had to tell himself to play it cool though, because he was out of his comfort zone, plus he wanted to touch base with his father first and see what the business was for real. He seriously doubted his pops would have him on some flunky shit.

Wink played it cool for the two days and agreed to keep things moving as planned. Nina was going to have 200 kilos waiting for him in the storage unit when he got back. She offered to front Wink an additional 200 kilos, but he declined, saying that he hadn't the clientele yet. But the real reason was that Wink didn't want to get into the habit of always owing Nina, especially since she had him on some "married to the mob" shit. Wink figured that as long as he was in her debt, it would be much harder to bounce when he was ready. In the meantime, he'd play the role.

Nina rode with Wink to the airport in a three-car convoy. She and Wink rode center in her bulletproof Lincoln stretch limo. "So when do you think you'll be ready to see me again?" asked Nina. The limo pulled into the airport and parked beside Wink's jet.

"Give me two weeks, maybe three, and I should be ready."

"You're going to make me wait that long?" Nina massaged Wink's dick through his jeans.

Wink had enough. "You gon' stop teasin' me. Matter of fact, the next time I'm out here, I'ma beat that pussy up, 'cause that's what you want."

"You really think you know what I want, huh?"

"I not only know what you want but also what you need. But don't worry. I'ma give you both of 'em." Wink opened his side door and climbed out of the limo, leaving Nina to chew on that. He wasn't stuntin' her ass for real. His mind was on getting back to his baby, Armeeah, and flipping the 200 bricks waiting for him.

He climbed the steps up to the plane and took his seat at the back of the jet. He kicked his feet up and closed his eyes. The jet's engine came to life and roared, making Wink's entire body vibrate. Within minutes, the plane had cleared the runway and was up in the air.

When Wink woke up, the plane was circling the tarmac at the Detroit City Airport on Connors and Gratiot Avenue. He stretched out his arms and yawned before getting up from his seat. The plane parked beside a black cargo van filled with Franko's people. They were there to unload the plane and make sure the kilos made it safely to the storage unit. Wink nodded but said nothing to the four heavily armed Cuban men as he stepped off the plane. He cut across the tarmac and caught the entry gate before the tanker truck could close it. "Thank you," he said to the driver as he made it through the gate into the front parking lot.

Willie was parked near the entrance in his El Dogg. Wink spotted him and picked up his pace. He tapped on the passenger window for Willie to open the door.

"What I tell yo' scared ass 'bout locking the door?" Wink joked as he settled into his seat. He reached over and gave Willie some dap. "What's up, my nigga? Why you look like you just seen a ghost? You good?" asked Wink.

Willie tried to straighten up his mug and hide his guilt. He tried to play it off by faking a yawn. "Nah, I'm just tired, that's all. I been up all night." He cranked the car up and pulled away from the curb.

"What, you was in them titty bars, huh?"

"Yeah," lied Willie. He was downtown at the federal building all day yesterday, being prepped by the DEA. They had him on some real secret squirrel shit. They installed a wire on his car, pager, and apartment, so everything he and Wink said, they could hear.

"Well, I hope you're all rested, 'cause it's time to get back on our grind. How many you need right now?"

"Uh, fifty," stuttered Willie. He was nervous as shit because there was no turning back. He had just locked Wink right into a conspiracy with the rest of them.

"A'ight, that's a bet. Drop me off at my apartment, and I'll have that for you in the morning," said Wink. He was already doing the math for the fifty bricks. He looked over at Willie, who was obviously lost in thought. "You sure you're a'ight, my nigga? You don't look too good."

Willie wiped his face, then pulled back a fake smile. "I'll be good once we get this money going."

"That's what I'm talking about. Look, after you feed the streets, we gon' take a trip down to Atlanta. I wanna see what's up. You know we gotta take ol' African Offy with us and let him play mob boss."

"Yeah, right," laughed Willie.

"That nigga had me fooled. His ass coulda been an actor for real," laughed Wink. "But yeah, though, it's time we start expanding and snatch up some of that outta-state money."

Willie just nodded as Wink went on to detail his plans. He didn't hear a word Wink was saying. His only thought was how long the Feds would wait until they moved in and indicted them.

Willie dropped Wink off at his apartment downtown. He parked at the entrance and turned to face Wink.

"In the morning, my nigga. Get you some rest, 'cause you lookin' like a zombie," said Wink.

"I got you. Just hit me up when you're ready," said Willie. He gave Wink some dap, then Wink got out of the car and walked inside the apartment building.

Willie pulled out of the complex, and not two minutes later his car phone was ringing. "Hello."

"Agent Defauw here."

Willie's heart sank because he already knew what the agent wanted. He told Willie to meet him downtown at the federal building. He wanted to talk about Wink.

Wink found Armeeah cleaning his apartment when he walked in. Well, he might as well have thought of it as their apartment, because lately Armeeah had been there more than he. Wink walked over to Armeeah and took the broom from her hand and set it against the wall. He wrapped her long black hair around her ear and looked deep into her eyes. "You miss me?"

"Of course I missed you." She smiled and gave Wink a long, wet, passionate kiss. "The Realtor called this morning. She wanted to make sure we were still coming to the closing."

"That's right, the closing is today. What time did she say?" asked Wink.

"One o'clock."

Wink looked at the clock on the wall. It was only 10:30. "So I guess we've got a couple of hours for you to show me how much you missed me." Wink let his hands slip down Armeeah's waist to her ass. His dick was rock hard and poking her in the stomach. "How bad did you miss me?" he whispered.

"I missed you really bad," Armeeah said in a soft, seductive voice.

Wink swooped her up into his arms and carried her into the bedroom. He laid her across the bed, and Armeeah slid out of the long white T-shirt she'd been wearing. Wink quickly undressed and climbed into bed after her. He playfully bit at her neck, then worked kisses down and around her thighs. Armeeah became soaking wet from the foreplay. She rolled Wink onto his back and proceeded to show him just how much she missed him. Wink had been trying diligently for weeks to get Armeeah to bless him with some head, but she would shoot the idea down every time he brought it up. But today was a new day.

"Damn," said Wink in a quivery voice as Armeeah softly stroked his dick with one hand and sucked him off with her eyes closed. *I guess you really did miss me,* thought Wink as he lay back, enjoying the toe-curling head.

Armeeah showed Wink in more than one way how much she missed him. She was really coming out of her good Muslim-sister roots that came from all those years of repression, constantly being told not to do this and not to do that. Being with Wink, Armeeah could experience all the *dunyaa* (world) and everything in it. Wink provided excitement in Armeeah's boring life, and she brought peace to Wink's. And for that they loved each other.

They met with a Realtor from Century 21 out in Farmington Hills. The Realtor had shown them over a dozen properties in the past weeks. Well, Armeeah anyway. Wink had given her a $500,000 budget to play with. He didn't have time to be house hunting and looking at boring catalogs about furniture and interior design. So he just let Armeeah and the Realtor handle all the formalities. Armeeah selected a beautiful mini mansion with a colonial front entrance situated on three acres of land, with a pond out back. The house was shaped like a Y, with two wings: a north and a south. The master bedroom was so big that it sat on one side all by itself. The house had cathedral ceilings, a family room, a den with library shelves built into the walls, a dining room that looked out on nothing but green pastures, a living room that set the whole house in motion, a big, beautiful gourmet kitchen, a five-car garage, and three bedrooms on the other side of the Y.

Wink paid for the house in all cash. The Realtor was an old friend of his dad's, Cynthia. She had sold Gunz several houses back in the day, dealing with straight cash. In fact, drug dealers were the only type of clientele she preferred to deal with because they were the only ones who could afford her fees. Cynthia was the best in the business when it came to hiding money and manipulating the paperwork. The house only sold for $420,000, but Cynthia was to keep $80,000 for her fee. The house was put in Wink's name under a land contract with the seller, but really the house was paid for in full. Cynthia would hold the deed in trust for Wink until the smoke cleared.

After Wink signed his name on the closing papers, everyone clapped and celebrated by popping bottles of champagne. The previous owners, an old white man and his wife, were celebrating because they had just unloaded their home of twenty years for a price well above the market value. Cynthia was $80,000 richer, and Wink had just bought his first piece of real estate.

"You like it, baby?" Armeeah asked with the biggest smile on her face.

"I'll love it once you lay it out and we're working on starting a family," said Wink. He toasted with a glass of champagne, then kissed Armeeah on the forehead.

Cynthia congratulated them on their new home and gave Armeeah the keys. "Now we are getting together to decorate your new home, right?"

"Girl, you ain't saying nothin' but a word. We are starting tomorrow."

"It's on." Cynthia smiled.

After everyone left, Wink and Armeeah walked through their new home, holding hands. Wink listened intently as Armeeah talked about her plans for each room. She had it all figured out, and Wink was just happy to see her happy. They cut out the dining room patio door into the back-yard. Armeeah snuggled under Wink's arm as they stood looking at their pond. Armeeah leaned her head against Wink's arm and sighed. "Isn't it beautiful?" she asked.

"Not as beautiful as you." Wink turned to face Armeeah, who was blushing from ear to ear. "See, that's what I mean. Your smile is as beautiful as it was the day I met you. When I'm away from you, Meeah, you're all I can think about."

Armeeah straightened up and listened to Wink closely because this was the first time he had ever let her in on his feelings. She knew that Wink loved her, but hearing it and knowing why he loved her was what she needed.

He continued, "From the moment I laid eyes on you, I knew you were special and that I wanted to be with you. Since that day, my feelings have not changed in the least, Meeah. Being with you has brought understanding and peace into my life, and I don't ever want it to leave." Wink dug in his pants pocket for the black ring box he'd copped before going to Miami.

Armeeah stepped back and put her hands to her mouth.

"Meeah, I didn't buy this place so we could play house. I want for us to make it a home. I love you and want you to be my wife." Wink got down on one knee, then pulled the lid back on the ring box. "Armeeah, will you marry me?"

Armeeah stared down at the five-carat diamond ring set in platinum. It was so beautiful it brought tears to her eyes. The feeling of confusion suddenly overcame her. Thoughts of her parents and her religion filled her mind. She couldn't marry Wink, not right now, because he wasn't a Muslim. Armeeah started blaming herself, because when she first met Wink, she told herself that she was going to *insha Allah,* bring Wink into the fold of Islam. Her plan was to get Wink to accept Allah as being the one true God, and for him to bear witness that Mohammad was the last messenger. But somewhere between Armeeah taking Wink to *jumah* services and trying to give him the *deen,* she got caught up being a gangsta's girlfriend and lost sight of her own obligations to Allah as a Muslim.

Armeeah shook her head. "Sorry," she said, then turned and walked back inside the house, leaving Wink down on his knee.

Wink dropped his head, like, "Ahh, I just played myself." He just knew she would say yes. *I mean, why wouldn't she?* He'd just dropped $500,000 on a crib and was trying to bun her up.

Wink reluctantly closed the box and picked himself up from the ground. He stood up and walked inside the house with his head down. He found Armeeah in the kitchen sitting on the floor, crying. Wink slid down the wall and took a seat beside Armeeah. For a few minutes they both stared off into the space of the kitchen.

"Armeeah, do you love me?" Wink asked as he turned toward Armeeah.

"Yes!" cried Armeeah. She sat up and wiped her tears.

"Then why won't you marry me?"

"I didn't say no."

"And you didn't say yes neither. Look at me, Meeah. Tell me what's wrong."

"Wayne, I love you, and I want to be your wife, but . . ."

"Come on, Meeah. Talk to me."

"Wayne, I am Sunni Muslim, and I was raised to be the wife of a Muslim man."

Wink leaned his head back against the wall. "I thought we talked about this already."

"No, we haven't. I've tried bringing up the subject many times, but you were never interested in talking about it. I invited you to *jumah* so that you may learn Islam."

Wink cut Armeeah off. "Baby, no disrespect, but that's your religion and belief. You grew up in a Muslim household and were taught to believe these things. Does that mean I have to believe the same thing?"

"Wayne, do you at least believe in God?"

"Right now it's hard to say." Wink got to thinking about the situation with his mother and how his life panned out. He wasn't thinking about God. He just wanted to be happy with Armeeah. "So what are you saying, Meeah, you're not going to marry me because I'm not Muslim?"

"That's not what I said."

"Give me your hand." Wink took it before she could offer it. He pulled the ring from the box and placed it on her finger. "Say yes."

"Wayne—"

"Say yes and save my life." He kissed each one of her fingertips, kissed her gently on the forehead, and whispered in her ear, "Save my life, Meeah. Don't force me to live in this world without you. I could never do that." He brushed her hair back out of her face and gazed into her eyes. "Say yes."

"Yes," Armeeah finally said in a low tone. "Yes," she repeated.

Wink smothered her mouth with kisses. "Thank you," he said between his kisses.

"For what?" asked Armeeah in a low tone. She was trembling, so Wink gathered her into his arms.

"For saving my life." Wink needed Armeeah. She was the one thing in his life keeping him sane. He had become the ruthless killer his father once was, and with every kill, his heart turned colder, but Armeeah had become his source of peace. He couldn't lose her.

Wink hadn't made any commitment to become a Muslim anytime soon, and it wasn't that he had anything against Islam. He just needed time. He needed time to find himself spiritually and time to understand what he was getting into.

Armeeah loved Wink and understood that he really needed her, so she said yes for the sake of not losing him to the streets. She told herself though that they were only engaged and would not marry unless Wink came into the fold of Islam wholeheartedly.

Chapter Five

Wink hated the long, depressing drive it took to get to Leavenworth USP from the Kansas City Airport. He would instantly become angry the moment his cab left Kansas and started on the miles-long deserted roads cutting up through the mountains. Wink's blood would boil at the very thought of how Uncle Cracker had his pops tucked away in the middle of nowhere on one of the government's many modern plantations. His dad had told him about the prisoner Unicor factory, and how it was a billion-dollar industry. Wink would look at all the pastures and think, *it's not about crime. These crackers use crime as an excuse to put a nigga's ass away in one of these slave camps until the end of time. It's all about money.* Wink felt justified in his life of crime. *These crackers think they 'posed to be the only ones rich.*

Wink had made the trip a few times already, but he still hadn't gotten used to the stomach-dropping "I gotta shit" feeling whenever his cab would pull inside the prison parking lot. So it came as no surprise when Armeeah scooted close to him and clutched the side of his arm tightly. The place was so scary that when you came to visit, you thought you were going to jail. It looked like a replica of the White House with a bunch of bars and gates. The prison was a level five, so it was surrounded by an eighteen-foot stone wall, five gun towers, and barbed wire on every inch of the wall. Wink noticed how tense Armeeah had become, so he caressed the back of her hand with his thumb. She was so nervous that when the cab stopped at the entrance, she didn't want to get out.

"Meeah, what's wrong?" Wink asked as he stood with the door ajar.

"Maybe I should wait for you out here."

"Baby, I'm not gon' leave you out here in no cab for four hours. Come on, I really want you to meet my dad."

"Wayne, what if he doesn't like me?" Armeeah folded her arms and lowered her eyes to the floor.

Wink reached for her chin and lifted it so she was looking him in the eyes. "Meeah, baby, of course he'll like you. You're beautiful. And if he doesn't, I'll beat him up." Wink waited for Armeeah to pull back a Colgate smile, and then reached for her hand. "Come on. I really need you to meet my dad 'cause, besides you, he's all I got."

Wink helped her out of the cab and kissed her forehead, assuring her that everything would be fine. Together they climbed the stairs and blended in with the rest of the visitors. They were herded along like cattle, stopping at checkpoints along the way. It felt like overkill to Wink and that it was just their way of making life miserable for the families of the prisoners. After being checked for contraband and showing their IDs at the last checkpoint, they were finally permitted into the visiting hall. The CO working the visiting booth took their passes and pointed to an empty section in the back.

Wink's stomach balled up at the sight of Nina staring him in the face. She and Franko were also situated near the back picture area. Wink quickly scanned the hall for another area. *Damn,* he thought, clenching his jaw because all the other seats were taken. Armeeah led him by the hand to their seats. On the way, Wink made sure to give Franko and Nina a nod with a closed smile. *Why couldn't she have picked another day to come see his old ass?* Wink knew exactly what Nina was over there thinking. Surely she was concerning herself with who Armeeah was to him. Wink sat, giving Nina his back, and tried focusing on his wife-to-be.

"You better now?"

"I guess so. It's just that I've never been inside a prison. Wayne, how much time is your father serving?" Armeeah sounded concerned. She had never met Wink's dad, and yet she felt bad for him and all the other men there because it seemed like a rough place and nowhere for any human being.

Wink sighed and looked off, then slowly said, "Two life sentences."

"Oh, my God," Armeeah whispered. She put her hands to her face, and with wide eyes she repeated, "Two life sentences. For what?"

Wink didn't say anything because he knew that Armeeah wouldn't understand his rationale of why his father was in prison. It had nothing to do with the fact that he was charged with drug conspiracy and a slew of murders. In his reality, the only reason his dad was in prison was because niggas snitched him out. The frustration in Wink's forehead released when he saw his father walk through the visiting room door.

"That's him right there," said Wink. He smiled and stood up to greet his pops.

"Son, how are you?" Gunz embraced Wink with a long bear hug just as a father would.

Wink turned his dad around to face a nervous yet smiling Armeeah. "Dad, I have someone very special I want you to meet. This is my wife-to-be, Armeeah."

Gunz opened his arms wide, and with a warm smile, he swallowed Armeeah into a hug. She was so nervous she didn't know what to do with herself. Wink motioned from over his dad's shoulder for her to calm down.

"Yes, son, you have done real well for yourself," said Gunz. He held Armeeah's hand while looking her over.

Armeeah couldn't help but blush. Gunz waved his hand at the chairs. "Let's have a seat."

"I am going to step over to the vending machine. May I get you guys anything?" Armeeah looked from Wink to his dad.

"Bring us some of those wing dings," ordered Wink.

"And you, Pa?" asked Armeeah.

"A bottle of water, please."

Armeeah smiled and excused herself so that Wink could speak with his father in private.

"I'm really proud of you, son. You make sure that you hold on to her, ya hear me?" Gunz met eyes with Wink.

"I'ma do my best. I proposed to her last week, so we're engaged."

"You're tellin' me you did it? You became Muslim?" Gunz asked proudly.

"Nah. That's the one problem."

"What's that?"

"Before we get married, she wants me to flip Muslim." Wink watched his father's mug screw up and the lines in his forehead take on some serious wrinkles.

"Wayne, first off, you don't flip Muslim. You take your *Al-Shahada* by bearing witness that there's no other deity except Allah, and that Prophet Mohammed is His messenger." Gunz paused a moment to let the frustration of Wink's ignorance of Islam pass. He faulted himself for not teaching Wink the *deen*. "Son, she's a Muslim woman. It's against Allah's commandment for her to marry a non-Muslim man, because as your wife she will be likely to lean toward your faith and way of life. She probably said yes because she loves you, son. But respect her beliefs, and if you love her, you'll do the right thing not only for the sake of marriage, but for the sake of your own soul. Have you been attending *jumah?*"

"Not like I should."

"Son, as your father, it is my obligation to offer you the *deen* of Islam. I didn't preach your ear off when we first united because I didn't want you thinking your old man was some burned-out Islamic extremist. But, Wayne, I gotta tell you that Islam is the most beautiful thing to ever come into my life. It literally has saved my life. Without it I don't know what I'd be around here doing. I'ma leave you with this, and I want you to think about it. In the holy Quran, Allah says, 'Die not except in the state of a Muslim.' Don't wait forever, son."

Wink nodded as his father went to church, or in his case the mosque. He was feeling all he was kicking, but deep down he knew that he was nowhere near ready to become a Muslim. He still had too many demons he was fighting with.

Wink looked over at Nina and Franko, then asked his dad, "What's the deal with Franko's broad?"

"What do you mean?" Gunz was confused.

"She gave me the impression we're now part of Franko's crime family and that there's no gettin' out."

Gunz threw his head back in laughter. "Is that what she told you?"

"In so many words, yeah. She basically threatened us." Wink was looking Nina in the face as she laughed with Franko.

"Yeah, Franko told me she's a real mess. But don't pay her no mind in nothing she says, 'cause she ain't runnin' nothing but her head. That was just her way of tryin'a spook you so you don't stop dealin' with her."

"Yeah, 'cause when and if I'm ready to leave the game, I'm not tryin' to be at war with the Cuban cartel," said Wink.

"Just remember to always keep your plans to ya'self. If you're going to get out of the game, get out. You don't owe anybody any two-week notice. Remember what I told you about everybody playin' for keeps."

When Armeeah finally came back from the vending machine, she was carrying enough food to feed an entire family. She had BBQ wings, cheese pizza, sandwiches, soda, and bottled water. She laid out the spread and watched as Wink and his dad pigged out on the finger foods. They talked some more, told jokes, took some pictures, and kicked it some more until the CO announced that visiting hours were over.

Wink and Armeeah hugged his dad goodbye and watched as he and the rest of the prisoners filed out of the visiting hall, each waving bye to their people. Every time Wink saw that door shut behind his father, rage would fill up his veins, then a feeling of helplessness would overwhelm him. There was nothing he could do for his dad.

Armeeah locked her arm around Wink's. "It's going to be all right, baby. Let's go."

Chapter Six

Back in Detroit, Trey was just waking up after a long night of drinking, smoking, and club hopping. He and his Money Squad Family were downtown at Legends nightclub, blowing money like it was going out of style. They all wore black tees with MSF printed on them, campaigning their name and trying to be seen. As hard as they were stunting, it was hard to go unnoticed. They pulled up back-to-back in six Benzes all sitting on chromed-out Hammers. When the valet parked their cars, everyone waited for Trey to lead the group inside, totally bypassing the long line of onlookers.

The moment Trey stepped out of his car, he turned into T-Money. The crowd outside was gawking, and as soon as he entered the club, everyone gravitated to him. You would've sworn it was his welcome-home party after serving a ten-year bid.

Trey spotted this five foot red bone out on the dance floor from his VIP booth. He locked eyes on her thick legs and forty-inch ass, and nudged Live to go get her.

Live pulled the girl from the dance floor. The guy she was dancing with started complaining until Live gave him a death stare. The guy shut up and walked away. Live escorted her by the hand over to T-Money's table. At first the girl had an attitude from the way Live was handling her, but as soon as she saw T-Money, she changed her tone. T-Money cuffed her for the rest of the night. They partied in the VIP, popping bottles and letting loose. When the club let out, she was by his side. T-Money gave his crew some dap and told them he'd see them tomorrow. He and the red bone got in his Benz and headed over to his apartment in the Jeffersonian. Trey was so high and buzzed from the drinking, he busted a nut as soon as he got in the pussy. He passed out with ol' girl lying beside him.

Trey had gotten into the bad habit of meeting chicks and taking them back to his apartment on the first night. Like in this case, he didn't even bother to ask ol' girl what her name was. He was living the dream and hadn't thought about the day when somebody would wake his ass up with a pistol staring him in the face.

That was exactly what happened when he rolled over onto his back and yawned wide, stretching his arms about the silk sheets. Trey smiled as he vaguely remembered how good the pussy was before he crashed last night. Trey felt around for her, then opened his eyes. When he looked up, four men were standing around his bed at every corner. The one at his side had a .44 Desert Eagle pointed dead at his grill while the other men all held their guns at their sides.

Fear filled Trey's entire body. He had the white-mouth look of death in his eyes. He didn't know how he was going to make it out of there alive, but he knew that he had a chance of living because the goons hadn't killed him yet. They obviously wanted something. Trey swallowed hard, but the nervous lump in his throat refused to digest.

"Nigga, you know what this is, so let's not make it a murder. Where that money at?" demanded the man of the hour.

Trey tried to speak, but the words wouldn't come out. He stared up the barrel of the man's gun at the bullet waiting to be released. "Please don't kill me," he managed to mumble.

The man cocked the hammer back and screwed his face up, then spat, "Bitch nigga, I'm not tryin'a hear that weak shit. Last night you was playin' big when you snatched my girl off the dance floor, so now we gon' see if you can afford the price of that pussy. Nigga, I want five hundred thousand dollars right now or I'ma paint these sheets red with yo' face."

This has gotta be a bad dream, Trey told himself, but he didn't wake up in a cold sweat. It was the real deal, and ol' boy was oh-so-serious.

"I only got half of that in my safe," said Trey, hoping that would be enough to save his ass.

"Where is it?"

"In my closet underneath my shoe rack."

The gunman nodded to two of his partners for them to go check it out. Trey sat up on his elbows and tried to get the dry taste of death out of his mouth. "Look, I didn't know she was your girl. No disrespect, my man."

"Shut your mouth. I don't want to hear no bitch-ass apology from you." He raised his gun at Trey.

Trey watched as the two goons carried the small safe into the bedroom. They poured all the money onto the foot of the bed for their leader to see. He nodded, and the men began bagging up the cash.

"That's half, you say. Where's the rest of it?"

"I swear that's all of it. Man, I'm not holding like that. I swear."

"Shut the fuck up!" yelled the goon. "I told you my price. If you ain't got but half, then I'ma half kill yo' ass."

"Come on, man," Trey pleaded. Tears welled in his eyes. He was too young to die.

"You got one phone call to get the rest of my money, bitch! I'm not playin' with yo' ass, so you betta make it happen." The man handed Trey the phone off the nightstand beside the bed.

Trey thought about his Money Squad Family, but not one of them had anything close to $250,000, Willie included. He proceeded to call the only person he knew could save his life: Wink. They hadn't been on the best of terms, but Trey knew that Wink wouldn't leave him hanging.

"What happened, you couldn't get through?" asked goon number one. He tightened up his mug as if he were about to splat Trey's ass.

"Nah, it's cool. I paged my man 911. He's gon' hit me back in a minute."

"You betta sure hope so, 'cause a minute's all that ass got before lights out." The gunman snapped his fingers, signaling his men to watch the front room in case it was a setup.

Trey crossed his fingers and toes and prayed the blood of Jesus that Wink hit him back. Otherwise, it was curtains.

Wink and Armeeah had just walked out of the Detroit City Airport terminal when Wink's pager vibrated on his hip. He held the back door open for Armeeah to climb inside their taxi cab, then climbed in behind her. As the cab pulled away from the curb, Wink checked his pager and saw Trey's number with 911 behind it. Wink knew that something serious must be wrong for Trey to page him 911. His first thought was that something might have happened to Willie.

"Is something the matter, baby?" asked Armeeah, noticing the distraught look on Wink's face.

"I hope not," said Wink. He used the cab's car phone to call Trey's crib.

"Hello," goon number one answered Trey's phone on the second ring.

"Trey, what's up? I got your page."

Goon number one tossed the phone onto Trey's chest. "It's for you. You got thirty seconds to get my money."

"Trey, are you there?" asked Wink.

Trey slowly raised the phone to his ear and cleared his throat. "Yeah, I'm here."

"What's this business? You paged me 911."

"Wink, these niggas got me hemmed up at my apartment, and they want two hundred fifty thousand dollars or they gon' kill me."

"What?" yelled Wink. He sat up and put his elbows on his knees. "Who are these niggas, and how do they expect to make it out of there alive?"

The goon had snatched the phone from Trey. "Easy. We're on our way outta here right now. And if you ever want to see ya man alive again, you'll have that bread ready in an hour. I'll call you with a drop-off place." He hung up.

Wink slowly lowered the phone from his ear and placed it back on its hook. He was shell-shocked. *Damn, Trey! How could you let them niggas get the ups on you?*

"Wayne, is everything all right?" Armeeah questioned with sincere concern.

"It will be."

Wink directed the driver to drop him off at his apartment at the Jeffersonian. He told Armeeah that he'd see her at home later. Wink went straight to his safe and counted out $250,000, put it in a Louis Vuitton traveler bag, then paced his living room floor while waiting for the drop-off call.

"Just hold on, my nigga. I got you," said Wink. He wasn't about to leave his main man stankin' over a little money. Even though they weren't hanging tough like the best friends they were, the situation made Wink realize how much he missed Trey. They were like brothers for real, and if anything were to happen to him, heads would roll.

Finally, Wink's pager vibrated. He nearly broke the clip snatching it from his hip. He raced for the cordless phone and dialed the phone number.

"You got my money, bitch?"

"Yeah, I got it. Where you want me to meet you at?"

"There's a grocery store on 8 Mile and Dequindre. Be yo' ass there in ten minutes, and don't make no pit stops." Click.

Wink looked at the phone for a second before hanging up. *This nigga don't know who he's fucking with.* Wink pushed his thoughts of sweet revenge to the back of his mind. Right now, he had to save his nigga's life 'cause he was down bad and needed him. Wink grabbed the Louis bag from the dining room table, cocked his .45, and was out the door.

When Wink pulled inside the Belmont Shopping Center, he scanned the parking lot for a place to park. He pulled into a space in the front row, figuring the niggas wouldn't try anything in front of all those people coming and going. As soon as Wink put the car in park, the passenger door swung open and a shit-black-faced man wearing all black slid into the passenger seat. He clutched a black short-dog .357 Magnum low at the waist pointed dead for Wink's stomach. The nigga had nuts though because he wasn't wearing a mask.

"Where's the money?" demanded black face.

"Where's Trey?" asked Wink.

"Mothafucka, you or that nigga ain't in no position to be asking no questions. Now where is it?" The man cocked the hammer back to let Wink know that he was serious.

"It's in the bag between yo' legs."

The man unzipped the bag and met eyes with a few familiar old dead guys, and then he zipped the bag shut and reached for the door handle. Wink grabbed the back of blackie's hoodie to stop him.

"You got your money. Now where's Trey?"

"Gon' be dead if you don't get the fuck off me." Black face snatched away, then slammed the door.

Wink watched as he maneuvered between the rows of parked cars, stopping at a blue conversion van. The side door opened, and seconds later, Trey was pushed out onto the pavement, and the van sped away. Wink hurried around to the empty parking space where Trey lay bound and gagged at the wrists and mouth with gray duct tape. Wink jumped out of the car and rushed to Trey's aid, peeling the tape from his mouth first, then from around his wrists. By this time, nosy shoppers were gathering, so Wink put him in the car and sped away.

"You a'ight, my nigga?" asked Wink.

Trey slapped the dashboard hard with both hands and yelled, "Fuck!" He had tears in his eyes. "I'ma kill them bitch niggas!"

"Calm down, Trey. We gon' get them niggas."

"Take me on Gallagher," ordered Trey.

"What's on Gallagher?"

"My team! We 'bout to go put this work in. I can't believe I let them niggas get the ups on me. Fuck!" yelled Trey.

"My nigga, just chill. I'ma take care of it."

"Nah, I'm good. Me and my Money Squad Family gotta handle this one."

Wink was getting furious. Here he was the one who'd saved his life, and all Trey could think about was a bunch of young punks calling themselves Money Squad. Wink knew that now wasn't the time to be bringing up the money, but he wanted Trey to know who really had his back.

They turned down Gallagher Street where Trey and his MSF hung out. Trey was using Wink's car phone to call inside their spot to let them know to gather up all the heat 'cause it was time to ride. Trey slammed down the phone and said, "Yeah, it's on!"

Wink could see Lee-Mac, Live, JT, and Dilla all come out of the spot, each toting Mack 11s at their sides. Wink pulled over and parked across the street. Before the car was good and stopped, Trey was pulling on the door handle.

"Hold on, my nigga. Let me holla at you," Wink said.

Trey stopped. Trey was anxious to join his young dummies on a blood-thirsty mission. "What's up?"

"Trey, don't go doin' nothin' with those young niggas who gon' get you a life sentence. 'Cause if one of 'em gets caught, they gon' tell it."

"My niggas is official. They know the business."

Wink shook his head, then looked out the window. "Trey, when we gon' get back to being crew? When are we gon' put all that money shit to the side and go back to the way it was, the way it 'posed to be?" Wink turned to face Trey.

"Wink, my nigga, you're not ready for that. You want me to work up under you instead with you. We tried that, remember? You doing yo' thang, and I'm doin' mine, and I'm good with that. Ain't no love lost."

Wink stuck out his hand for Trey's. "I wish we could be a family again. But I'ma let you do you, my nigga. And you're right, ain't no love lost. Just remember that if you ever need me, I'll always come runnin', guns blazin'."

Trey smiled, then said, "No doubt."

"Be careful out there," said Wink.

"You too. And, Wink, thanks, man."

Wink nodded. Trey climbed out of the car to join his Money Squad Family.

Wink pulled away from the curb and headed home to his beautiful fiancé. He was fucked up that Trey would choose them little niggas over him, but then again, it had nothing to do with them. It was about the power they both wanted.

Wink chalked the $250,000 up as a loss to the game. He had 200 bricks to move and millions to make. He wasn't about to share that with Trey or anyone else.

"See you at the top, my nigga," Wink said, looking in the rearview mirror.

Chapter Seven

1993

Krazy carried his name and reputation from the grimy streets of east Detroit with him through the treacherous penitentiaries of the Ohio state prison system. Fresh off the bus, he had to bust a nigga's ass for trying to play him over the phone. Being from Detroit, quite naturally he was outnumbered by all the Columbus, Toledo, Akron, Dayton, and Cleveland niggas. They ran everything in the joint, from the TV to the phones, so it wasn't unusual for one of those O-town niggas to roll up while an out-of-town cat was using the phone, and hang up. That was exactly what happened the first day Krazy got to MR reformatory. He was trying to call Wink to let him know they'd moved him from the county jail. The phone started ringing, when out of nowhere, this muscle-back nigga named V reached over Krazy's shoulder and pressed down the receiver.

"Phone check, fool! This here jack is off-limits unless you pushin' da Cleveland line."

Krazy slowly looked up at V like, "I know this nigga didn't just hang up on me."

"Nigga, you hard of hearing?" yelled V. He reached for the phone while saying, "I said this here—"

Smack!

Krazy cut V's words short when he slapped the cowboy shit out of him with the phone. By the time V recovered from the first lick, it was followed up with an overhand swing with the phone. Krazy got a few more swings off, cracking that niggas shit to the green meat, before his boys called themselves trying to rush over and help V's punk ass.

Krazy quickly dropped the phone and snatched the mop ringer from a bucket sitting next to the phones. "Come on, mothafuckas!" snapped Krazy. He bucked his eyes to show them niggas that he was crazy for real. He held the ringer up and took a few quick steps forward, and all five of them pussies gave him their backs, tripping over one another trying to get somewhere.

By the time the prison emergency system had sounded, the guards' keys could be heard jingling at their sides as they neared the scene. All the prisoners in the dorm got quiet and stopped what activities they were doing while Krazy finished V off with the mop ringer. He figured, *hell, why not?* He was going to the hole anyway. At least when he got out, the word would beat him to the compound that he was about his work. *Yeah,* Krazy thought as he continued the bloody onslaught, *take this with you to the infirmary.*

Two guards tackled Krazy from behind, knocking the mop ringer from his hand. They wrestled him down and restrained him with handcuffs and shackles, then stood him up, and off to the hole he went. He fucked up V so badly they had to medevac his tough ass out of there.

For the assault, the disciplinary hearing officer at the prison sanctioned Krazy to ninety days in the hole, but he ended up doing six months altogether because he had to fuck another nigga up out in the recreation cages. He beat him with a sock full of soap. During two and a half years, he'd spent two years in the hole. Krazy didn't want for anything the whole time he was down, because Wink kept at least $5,000 on his books for commissary and whatever else he wanted to do in there. But Krazy didn't care about having a locker full of zoom zooms and wam wams. He couldn't get over the fact that those crackers had parked him for the next twenty-five years, so in no way was he trying to get comfortable.

In his crazy way of thinking, he thought bucking the system would somehow change facts. And if not, then fuck it. He would at least blow off some steam by giving them Cracker Jack mothafuckas hell on a daily basis. He would start false arguments with the guards just to have a reason to spazz out on them. Not that he needed one, but he got his rocks off by knowing they were taking the shit to heart. It was his way of pulling them into his world.

When the guards used to talk shit back, Krazy would come alive and snap into his "go hard" mode. He'd wait for a guard to open his food trap and shit 'em down, literally. He'd have 2-day-old shit saved up in milk cartons with some sour milk and a little piss mixed together. That was a mean concoction, and even more vicious when he would douse one of their asses. That shit was like a war bomb. Within seconds, the entire tier would be hummin' like a mothafucka. And all the while, the guard would be standing there stuck and melting, trying not to swallow any of the feces.

Krazy would be standing there laughing his heart out. He didn't care when it came to them pigs. He once shit the warden down. As soon as the guard would walk off, Krazy would get ready for war, because he knew they were coming deep to fuck him up, but never did he go out without a fight. Each time he fought the sort team, he got better at it. His latest tactic was to strip buck-naked and cover his entire body with grease and baby oil and put water on the floor, so when they ran in his cell, they'd be slipping and sliding everywhere.

Krazy found a bunch of ways to equal out the fight, and sometimes he'd win by sending one of them to the hospital. Other times he was not so lucky. They'd pepper spray his ass first and shoot pepper balls into the cell. All the while, all the other prisoners on the tier would root Krazy on. "Go hard!" And hard he would go every time the sort team would eventually drag Krazy out of his cell buck-naked and gleaming from the grease. He had all kinds of akas jumping off in the piece, everything from Krazy to Go Hard to Buck-naked.

Krazy was at it one afternoon, back on his bullshit trying to get something cranked up with a rookie. The young white officer refused to buy into Krazy's daily entertainment as he jacked his food slot and commenced cussin' and calling him every kind of cracker in the book.

"Please close the food slot," pleaded the guard. His heart was racing because he feared the hell out of Krazy. The guard made sure to keep his distance from Krazy while he continued to plead for Krazy to take his arm out of the slot. The warden and commander bent the corner, and the guard stepped aside.

"And just what the fuck you two cracker bitches want, huh? Ya ass ain't learned from the last time I gave you a shower, I see. Well, just wait right there." Krazy went to reach for his milk carton, but Warden Bledsoe's stubby ass held out a piece of paper for Krazy to read.

Krazy squinted as he read the memorandum. He saw the word "appeal," but his eyes bucked and his dick got rock hard when he read, "Your appeal has been granted! And your release is effective immediately!" He looked up at the warden and commander, who were both cheesing because they could finally run their institution Krazy free.

"That's right. You've won your appeal. So please pack your shit, and be ready in five minutes," said Bledsoe.

"I'm ready now!" Krazy jumped up from the slot and rushed to put his orange jumper on. "You bitches betta not be lying, 'cause I swear on my mammy I'ma shit all y'all asses down."

"Oh, believe me, it's the real thing," Bledsoe gladly assured Krazy.

"Yeah, well, I'm ready." Krazy put his arm through his sleeve and straightened his jumper. The rookie hand-cuffed him, then opened his cell door. Krazy didn't look back or acknowledge the hollering of his fellow prisoners on his way out of segregation.

The warden himself and the commander walked Krazy over to R&D to see him off. It was like a celebration for all the staff and MR. They were all clapping and whistling. But for Krazy it was like awakening from a nightmare that had lasted two and a half years. He'd been in the hole so long that when he walked out the front door of the prison, the daylight nearly blinded him. He stood there for a minute taking it all in: the air, the grass, and his freedom. The sound of a horn brought him back.

"You gon' just stand there, or you gon' come take a ride with ya boy?" Wink hollered from behind the wheel of a sapphire blue drop-top BMW. He threw both hands up, and Krazy broke out running with a huge smile on his face. Wink got out of the car and opened his arms wide for his best friend.

"My mothafuckin' nigga," Wink said into Krazy's ear as they rocked side to side with their embrace. "It's finally over," said Wink. He held Krazy a moment longer, then stood him back so he could take a look at him.

"First stop, the barber shop," joked Wink as he dug his fingers into Krazy's unkempt 'fro.

"No bullshit, right?" Krazy smiled.

Wink had no idea what he had been doing in there.

"Is this shit for real?" asked Krazy.

"Betta believe it's real. I told you, my dawg, that you weren't forgotten."

"Well, let's get the fuck outta here before I wake up in my cell."

"My nigga's home!" yelled Wink.

They jumped into Wink's BMW and peeled out of the prison parking lot. It didn't get no realer than that.

Chapter Eight

Wink laid down the red carpet for Krazy's homecoming. As soon as he got the word from Krazy's attorney that the district court had granted Krazy's appeal, he went all out for his boy. Wink copped a $270,000 crib in Oak Park, Michigan. The house had an in-ground swimming pool and guest quarters, with a three-car garage for Krazy to park his new Benz 500, Lexus truck, and '94 Impala, all of which were cocaine white.

After they visited the barber shop and hit Somerset Mall, Wink surprised Krazy with his new house. Wink had the Benz, Lexus truck, and Impala all waxed up and posted outside the house's circular driveway. When they pulled up and got out, Krazy was astonished, thinking that the crib belonged to Wink.

"I knew y'all niggas done came up, but damn, my nigga, I ain't know you was doin' it this hard," said Krazy. He followed Wink up the driveway, eyeing each car along the way.

Wink smiled as he put the key in the front door. He unlocked it, pushed it open, and stood aside for Krazy to walk in first. Krazy stepped inside the crisp, cool central air and stopped in the foyer, admiring the white marble floors he was standing on. He took a minute eyeing all the expensive fixtures that made up the house, including the all-white living room. When he finally snapped out of his trance and turned around, he said, "Yo, this is nice."

Wink was smiling and holding out a key ring. "Take it," he said.

Krazy squinted in confusion. Was Wink saying what he thought he was saying? He had to be dreaming.

"These two are the house keys, and the other three are to your whips outside," said Wink. He waited for Krazy to say something, but Krazy was on cloud nine.

"You're home, my nigga. And from now on, this is what it is. Come on, let me show you around your crib." Wink put his arm around Krazy's neck and led him through the three-bedroom house.

Krazy walked around the home in shock as Wink showed him the rest of the house.

They stood alongside the pool. "So what do you think?" asked Wink.

"I think I'm dreaming and I'ma wake up any minute back in my cell."

Wink pulled back a smile and stuck out his hand for Krazy's. "I assure you that this is the real thing. All of this is yours, and there's more to come. This here ain't but a starter kit."

"Thanks, Wink. This is more than I expected."

"It's nothin'. You my brotha. I got nothin' but love for you."

"I love you too, my nigga." Krazy pulled Wink in for an embrace. He was so grateful for Wink's friendship it was the only thing he could think to do at the moment.

They broke their embrace. "A'ight. I'ma let you get settled, you know, take a shower and knock the cheat off that ass. I'ma go get ready for tonight."

"What's tonight?"

"You know it wouldn't be official if I ain't bring the city out to celebrate you coming home. We gon' do it real big. Just be ready by, like, ten o'clock."

"What's up with Trey and Willie?"

Wink shook his head like, "You don't even want to know." "You gon' see for ya'self. G'on and get straight. I'ma holla at you tonight."

"A'ight, my nigga." Krazy gave Wink some dap, then followed him around the side of the crib to his Beemer.

"Oh, yeah, I forgot to tell you. Two hun'd stacks are in the top dresser drawer. That should hold you until we can get you back on ya feet."

"Good lookin' out. I'ma see you tonight." Krazy closed Wink's car door. Wink pulled off as Krazy stood there and watched him go.

Krazy turned around and looked at his house and cars. *It's funny what twenty-four hours can change,* he thought as he started for the house. Krazy still couldn't believe how his luck had changed for the better.

He entered the house and stood in the middle of his living room. The first thing he noticed was the quiet. It had been years since he was surrounded by real quiet. Prison wasn't easy for Krazy. Being surrounded by silence made him realize that he was safe, and it was the first good thing to happen in his life in a long time. He was so used to getting the short end of the stick that the shit just didn't seem real. He ain't never had nothing except two strung-out parents and a pocketful of dreams. He was so thankful to have Wink as a friend. Since they were younger, Wink had held him down. When he didn't have anything at home to eat, which was almost always, it was Wink who made sure he put a plate to the side for him.

Krazy smiled as he stood in his bedroom trying on the gold Rolex President he found in the dresser drawer on top of the $200,000. Wink was still taking care of him.

Krazy stripped out of the tight Wrangler jeans the prison sent him out in. He balled them shits up and threw them in the garbage, and he finally started accepting that he was really home. He walked into his master bathroom and ran a hot bubble bath. It had been almost three years since he took a bath, so he wanted to indulge in a long, relaxing bath until his skin got soggy.

After knocking the cheat off his ass, Krazy popped the tags on a Pelle-Pelle outfit and some white Air Force Ones. He stuffed his pockets with two handfuls of money, put his Rolex on, then stood in the floor-length mirror, taking a B-boy stance.

"Bitch, I'm back."

Chapter Nine

Trey and Willie hadn't done shit for Krazy the whole time he was down. When they all took their money out of the pot and started doing their own thing, Wink was the only one making sure Krazy kept money on his books and that his lawyer fees got paid on time. If it weren't for Wink, Krazy would still be parked doing the rest of that twenty-five-year sentence. Still and all, Wink didn't hold that against Willie and Trey, nor did he salt them to Krazy like, "Yeah, I was the one doing this, that, and the third." He just didn't see what good could come from it.

That was why, when Trey pressed the issue about being the one to throw Krazy's homecoming party, Wink didn't veto the idea, because he knew the nigga was feeling guilty. For Wink, the important thing was that Krazy was home, and as far as he was concerned, Krazy wouldn't want for anything, because he was going to be the one to make sure he was straight.

The party was to be held at Geno's, a nightclub Trey bought from this old hustla Mark Bell right before he got indicted. Trey had bought the club and turned it into the headquarters for his Money Squad Family. Right after Trey had his brush with death, waking up buck-naked with a gun in his face and being robbed of everything, he and his MS Family turned up the heat and started taking niggas to war over drug territory. Trey had to save face in his own eyes because the shit was causing him to have nightmares, so the only way to fix things was to kill any and all opposition.

After much bloodshed and hundreds of bodies, niggas finally started getting the picture that Money Squad was taking over. So instead of being added to the massive body count, niggas got on board. Pretty soon, in almost every hood you went to, there were some niggas reppin' Money Squad and warring any nigga who wasn't.

Trey had king status in the city and could go anywhere and do whatever he wanted. He was the unofficial mayor of Detroit in the eyes of the streets, and his MS Family was like the city council. They had the shit in the chokehold. In all, there were over 500 MS associates throughout Detroit. Only the founding members had the right to call themselves family: Trey, Willie, Live, Lee-Mac, JT, and Dilla. And Trey treated them all like family in every sense of the word, like they were a real-life Mafia. All of them had four cars, mansions, jewels for days, and money to blow.

Wink picked Krazy up at his crib, and they rode back-to-back in their white Benz 500s downtown off Woodward and Jefferson where Geno's sat. They pulled up looking like two boss players and had the valet park their cars. Wink met Krazy at the curb, and together they read the marquee outside the club. WELCOME HOME, KRAZY, the sign read. Krazy smiled, realizing that the long line of onlookers was there to celebrate his homecoming. FM 79 Jamz was out there broadcasting live. Trey had made a few power moves to make sure there was a big turnout for Krazy's party. He had flyers printed and posters with Krazy's picture hung all around the city. With all the hype, everybody who was somebody was planning on hitting the party. There was so much talk about the party that you would have thought they found Jimmy Hoffa alive and this was his party.

Wink put his arm around Krazy's shoulder, and they made their way up to the front door. Trey was standing at the door doing what he did best, flodging for the public eye and talkin' trash. He ceased his ghetto campaign at the sight of Krazy standing before him.

"My niggaaaa! Ahh!" Trey rushed over to Krazy and gave him a bear hug. "Welcome home, baby!" Trey was so excited to see Krazy.

"What up doe," said Krazy. He couldn't stop smiling.

"You what's up. Come on, let's get up in here to your party." Trey put his arm around Krazy's neck and walked him inside the club. They stopped under the EXIT sign, and Trey signaled DJ Shaun.

DJ Shaun put the strobe light on Krazy and cut the music. Everyone in the club stopped and faced the light. Trey went on to present the man of the hour.

"Ay, y'all. This here is my brother from another motha. My nigga, my mothafuckin' nucca. He just comin' home from doin' a bid, so I want y'all to show him nothin' but love, and let's turn this bitch out tonight. Welcome home, Krazy."

Trey kissed Krazy on the cheek, and everyone went nuts hollering, "Welcome home, Krazy!"

Trey signaled the DJ, and he cranked up Biggie's new cut, "Big Poppa." There couldn't have been a better song on, because that was exactly how Krazy was feeling as Trey showed him off to everybody. Chicks were putting their bids in, slipping him their numbers, trying to be the first bitch to get some of the penitentiary dick.

"Never mind them skanks. I got some models lined up for you tonight. I know you wanna get ya nuts outta pawn," said Trey. He led Krazy around the back of the bar. They walked with Wink up to Trey's office, which overlooked the entire club. "Close that door," said Trey as he walked around his desk and opened the bottom drawer.

Wink took a seat on the leather sofa and watched as Trey tried making up for lost time. He placed a black briefcase on top of the desk, then pushed it toward Krazy. "That's yo' homecoming present."

Krazy clicked open the flaps on the case, then raised its lid.

"That's a mill ticket," said Trey.

Krazy's eyes bulged. "Thanks, Trey."

"Welcome home, baby." Trey knew that Wink had already blessed Krazy, but he was set on outdoing Wink, not because he felt guilty, but because he wanted Krazy on his team. He needed another head hitter on his side, and who better than Krazy?

There was a knock on the door, then without warning it opened. JT stuck his head inside. "Excuse me, but T-Money, you're needed downstairs. It's kinda important."

"It betta be important enough to interrupt me welcoming my man home," said Trey. He stood up and walked around the desk. "I'll be right back," he told Wink and Krazy before closing the door.

"Did I hear that nigga just call him T-Money?" asked Krazy.

"Oh, you ain't seen nothin' yet. Just give it a couple of days, and you gon' see all kind of shit." Wink pointed to the Money Squad Family emblem hanging on the back wall.

"What the fuck is Money Squad Family?" Krazy asked with his face screwed up.

"Let's just say that the Trey we once knew is no more. He's on some Nino shit, and all these little niggas is his flunkies."

Krazy looked down at the money for a minute. He still couldn't believe he wasn't dreaming. There were moments in prison when he thought he'd never get out.

He was grateful for Trey giving him the cash, but it didn't feel right. He closed the case. He walked around the desk and put the case back in the drawer and closed it.

"What are you doing?" asked Wink.

"My nigga, I know who was down for me when shit wasn't right. I don't care if there was ten million in that case. I'm on yo' team." Krazy stuck out his hand, and Wink smiled, then met his embrace.

"I didn't want to say nothin' 'cause I wanted you to see for yourself."

"Wink, I'm not slow. I know the score." Krazy stopped talking when Willie walked through the door.

"My nigga!" yelled Willie. He rushed over to show Krazy some love. "Damn, boy, you done got big as shit," said Willie after he finished hugging Krazy.

"What y'all gon' do, stay up here all night? We got a club full of people waiting to see you. Come on and let's get to the party," Trey said from the doorway. "Plus, I wanna see if y'all still got it."

"Oh, nigga, you know I still got it," said Willie.

"A'ight then, well, let's see."

They all filed downstairs, and Trey signaled DJ Shaun for his music. The crowd parted like the Red Sea as the original B-boys made their way onto the dance floor. As soon as Rakim's "Paid In Full" dropped, they broke off into one of their old routines. They pop-locked, ticked, jitted, and brake-danced, not missing a step. The crowd cheered them on to keep going, but after three songs they were all good and tired. They ended their set in a B-boy stance just how they used to do it back in the day at the high school icebreakers. The crowd went wild, and some other old-head, washed-up B-boys took the floor while Trey led the way to their VIP table.

"Ah, man, I ain't had this much fun since our prom," said Trey, sliding into the booth. He introduced Krazy to all his MS Family members. JT, Live, Dilla, and Lee-Mac all nodded in Krazy's direction, then Trey dismissed them so he could chill with his original crew. Trey ordered four bottles of Dom P and a couple bottles of Rémy Martin. He did most of the talking, pointing, and nodding at all the money-gettin' niggas in the club.

While they were chilling and drinking, two Mexican men walked up to their table, and right off the bat, Wink recognized the short, old, bad-body one. There was a picture of him with his dad in their old house.

Trey leaped from the table, bearing a huge Kool-Aid smile. He hugged the old man like he was the last don himself. "I thought you couldn't make it," said Trey.

"I decided to send my son to handle the business. You sounded like the party was important to you."

"And it is. I want you to meet some very good friends of mine." Trey introduced Wink, Willie, and Krazy. "Y'all, this is ol' Sammy," said Trey.

They all nodded at the old man and his bodyguard, who stood well over six feet and looked like he was ready to kill on command. Trey excused himself from the table and escorted Sammy and his watchdog up to his office. Trey did this because he didn't want Wink rubbing elbows with his connect. He didn't want Wink within a hundred yards of Sammy.

Wink knew damn well who Sammy was, but he wanted to hear it from Willie because he was with Trey when he met Sammy down in Texas.

"Ay yo, who ol' boy is?"

"That's his plug," advised Willie. He was still playing the fifty-yard line with Trey and Wink, selling keys for both of them.

"Yeah, I figured that's why he hurried up and got his old ass away from here," said Wink. *It's a small world. Yeah, a real small world.*

Wink could no longer enjoy himself after seeing Sammy. All he could think about was the old photo album he took from Gary's closet the day he killed him. Wink knew for a fact that he was the same man in the picture with his dad and Gary, but he still wanted to be absolutely certain before he jumped the gun.

Wink played it cool for the rest of the night, not letting anyone in on what was about to go down. When the party ended, it was damn near 4:00 in the morning, but Trey packed everybody into a few limos and headed over to the DoubleTree hotel so they could crank up the after-party.

Wink said he would follow them over in his Benz, but he turned off on Jefferson and raced over to the Jeffersonian, where he still had an apartment. He dug out the photo album from his walk-in closet, then took a seat on the edge of the bed while flipping through the pages. Wink stopped on the page where he remembered seeing the picture. He used his finger to scan the Polaroid. "I knew it was you, bitch." Wink removed the photo from the sleeve and held it up. Without a doubt it was Sammy. He had aged a lot and put on some weight, but that was definitely him standing in front of his father in the photo, with a big-ass smile on his face. "Rat bitch."

Wink became furious just knowing that this slimy mothafucka was out running around like he hadn't helped get his dad two life sentences. And to top it off, he had the balls to be in Detroit like shit was sweet, like nobody remembered.

"I remember, mothafucka." Wink stood up and closed the photo album. He tucked the picture of Sammy in his pocket, then returned to his closet to suit up.

He came out dressed in black from head to toe. He flipped up the mattress and grabbed the two .40-cal Berettas. He cocked them, then tucked them under his hoodie and was out the door.

Chapter Ten

When Wink got over to the hotel, the party was still going strong. Trey had some of the baddest strippers known to mankind in there, and they were all in their birthday suits doing the damn thing. Trey had flown chicks in from Atlanta, Chicago, New York, and of course Detroit. He had it lookin' like the Stoker's up in that piece.

Wink blocked all that out though. He was dead set on a mission to kill Sammy and anybody else who wanted to die with him. He was tempted to just pull out right there in the room in front of everybody and push Sammy's shit back. That was how badly he wanted to kill him. Sammy was sitting on one of the sofas enjoying a lap dance. His old-ass dick probably couldn't even get hard anymore, but the fact that he was able to enjoy himself while Wink's dad sat in prison forced to jack off to memories, the shit made Wink's blood boil. Wink stood over in the corner next to the bar watching Sammy like a lion stalking its prey.

"What's good, my nigga?" asked Krazy as he leaned against the bar and ordered a drink from the sexy barmaid. Krazy turned to face Wink. "Wink, you hear me? What's up with you?" Krazy thanked the woman for the drink, then stepped over to where Wink stood.

"You see that old bitch right there?" asked Wink. He hadn't broken his fixed stare on Sammy.

Krazy locked eyes on Sammy. "Yeah, what's up with him?"

Wink thought about what his dad told him. *"Never tell anyone what you're thinking, and only kill by yourself."* Wink felt like that rule didn't apply to Krazy because he was tested and approved. Under pressure he wouldn't fold. That much Wink was certain of.

"You my nigga, right?" asked Wink.

Krazy downed his glass of Rémy, then slammed the glass down on the bar. "Of course I'm yo' nigga. Now tell me what's up. Who gotta die tonight? 'Cause you got that look in yo' eyes," said Krazy.

"Step over here," said Wink. He led the way out onto the balcony. He nodded at Lee-Mac as he and two strippers were on their way in. Wink slid the balcony door shut, then walked over to the ledge where Krazy stood overlooking the city.

"Here."

"What's this?" asked Krazy, taking the photo from Wink.

"You recognize anybody in there?"

"This looks like Gary right here." Krazy squinted at the other two men in the picture but didn't recognize them.

"Yeah, that's his bitch ass. But tell me that's not that wet-back mothafucka sittin' in there on the couch right now."

"Sho' is. So what's up?" Krazy asked, handing Wink the picture back.

"What's up is that used to be my dad's connect back in the day. This is my pops right here." Wink showed Krazy his dad in the photo. "Anyway, his ass snitched on my pops twenty years ago and got him two life sentences. So you already know what time it is."

"My nigga, let me do it. I'll push his shit back right now. I swear to God!" yelled Krazy. He was getting hyped just thinking about it, not to mention the liquor was starting to talk.

"Nah, chill, Krazy. I can't have you on no murder shit. You just came home."

"Fuck that! For you, my nigga, I go out in a blaze of glory, so I'm not tryin'a hear that shit 'bout I just got out. Does Trey know he's fuckin' with a rat?"

"Nah, and that's how we gon' keep it."

"I wish you would let me handle the shit. I need to get my hands dirty anyway," pleaded Krazy.

Wink thought about Sammy's bodyguard. His ass was definitely going to pose a problem when it came time to kill Sammy. "You know what? I do need you to handle something." Wink pulled up his hoodie and gave Krazy one of the Berettas.

Krazy flashed a sinister grin as he looked the gun over. It was as if the power to take life had just been vested in him. "I'm listening. What do you need me to do?"

"You gon' take out big-boy bodyguard for a nigga. These two ain't makin' it outta the D alive. Trey gon' have to find a new connect." Wink watched Sammy through the sliding glass door enjoying his lap dance with a shit-eating grin on his face. *Yeah, that's right. Have the time of yo' life, 'cause it's gon' be ya last,* Wink promised.

It was going on 8:00 in the morning, and the last of the strippers were just leaving. Some had already either passed out in the hotel room or left with one of the many tricks who made up Trey's Money Squad Family.

Trey was walking Sammy and his bodyguard to the door. They were all laughing and saying how much fun they had. "You gon' stay another day? 'Cause you know I got the suite for the whole week, and I got some more strippers flying in," said Trey. He stopped in front of the door and stepped to the side so the other people could leave.

"I wish we could stay a couple more days, but I really have to get back to Dallas. You know things will fall apart if I stay gone too long," said Sammy.

"A'ight, well, I'll be down to see you in about a week. I'm 'bout out," said Trey.

"I'll have things ready when you get there, and thanks again for the party." Sammy slapped Trey on the back, then walked out of the room with his bodyguard in tow.

Wink and Krazy were waiting over by the elevators when Sammy and his bodyguard bent the corner. Wink tapped Krazy, who was fighting to keep his eyes open. He had been up since they released him from prison. But seeing his target coming their way, he quickly straightened up. Wink wasn't sure if they were on their way to a room or leaving the hotel. It didn't make a difference either way, because they wouldn't make it there alive.

Wink put his hand inside his hoodie, clutching the butt of his .40-cal, then caught the elevator door before it could shut all the way. Sammy met eyes with Wink and nodded with a closed smile as Wink and Krazy stepped on. They stepped to the back of the elevator behind Sammy and his watchdog.

"Nice party, huh?" asked Sammy. He pushed the button for the ground floor, then turned around to face Krazy and Wink.

They both had their guns drawn and pointed at their targets' heads. Krazy didn't waste any time splattering Sammy's bodyguard's brains all over the elevator walls. His large frame slammed hard to the floor, DOA before he got there.

Meanwhile, Sammy was lookin' like a thief caught with his hand in the church collection plate. His eyes bucked with the look of death Wink needed to see before killing him.

"What is this about?" asked Sammy, backing himself into the corner. "Please," he begged.

Wink reached for the stop button. The elevator came to a stop between floors. Wink pulled the picture from his pocket and shoved it in Sammy's face.

"This is what this is about. You rat mothafucka, you snitched on my father!" Wink raised his gun to Sammy's head and waited to see the realization on his face that his past had finally caught up with him. Sammy closed his eyes and squeezed them tightly in anticipation of his death.

Wink pumped four slugs into the side of his head, and then squeezed four more shots into Sammy's chest as he lay slumped over his dead bodyguard.

Wink picked up the picture and tucked it back into his pocket.

"You ready, my nigga?" asked Krazy, as he stood with his finger on the open button.

Wink nodded and Krazy opened the doors. They got off on the second floor and took the stairs down to the lobby. They cut out of the hotel and jumped in Wink's Benz, fleeing the scene totally unsuspected.

Krazy was all amped up. To him, killing was like crack to a crackhead. That was his high. And to get away with it was sheer ecstasy. He sat up in his seat once they made it onto the Lodge Expressway.

"Did you see how I knocked the nigga's shit loose?" Krazy asked, looking over at Wink.

"Krazy, let's leave them two wet-backs in the elevator, a'ight? I don't ever wanna talk about it," Wink said with a dead serious tone. He held his stare at Krazy until he promised never to bring it up again.

"I got you, my nigga. We ain't gotta talk about it no more."

Wink knew he could trust Krazy with his life, so he relaxed. He stretched out with one hand on the wheel and rejoiced in knowing that in a matter of minutes someone would find Sammy's rat ass stretched out dead on the elevator floor. He couldn't wait to tell his dad that he evened the score all around the board.

Chapter Eleven

When Wink got home, he found Armeeah in the living room curled up on the sofa. She was cradling her pooch, Champ, as if he were their baby. Lately, Champ had been Armeeah's only company because Wink was always out in the streets or taking trips out of town working to expand his business. Her parents were on the verge of disowning her if she didn't get her act together, which meant leaving Wink's hoodlum ass and finding herself a Muslim man.

"You just getting up?" Wink asked, pulling his hoodie over his head.

Armeeah didn't bother answering. She just continued to rub Champ's soft coat. She was pissed.

"What, you didn't hear me? I asked you a question, Meeah." Wink stood in front of Armeeah, impatiently waiting for her to answer him. Lately she had been acting shitty, giving him the silent treatment, and the shit was starting to bother the hell out of Wink. They were supposed to be happy. "I'm not gon' repeat myself, Meeah."

"Okay, then don't, Wayne, okay?"

"I know one thing. You betta check yo' li'l funky-ass attitude."

"Or what, Wayne? What are you gonna do, huh? Hit me?" snapped Armeeah.

Before Wink knew it, he had snatched Armeeah's ass up from the sofa and had her hemmed up.

"Let me go, Wayne!"

"Shut yo' ass up." Wink ordered, then he shoved Armeeah against the wall beside their fireplace. He held her arms above her head by the wrists.

"Let go of me. Wayne, you're hurting me."

"I'm not letting you go until you tell me what your problem is. Why are you disrespecting me, huh? Since when did we start talking to each other like that?"

Armeeah turned her head so she wouldn't have to look him in the eyes.

"Talk to me, Meeah."

Tears welled in Armeeah's eyes, and she dropped her head. "I'm pregnant, Wayne."

Wink slowly released his grip from Armeeah's wrists. He pulled her close to him and caressed her back while she cried into his chest. The news came as a surprise to Wink. Pregnancy was the furthest thing from his mind.

Armeeah had been keeping her pregnancy from Wink for over a month. She was six weeks and scared to death because she knew Wink would want to keep the baby. Although she had no plan to have an abortion, she was still torn on whether she should tell Wink, because she was seriously contemplating leaving him. Having an abortion was totally out of the question because it was against her religion. Hell, everything that she was doing was against her religion. Her entire life with Wink was against her beliefs, and it had gotten to the point where she no longer believed he would come into the fold of Islam. Armeeah felt like she had betrayed her covenant with Allah, and she resented Wink for that. He was to blame.

"Meeah, don't cry. It's going to be all right." Wink caressed Armeeah's head.

"No, it's not, Wayne." Armeeah pulled herself up and pushed away from Wink. She walked over to the sofa and took a seat.

"Of course it'll be okay. What, you think that I'm not going to man up and take care of my child?" Wink followed Armeeah to the sofa.

"That's not what I'm worried about. I'm worried about our child being raised in a non-Muslim household. When are you going to get yourself together, Wayne?"

"Meeaha, I have myself together. Look around you. I know that I'm not doing all this for nothing." Wink waved his arms around at all the expensive furniture.

"You know what I mean, Wayne."

Wink handed Armeeah a Kleenex, then took a seat on the sofa beside her. He took a deep breath and then exhaled. Yeah, he knew exactly what she was talking about.

Armeeah faced Wink and tried to gain some understanding as to why he didn't want to submit his will to Allah. "Wayne, what are you running from? Why won't you accept Allah into your life?"

Wink had been struggling to answer that question himself. The truth was he didn't know how to. He was afraid because he knew he wasn't living right. But deep down, Wink wanted to change and start living on the right path before it was too late. He thought about their newborn child and then his dad. He didn't want history to repeat itself and his child to grow up without a father. Wink told himself that he had enough money put up and that he didn't have to hustle anymore. And he had avenged his father by killing everyone who snitched on him.

"I'ma do it," Wink softly said.

Armeeah looked up in disbelief of what she was hearing. She hugged Wink around the neck and began kissing at his face. "You mean it, baby?"

"Yeah, I'ma do it. And not because you want me to, but for me."

"I love you, Wayne," said Armeeah. She gave Wink another peck on the lips, then jumped up from the sofa. She raced off to call her mom and tell her the news. They could finally start planning her dream wedding.

Wink kicked back on the sofa trying to get his head together. *How bad could it be becoming a Muslim?* he asked himself. It wasn't like he had to be on some perfect priest stuff. Wink told himself it was for the best, because lately he found himself needing more than just Armeeah to keep him grounded. He thought about the drug empire that he'd built, ranging from Detroit to Atlanta to Mississippi to St. Louis. He figured he'd make one or two more runs just to snatch up a few more million, and then he would put Willie and Krazy down with the connect maybe.

The game had been good to him, and now it was time to hang his jersey the way every hustla dreamed of doing: retiring on a yacht with money to blow and not a worry in the world.

Wink smiled at his newfound plan. It wasn't a bad idea at all. He could hear Armeeah upstairs celebrating with her mom and sisters on the phone. Hearing the joy in her voice made him think about his mom for the first time since he killed Gary on her kitchen floor. Wink missed his mom and wondered how she was doing. He kicked off his shoes and dozed off to sleep while contemplating whether he was ready to see his mom. And more importantly, did she want to see him after what he had done?

Chapter Twelve

Wink woke up the next morning to Armeeah standing over him with her Quran in one hand and the cordless phone pressed to her ear. She was talking very fast in Arabic with her mom. Her mother was giving her the proper instructions how to give Wink his *al-shahada*. Armeeah wanted to hurry up and give it to him before he changed his mind.

"Okay, bye, Mommy. Yes, I will." Armeeah promised her mother she would call as soon as she was finished with Wink. She set the phone down on its charger, then took a seat on the sofa next to Wink.

Wink sat up on his elbows and wiped the sleep from his eyes.

"Good morning, baby," said Armeeah. She gave Wink a peck on the mouth, then cut straight into it. "Baby, I was figuring that since you're home, we could go ahead and do your *shahada*. It's really easy, and it won't take long."

For the sake of avoiding any further arguments, Wink nodded. He knew that he might as well get it out of the way now, because otherwise he'd be waking up every morning with Armeeah standing over him, looking like a mad medicine woman.

Armeeah jumped up from the sofa, excited. She grabbed Wink by the hand and dragged him through their dining room and upstairs to the master bathroom.

"What do I have to do?" Wink asked in a not-so-enthusiastic mood.

That was okay though, because Armeeah had more than enough enthusiasm for both of them. She stepped over to the double sink where she had everything they were going to need already laid out.

"Go ahead and strip down," she said, picking up a pair of hair trimmers.

Wink hesitated because he wasn't with no bikini waxing or any other feminine-type shit Armeeah had planned. "What are the trimmers for?" he nervously asked.

Armeeah explained that it was obligatory for all Muslims to keep their pubic hair groomed to a low level, and that it was something they could not overlook while taking his *shahada*. "You don't have to go bald, baby, just knock it down, that's all."

Wink shook his head while reluctantly taking his clothes off. *I don't know how I let her sit up and talk me into this.*

Armeeah did the honors of shaving Wink down. She not only shaved around his pubic area, she got into the nooks and crannies of Wink's ass. All the while he was standing there feeling violated and whatnot. He told himself, *after today she better not say nothing else to me about nothing concerning Islam. Not for a minute anyway.* After Armeeah finished shaving Wink's dick, ass, and underarms, she started him a nice, hot shower.

"You know this is crazy, right? You got a nigga standing here like a shaved poodle."

Armeeah tried to hide the smirk fighting to show itself. "It is not that bad. In fact, I think it's sexy." She smothered Wink with kisses while she waited for the water to heat up.

"Why don't you show me how sexy you think it is and get in with me?" Wink almost had Armeeah sold on the idea of joining him for a shower as he passionately treated himself to her spot, kissing all around the sides of her neck. The steam rising from the shower wasn't making matters any better.

"No, I can't. Maybe later after we're done." Armeeah regained her focus as to the purpose of the shower in the first place. She pulled back the curtain for Wink to step in.

"Now what?" Wink asked from under the hot shower water.

"You're going to perform *ghusal*." Armeeah explained what *ghusal* meant and how to perform it. She explained to Wink that it was a Muslim's way of purification, and that they had to purify themselves before coming into the presence of Allah, whether it was for the five *salat'a, jumah,* or in Wink's case, his *shahada.*

After Wink finished making *ghusal,* he dried off and put on a fresh white long bathrobe Armeeah laid out for him. He followed her into their bedroom, and she sat him down on the corner of the bed while she stood. Reading from her noble Quran, she did everything her mother told her to do, having Wink repeat the following: "*La illah illallah.* I bear witness that there is no other deity but Allah, the most high magnificent, merciful, master of the day of judgment, creator of the world and universe. I bear witness that Mohammed is His slave and messenger."

Armeeah walked Wink through the five pillars of Islam and the seven articles of faith and explained each condition, how it was obligatory for all Muslims to pray the five *salat's,* pay *zakat,* make the pilgrimage to Meekah if possible at least once in one's lifetime, fast the month of Ramadan, and attend *jumah* for assembly of prayer.

By the time Armeeah finished running down all the do's and don'ts of Islam, Wink felt like he had joined the Army there were so many rules. It was all good though, because Armeeah would help him along the way with learning his prayers and the basics. She told him that she didn't expect him to learn everything overnight, and to just take it one day at a time, that they would do it together.

"*Asalaam alikum,* baby. You are now a Muslim." Armeeah smiled. She set her Quran down and took a seat next to Wink. "You're supposed to return my greeting by saying, '*Wa alikum salaam.*' Say it with me."

"*Wa alikum salaam,*" said Wink. He didn't feel any different from before he took his *shahada,* other than the fact that he was happy it was over and done with. Maybe now they could move forward with their life. Wink promised himself though that he would at least try to be a good Muslim, especially since they had a child on the way. He didn't want to be looking stupid when his son or daughter asked him a question about Islam and he didn't know the answer.

"I am so proud of you, Wayne." Armeeah hugged Wink, squeezing him tight. She kissed the side of his face, then said, "I'll be back. I'm going to call my mom." Armeeah raced for the cordless phone on the nightstand. She dialed her mom's number, and within seconds she was gushing into the phone.

Wink grabbed the Quran and flipped it open to Surah 1 Al-Fatiah. He lay across the bed and began reading what he had just committed himself to.

Chapter Thirteen

Meanwhile, Trey had called a mandatory meeting for all his Money Squad Family members and its 500 associates to discuss the murders of Sammy and his bodyguard. Trey called every one of his underbosses: JT, Live, Lee-Mac, Dilla, and even Willie's hot-rat ass. He told them to put the word out about the meeting, and within a matter of an hour, Geno's was packed to the brim with MSF members and associates. The place was so thick that a lot of people had to stand dick to booty just to fit inside.

When the front door closed, all that could be heard were the screechy whispers surrounding Sammy's murder. Everybody had heard something different from the others. Some said it was a hit by the Italian Mafia. Others were saying it was a robbery gone bad. No one knew the truth. The reason Trey had called the meeting was to cease the speculation. The only way he'd uncover the truth was by the almighty power of the dollar. Money always made niggas do three things: talk, listen, and kill. Trey was only interested in the last one.

Trey was upstairs in his office talking on the phone with Sammy's eldest, Sammy Jr. He was trying to calm Junior down and convince him that he had nothing to do with his father's murder. From the way Junior was yelling into the phone, Trey could tell that he wasn't buying it. Finally, Junior just snapped.

"You fucking nigger! I'm going to have your head and nuts chopped off!"

Trey flinched from the sound of the receiver slamming in his ear. He slowly lowered the phone and hung it up. Willie was impatiently waiting for Trey to give him the news.

"What he say?" asked Willie.

"He's mad as shit, what do you think he said? He wants blood. My blood," said Trey. He walked over to the window in his office and peeked through the blinds at his MS Family.

"Is everyone here?" he asked.

"Yeah. They're all waiting for you," advised Willie. He walked over to join Trey at the window.

"Good. Come on." Trey opened his office door, and Willie followed him downstairs.

All the conversations stopped at the sight of Trey. He climbed on top of the bar and stared down at his men.

"As you all know, there was a murder the other night at an after-party I threw for my man comin' home. Anyhow, the men who were murdered, they were very close to me and the lifeblood of our Money Squad Family. As of right now I am not certain what happened, which is why I called this meeting. I have two million dollars up for the heads of those responsible. That's cash! You can get it however you want it, big bills or all ones, but I want blood! Y'all get out there and comb these streets until we find our man. Show me we still own this city. Let's go!"

Trey clapped his hands together, dismissing the 500-something members and associates. They all filed out of the club, whispering, some making calls on their cell phones. One thing was for sure, for $2 million, blood was going to spill.

Trey hopped down from the bar, and Willie, along with Live, JT, Dilla, and Lee-Mac, followed him back up to his office. They all stood around with their backs to the wall watching as Trey paced the floor. Trey couldn't get his thoughts in order with everybody standing around staring at him. He stopped in his stride and snapped.

"What the hell are y'all waiting for? Get the fuck out!" He pointed to the door. As his top enforcers began to file out of the office, he continued in his tongue-lashing. "Where the fuck all y'all asses was at when they killed Sammy, huh? Don't come back unless you got blood on yo' hands." Trey slammed the door in Willie's face as he tried to explain his case.

Trey wasn't trying to hear any excuses from anyone. He walked around his desk and flopped down in his plush leather chair. In a sudden rage, he knocked everything from his desk, sending it crashing to the floor. He was not only pissed, but he was also scared. Junior sounded dead-ass serious about having Trey's head and nuts chopped off. And even if he were to escape the long arm of the Mexican Mafia, he still lost a 1,000-kilo-a-month connect.

Trey hoped that if he could find whoever killed Sammy and have their blood on his hands by the time Junior and his peoples caught up with him, just maybe Junior would let him live and they could continue business as usual. It was a long shot, a hope, and a dream. But it was the only hope Trey had.

As soon as Willie left the club and got into his Benz, his cell phone rang. He let it ring and ring, hoping that the caller would leave him the hell alone. But there was no chance of that happening, not unless he just said fuck it and reneged on his deal to cooperate with the government. He finally snatched the phone up to his ear, figuring that they were watching him anyway and knew he was in his car.

"Agent Defauw here. I need you to meet me down at the federal building."

"I'm on my way." Willie hung up the phone before Defauw could say another word. He knew what he wanted. He'd heard Trey's speech from the wire he was wearing.

Chapter Fourteen

Wink finally met Armeeah's family. Her mom invited them over for dinner to celebrate Wink's coming into the fold of Islam. Her mom laid out a feast with lamb and fish as the main course. Wink passed on a lot of the dishes because they smelled peculiar and had names he couldn't pronounce. Instead of asking what the dishes consisted of, Wink stuck to what his eyes could identify.

He sat quiet and nervously during dinner. He kept his back straight, one hand in his lap, and his eyes glued to his plate. He could feel the piercing eyes of his soon-to-be father-in-law penetrating a hole through the side of his face. He knew that there would be a blizzard in hell before the day came that Armeeah's father would really accept him. Armeeah's mom, Sole', was good people though. Her only concern was that her daughters marry Muslim men. The Quran said nothing about the men having to be Arab, so to Sole' it was all the same. She made sure to let Wink know it, too. She went out of her way to make sure he felt comfortable and not out of place the way her husband, Abir, was set on doing. Sole' made sure to include Wink in the dinner table conversation as well. She wanted him to know that he was family.

After dinner Wink kicked it with Armeeah's male cousins while she joined the women in the kitchen to talk about the wedding and God knows whatever else they were in there giggling about. To Wink's surprise, her cousins were cool as shit. They weren't on any extreme

Islam type of time. They were regular people who had dreams, problems, and vices just like the next man. The only difference was that they were Muslim. They smoked cigarettes and sold liquor at their many stores, and her uncles even had a hand in the game. The only one acting reserved was Armeeah's dad. He excused himself and retired for the night after dinner.

Bazzi, Armeeah's youngest cousin, seemed to be the coolest of everyone, so he and Wink chopped it up outside on the porch. Bazzi was only 24, but he was focused like he was 50. He already owned six strip clubs around Detroit called Starvin' Marvin's, and he had plans to open more soon. Bazzi put Wink down as to how he came to own his clubs. He used the money his older brother Marwan left him to jumpstart his growing empire. Marwan was in federal prison doing thirteen months for embezzling $1.3 million. He left the money with his baby brother, and Bazzi wasn't wasting any time flipping it.

Bazzi was buying dilapidated clubs and inking agreements with owners to renovate and manage them while awaiting sale approval from the city and the Michigan Liquor Control Commission. That could take years. All the while, Bazzi was getting filthy rich.

By the time Wink finished listening to him, he wanted to invest in his idea. The boy was hungry and a genius. Wink was starting to like this new family already. His transition from the game wouldn't be as hard as he'd thought now that he had the Arab connection behind him.

Armeeah and Wink said their goodbyes. He had to get up early the next morning because he was going to catch a flight out to Miami to see Nina. Armeeah invited her entire family out to their house for dinner next week after *jumah*. She was so excited that everyone, with the exception of her dad, loved Wink. She figured her dad was just refusing to let her go, but he'd come around eventually when her little sisters brought someone home. That would give him something else to focus on.

Wink and Armeeah waved bye as they pulled out of her parents' driveway in his new Jag. He put the car on cruise control and laid his seat back as they drove through Dearborn. Wink had been through there a few times before, and he knew how racist the police were out there, so he didn't want to be seen.

"You enjoy yourself, baby?" Armeeah asked, then turned to face Wink. She was wearing the biggest smile her face could form.

"I have to say I did. Your cousin Bazzi and I are thinking about making some business moves in the future."

"Well, I'm glad you enjoyed yourself. My family really likes you." Armeeah leaned over the console and kissed the side of Wink's face. She reached for his free hand and interlocked her fingers with his. "Baby, when am I going to meet your mom?" asked Armeeah.

The question of his mom caught Wink off guard because they had never talked about her. Wink wanted it that way, or at least he thought he did at first. But lately he had been missing his mom.

"You hear me, baby?" Armeeah asked, breaking Wink's trance.

"We'll do it soon, Meeah."

Chapter Fifteen

The next morning, Willie picked Wink up and drove him to the Sheraton to drop off the re-up money in the room Nina had set up. After dropping off the money, Willie drove Wink across the street to the airport. They parked close to the entrance and kicked back because they were early and Wink's jet hadn't landed yet.

"Yeah, we made it a little early. They should be here in about twenty minutes," Wink said, looking at the clock on Willie's dashboard.

Willie wasn't saying much. He really hadn't said two words since he picked Wink up from his house. He didn't want to talk details because he had a wire on, and the Feds had his car bugged up with wires everywhere. If they farted in there, the Feds would hear it. Willie just stared blankly ahead at the empty parking lot. How badly he wished he'd told those two cracker DEA agents to suck his dick when they first caught him in Memphis. But it was too late to turn back now. They had too much on him. Willie wondered what his life would be like ten years from now, and how much time the Feds would give Trey and Wink after they brought them down. He just wished there were a way he could tell Wink and hope he would understand. They could work together and bring down the real bosses. That was who the Feds wanted anyway.

"You a'ight, my nigga?" asked Wink. He noticed how distant Willie had been acting.

"I'm good. Just got a lot on my mind right now," said Willie, wiping the invisible frustration from his face.

"Shit, holla at me."

"It's Trey. He's goin' nuts about what happened to ol' boy at Krazy's after-party," Willie lied, figuring he'd throw Wink off.

"Yeah. . . ." Wink flashed back to killing Sammy in the elevator. "They still ain't found out who did that?"

Willie shook his head no. "That could've been anybody. But you know Trey. He's set on finding who did it, and he's trippin' real good."

Wink saw the nose of his jet descending through the air, preparing to land. "That looks like me right there. We gon' chop it up when I get back. Do me a favor and keep an eye on Krazy. Why don't y'all hang out and put him down with the business?" Wink reached over and gave Willie some dap, then reached for the door handle.

"A'ght, my nigga. Hit me up when you 'bout to touch down so I can be here to pick you up."

Wink nodded as he crossed around the front of the car. Willie watched Wink walk inside the terminal before starting the car and pulling away from the curb. He did as Wink told him and called Krazy so they could hook up and hang out.

Nina was seated at the back of the plane in her comfortable nook. She avoided eye contact with Wink and turned away as he tried to steal a kiss on her cheek. Wink fell into his seat and kicked back. He wasn't about to jog his brain trying to figure out what Nina's trip was today. He charged it to the possibility that she might just be trying to keep him off-balance as usual.

Wink buckled his seat belt and returned the silent treatment Nina was throwing his way. It was funny to him, because they were like an old, feuding couple, only not. The plane began inching down the runway, preparing for takeoff. Wink closed his eyes only to be popped upside his head by Nina. When he opened his eyes, she held out the roll of papers she'd popped him with.

"Read it," she ordered.

Wink unrolled the three pieces of paper and sat up in his seat. Nina spoke as he read with buck eyes.

"You are being investigated by the DEA and FBI in Detroit. You along with a long list of names," Nina informed.

Wink scanned through the papers. There was indeed a host of names, too many to count. Wink's name was right under Trey's number two. The title read, "MSF." Wink wondered how his name got on there. It had to be a mix-up, because he wasn't down with Trey's Money Squad Family. He made sure to keep his distance from Trey because he knew sooner or later the Feds would be knocking down doors with indictments. Wink wanted no part of the alphabet boys, which was why he had set up his own operation the way he did with Offy as the front man.

"Do you know what this means?" Nina continued before Wink could answer, "If they're watching you, nine times out of ten, they're on to us. They probably were at the airport and watched as you got on the plane."

Wink's heart started speeding up as he jogged his memory. He hadn't recalled being followed. He was convinced that the Feds had him mixed up, guilty by association. And besides, the paper only had names on it. There was nothing that said he or anyone else did anything. Still, the fact that the Feds knew his name didn't sit well with him, or with Nina for that matter. She was obviously pissed.

"I need a drink," she said, leaning forward to the minibar. She poured herself an almost-spilling Scotch, and then gulped down half the glass. "Wink, I am going to tell you where we stand, and this is coming straight from Franko."

Yeah, right, bitch. The last time yo' ass said that, you were lying. But he let her carry on in her mob-bitch fantasy.

"We are prepared to continue business as usual. Our family is no mystery to the government. They have long wanted to dismantle us and our business, so it is no secret who we are. With the exception of Franko, my family has been able to elude the Feds for over twenty years, and we're prepared to do so again for another twenty years. Wink, when the Feds indict you and your friends, I must warn you not to mention our family."

Wink cut Nina off, because she was insulting his gangsta and disrespecting him as a man. "First off, I'm not a rat! So be clear on that. And let that be your last time threatening me on the sly. You warn kids and bitches, not men." Wink looked toward the front of the plane at Nina's bodyguards. They were all looking at Nina, waiting for her to give the nod of approval to spank Wink's black ass. Wink realized after coming down off his sudden high that he was unarmed and over a thousand feet up in the air with the Cuban cartel. He was in no shape to be talking shit. He swallowed the dry lump in his throat and kept his poker face at the men.

To Wink's relief, Nina gave the "it's okay" signal, shaking her head no, instead of giving the nod of death. "Are you finished?" she asked.

Wink nodded while keeping his eyes to the front of the plane.

"Well, good, because I never said you were a rat. I just wanted to make sure that we understand each other."

"Yeah, we cool," lied Wink. If he'd had his gun with him, he would've killed all their Cuban asses.

Wink blocked Nina out for the rest of the flight as she continued to talk his ear off about the Feds. Wink wasn't the least bit worried, because right then he had made his mind up that this would be his last run. *So fuck the Feds, and fuck Nina!* After this, he was going into business with Bazzi to open up some strip clubs. The Feds could kiss his ass. The game was over, and he had won!

Chapter Sixteen

Willie had been downtown at the federal courthouse all morning debriefing with Agent Defauw and his partner about Trey's Money Squad Family, Sammy's murder, and Wink's connection to Nina. They had been going at it for over two hours, and both Willie and the agents were equally frustrated.

"How much longer we got before we're done?" Willie looked at the clock on the wall. It was almost noon.

"The only place your ass is going is jail if you don't stop holding out," snapped Agent Defauw.

Willie tucked his head back and squinted. "How am I holdin' out when everywhere I go, y'all got me wired for sound? Hell, I can't take a shit without wearing this fuckin' thing!" Willie snapped back, pulling his collar down so that Defauw could see the wire taped to his chest.

"You're going to need more than that. We've been working on this case for almost two years, and we still haven't made contact with anyone outside of Trey or Wink. I suggest you start making some things happen and stop tiptoeing around this, because the day is coming. And so far you haven't done anything to keep your ass from going to prison. I want Wink's connection! I want a buy! Something solid, you hear me? Damn it." Defauw slammed his hand down hard on the table between them, leaning his heavy frame forward.

The look in his eyes let Willie know that he was serious. He had to stop half-stepping and get them crackers what they wanted before they decided to set their sights on him. Willie was too deep in the pussy to pull out now.

"I'll make it happen," he assured Defauw.

"You damn sure better not waste any more time. Now g'on and get the hell out of here." Defauw jerked his fat neck, motioning toward the door.

Willie got up and left feeling like a cheap suit caught out in the rain. Defauw had treated him like a $10 snitch back there. *Truth be told, no one likes a snitch, not even the police.* Willie didn't have the respect of the DEA, and he would soon lose the respect of the streets when it was all said and done. He was a RAT, all capitals!

Willie left his rathole federal building and jumped in his Benz on his way to scoop Krazy. He had called him earlier after dropping Wink off at the airport. He was supposed to have picked Krazy up, but he had no idea the meeting with Defauw would take so long. When Willie pulled up to Krazy's house out in Oak Park, he had just caught Krazy about to pull out of the driveway in his Impala.

Krazy rolled down the window and hollered first. "Shit, my nigga. I thought you weren't comin' or maybe you went back to sleep on me. What up doe?"

"Shit. I had to shoot this bitch down to the abortion clinic," lied Willie.

"Word! You mean to tell me somebody finally gave yo' ugly ass some pussy?" laughed Krazy.

Willie laughed too. "Nah, seriously though, follow me downtown to Trey's club. I want to see what's up with his scared ass. Plus, we can drink up all that free liquor."

"I'm right behind you," laughed Krazy. He rolled up his window and got behind Willie. Krazy wanted to see what was up with Trey too. He hadn't seen him since his party and wanted to see if Trey had heard anything about Sammy's murder.

When they pulled up to the club, four men all dressed in black were standing with their backs against the wall, eyes straight. They looked like the Black Panthers standing out there.

"You see these fools?" Krazy joked as he met Willie at the curb.

"I told you Trey was scared to death," said Willie.

"Scared of what?" Krazy asked as they reached the front door.

"It's a long story. I'll tell you later."

Two of the Black Panthers stepped forward while the other two brushed back their trench coats revealing sawed-off pumps.

"Who y'all tryin'a see?" one of the men asked, holding his hand out between Willie and the door.

"Nigga, if you don't get yo' Malcolm X ass outta my way . . . It's me, Willie!"

The man didn't budge. He nodded to the other man, who in turn pulled a radio from his coat pocket. "Uh, boss. Got a guy out here named Willie. He has someone with him, too." The man put the radio to his ear and waited for a response.

"I see him. It's cool. You can let 'em in." Trey said, coming over the radio.

The Panthers took their positions back on the wall, eyes straight forward. Willie shook his head while Krazy laughed.

"What the fuck is really going on?" Krazy asked, still smiling. Trey buzzed them in, and Krazy held the door open for Willie.

Trey wasn't taking any chances on getting his shit pushed back. After Junior threatened him, Trey had security cameras installed at every angle of the club: front, side, back alley, and the inside. He put four men in the front, two in a van at the end of the alley, and two snipers on the roof. Meanwhile, Trey was living inside the club. He had built himself a nice little fortress. It would take the National Guard to get in there, and yet he still was on pins and needles. Trey was pacing the floor behind the bar when Willie and Krazy walked up.

"What's with the Secret Service outside and the buzzard?" asked Willie. He and Krazy slid onto two barstools.

"I'm not taking no chances. They'll never call my momma, tellin' her to come down to the morgue," said Trey. He hadn't looked up from the floor. He paced that bar like a war general planning his attack. Only he was hiding. The club was his manhole.

"Damn, my nigga. You gon' walk a hole in the floor. Pour me a drink, and tell me what's up," said Krazy.

The phone mounted on the wall behind the bar started ringing. Trey raced over and snatched the phone to his ear like he'd been waiting for that call all day.

"Fuck this. I'ma get my own drink," said Krazy. He hopped over the bar and grabbed a bottle of Bombay from the shelf.

"You tryin'a get fucked up early, I see," Willie said, referring to the fifth of gin Krazy was turning up.

"Ahhh," sighed Krazy as if his chest were on fire from the long gulp.

"Pass me that Henny right there," said Willie. He and Krazy helped themselves while Trey excused himself up to his office to finish the call.

"I don't know what's goin' on, but I ain't runnin' from no nigga. You know why?"

"Why is that, Krazy?"

"'Cause 'I ain't no track star, Goldie,'" Krazy said, imitating Richard Pryor from the classic movie *The Mack*.

"You a fool, you know that?" laughed Willie.

The front door buzzed open, and Live, JT, Dilla, and Lee-Mac all walked in. They came over to the bar, each giving Willie a pound. Krazy just nodded at them. He wasn't with all that friendly shit. Hell, to be real, he didn't even like them niggas just because. There wasn't a real reason. Krazy didn't need one. It could have been the liquor taking its effect, but either way, Krazy wasn't feeling them little niggas. He was sizing them up as they sat around the bar, Live's big ass especially. *Yeah, you think you tough,* Krazy thought while he looked Live over. He turned up his bottle of Bombay, keeping his eyes locked on the four of them.

These the niggas you call ya'self runnin' with while leaving me down bad in the joint, huh? The liquor was really starting to work its mojo on Krazy. He was asking Trey questions as if he were standing right there in front of him. Krazy had been feeling like Trey played him. *You too, bitch!* Krazy thought as he focused on Willie. He and Trey had played Krazy while he was down bad.

Trey came back down from his office. The distraught look he had in his eyes earlier before he took the phone call was no longer there. He had talked to Junior and managed to calm him down. They had set up a meeting for next week to sit down and talk things out. Trey promised to have the blood of Sammy's killer on his hands by the time they met. He had a week to make something happen, so Trey was a little relieved knowing that Junior had called off the wolves.

Trey grabbed a bottle of Moët from the refrigerator and popped the cork with a celebratory smile on his face. "What up doe," he said, excited.

"Damn, just ten minutes ago you was in this bitch lookin' like you was 'bout to cry. That call must have been good news," said Willie.

"Don't watch me, nigga. Here." Trey tossed Willie the remote control. "Watch TV." He pointed to the flat screen mounted behind the bar.

"I like that one. That's a good one," laughed Willie.

They all laughed except Krazy.

"Yeah, well, since you in such a good mood, can we get the keys back to our Benz?" asked Lee-Mac.

"Yeah, for real we gon' start calling yo' ass the repo man," said JT.

Trey nodded. He had taken all their cars after Sammy got killed. Trey wanted them doing nothing except hunting down Sammy's killer. Since things with Junior were straight, Trey figured he could let them have their cars back.

"Yeah, I'ma give y'all shit back. But I still want blood," Trey said, losing the smile for a moment as he gave his men a stern look. His face lit up again as he turned to face Krazy. Trey set his champagne bottle on the bar, then walked over to Krazy. He put his arm around Krazy's neck and pulled him close. "What's up, my nigga? Why you over there zoned out?"

Krazy's blood started boiling because he wasn't never with the fake shit, and the gin wasn't doing anything but stirring up ill feelings.

"You know you forgot the briefcase in my desk drawer. I saw it this morning," said Trey. He was referring to the $1 million he gave Krazy as his homecoming gift.

Krazy turned his bottle up for a long swallow, then said, "I ain't forget. I don't want it."

"Why not?" Trey asked with a confused look.

"'Cause, nigga, you can't buy me like the rest of these bitch niggas," Krazy snapped. He waved his gin bottle at Live, JT, Dilla, and Lee-Mac. They all stopped talking and looked at Krazy with their faces all torn up. Krazy screwed his mug up and grilled their asses right back with a daring look in his eyes.

"Damn, my nigga. Where all that come from?" asked Trey.

"That bottle of gin he holdin'. Don't pay that shit no mind. Y'all let that be." Willie hoped to defuse the situation, because the tension got thick real fast.

Krazy slammed the rest of the liquor back, then set the empty bottle on the bar. He glared at Willie. "Nigga, I'm not drunk, so don't be making no excuses for me." Krazy slowly pointed Live, JT, Dilla, and Lee-Mac out one by one. "I meant what I said. These niggas is bitches."

Live jumped from his stool and pulled his .45 from his hip. He reached over the bar, pointing the gun straight at Krazy's head. But Trey quickly stepped forward with his arms extended to block Live from killing Krazy. He looked from side to side. It was like the Wild West in that bitch. JT, Lee-Mac, and Dilla slid off their stools and stood with Live, while Willie's scared ass stayed put. He was so used to playing the fifty-yard line he didn't know what side to choose.

"Y'all chill!" ordered Trey. He knew that shit would get ugly in there if Live started shooting, because JT, Lee-Mac, and Dilla were riding with Live. Trey didn't want it to go down like that, because he and Krazy were like brothers.

"Fuck that, nigga. Let 'em shoot. Lord knows—"

"Krazy! That's enough!" yelled Trey. Silence lingered through the bar as Live kept his gun aimed at Krazy. He wanted so badly to kill Krazy for calling him a bitch.

"Live, do this for me. Put the gun down. I can't let it go down like that. We all 'posed to be family."

"Man, I'm not related to you niggas in not blood or thug," said Krazy. "That goes for you too, Trey."

"What are you talkin' about, Krazy?" Trey asked, spinning around.

"I'm talkin' 'bout us. These niggas ain't family, and neither are you anymore. You stopped being family when you started fuckin' with that rat-ass Mexican mothafucka. What's his name, Sammy?"

"What about Sammy?" asked Trey, raising his eyebrows.

"He was a rat just like these niggas. They gon' get caught and snitch, wait and see."

"Fuck all that!" snapped Trey. He wanted to know about Sammy. He stood closer to Krazy. "What about Sammy? How was he a rat?" he demanded.

"Like you don't know he snitched on Wink's dad back in the day. Got that man two life sentences." Krazy started crying. "Just like these niggas is gon' do to us," he cried.

Trey stared blankly into the distance of the club. His veins became full of rage because he realized what Krazy was telling him. It was Wink who killed Sammy.

"What you want me to do, Trey?" asked Live. He had the trigger halfway back, ready to put a hole in the back of Krazy's skull as he stood slouched over the bar in his drunken crying.

Trey waved the gun down, then returned to his thoughts. Sammy snitching on Wink's dad was bullshit. Trey was certain of it. He told himself that Wink was jealous and couldn't stand to see him doing better than him, so he killed his connect.

"You want it like that, huh? Well, I'ma give it to you." Trey had every intention of having Wink's blood on his hands when he met Junior next week.

Chapter Seventeen

Wink's plane had just landed at Detroit City Airport. Wink glared into the distance of the empty airstrip. Nina reached for his hand, breaking his deep train of thought.

"What's up?" He turned to face her.

"Wink, I want you to be careful out there," Nina said.

But Wink knew better than to believe for one second that Ms. Boss Bitch was capable of being sincere. He knew Nina didn't care for real whether his black ass went to prison, as long as he didn't snitch and take her with him. Nina had already revealed her true colors. All she was interested in was selling Wink cocaine. But fair exchange ain't never been no robbery. The feeling was mutual.

"So watch yourself, because right now we still don't know who's helping them."

Wink nodded like he agreed, but deep down he had other plans, none of which included Nina or her Cuban cartel family. Little did she know that today would be the last time she saw Wink.

Wink leaned over to kiss Nina's cheek and then slid out of his seat to the aisle. "I'll see you in a couple of weeks," he lied, leaving Nina with the impression that they would be proceeding with business as usual.

As soon as Wink stepped down from the jet, his mind went into overdrive with thoughts about the Feds' investigation. He couldn't help but look around as he crossed the tarmac, thinking that he was being watched. He tried telling himself they wanted Trey, not him. *They ain't got nothin' on me,* Wink tried convincing himself as he cut through the terminal. But still, knowing that some federal agent had his name, and perhaps his picture, too, didn't sit well on Wink's stomach. He tried to stomach the sudden paranoia that struck him on his way out the double entrance doors. It felt like there were eyes touching him all over as he stood at the curb looking for Willie. Wink spotted Willie's silver Beemer parked in the third row. He rushed the short distance, banging on the hood of the car as he walked around the passenger side.

"Wake up and unlock the door," Wink said. He kept a watchful eye on the traffic in the parking lot. He tugged on the door handle after hearing Willie pop the locks. Wink slid into the car and closed the door quickly. He hadn't acknowledged Willie or Krazy, who was in the back seat, snoring.

"Wink, you hear me talkin' to you?" Willie asked for the third time.

"Yeah, I heard you," said Wink. He leaned forward, squinting at the two white men parked directly in front of them in a navy blue Ford Taurus.

"What are you lookin' at? You a'ight, my nigga?" asked Willie.

"Yeah, I'm good," lied Wink. "Just pull off." He kept his stare locked on the Taurus. *Yeah, that's definitely the Feds,* Wink thought as Willie pulled out of the parking space.

"I wish you'd chill out and tell me what's wrong," Willie said. He looked over at Wink, who was turning every which way in his seat and looking in the mirrors and out the back window.

Wink sat back in his seat as they turned down Gratiot. Still he kept his eyes on the side mirror. "You see them two white boys back there in that Taurus?" asked Wink.

"Nah, I didn't." Willie's stomach and ass dropped because he knew Wink had spotted the Feds.

"Yeah, well, I know them people when I see 'em."

"What does that have to do with us? They not on us," said Willie.

"I wish that were the case, but it ain't." Wink pulled from his coat pocket the list of people who were under federal investigation. "You see that?" Wink handed Willie the papers and pointed to his name right up under Trey's.

Willie was scanning the list quickly with an eagle eye in search of his own name. He gripped the wheel with one hand while shuffling the pages. His nerves rested with ease after seeing that his name was not on the government's hit list. The nervous feeling returned to the pit of his stomach once he handed the list back to Wink, because Wink hit him with a question he wasn't ready for.

"Why you think yo' name ain't on here?" Wink asked.

Willie knew he had to come back quickly, so he played the defensive role. "Damn, that's fucked up you would even say some shit like that. What, you want my name to be on there?"

"You know that's not what I was saying. I'm just tryin'a figure out why my name is on here!" Wink said, raising his voice with every syllable.

Silence filled the car for a long moment.

"That's Trey silly ass with this kiddie-ass Money Squad shit. I know one thing: when them people start roundin' nigga's asses up, I betta not be one of them," warned Wink.

Willie waited a few seconds before saying, "I think that's gon' be the least of your worries."

Wink balled his face up, then turned in his seat. "Willie, what the fuck you talkin' 'bout the least of my worries? You know something 'bout this that I don't?"

"Trey found out you killed his connect, Sammy."

Wink's mouth hung open, and his eyes gleamed with guilt. But he kept his silence.

Willie glanced over from the road to meet eyes with Wink. He was waiting for an answer that Wink was never going to give. There was nothing to talk about except how Trey found out.

"What makes Trey think that I killed his connect?" He was going to the grave with Sammy's murder.

Willie nodded at the back seat. Krazy was stretched across the seat, dead asleep and snoring like a bear. Willie explained to Wink how it went down, how Krazy got drunk and blacked out.

"The nigga broke down crying and some mo' shit. Trey didn't say what he was going to do, but knowing him, he's gonna—"

"He gonna what?" snapped Wink. "That nigga ain't gon' do shit to me, him or them crash dummies he out here runnin' around with. Shit, they the reason the Feds got me under investigation. So fuck them niggas, and fuck his connect!"

Willie just let Wink go ahead and vent. He was relieved that Wink hadn't claimed killing Sammy because he and his car were wired for sound. Agent Defauw had given Willie a list of questions to try to get him to admit that he pulled the trigger on Sammy. Had Wink confessed, it would have cost him the rest of his natural life in prison.

As Willie pulled into the Jeffersonian apartments, his pager vibrated on his hip. He discretely looked at the screen. It was Agent Defauw's pestering ass. He'd put in their code, which was the address of the federal building, letting Willie know to meet him there.

"I gotta bust this move, so I'ma get with y'all later on," Willie said. He pulled up to the entrance of Wink's apartment.

"Yeah, a'ight. Make sure you do that, 'cause there's too much shit going on right now. We need to sit down and chop it up." Wink reached over and gave Willie some dap. Then he looked in the back seat at Krazy. *I can't believe this nigga.*

"My man, get yo' ass up!" Willie yelled into the back seat.

Krazy sat up with a look of delirium in his eyes. It took him a few moments to recognize who he was staring at and where he was.

"Come on, my nigga," Wink said, holding the back door open. He helped Krazy out of the car, wrapping his arm around his shoulder.

"Yeah, take care of yo' son!" Willie yelled at the back of Wink's head as he ushered Krazy inside the building.

Wink put Krazy on the elevator and leaned him against the wall. He didn't know who he was more pissed at, Willie or Krazy. Willie had let Krazy get sloppy drunk. When the elevator stopped on Wink's floor, he hoisted Krazy back under his arm and carried him the rest of the way.

When they made it inside the apartment, Wink carried Krazy straight into the bathroom and put him in the tub. He turned on the cold water, then hit the shower nozzle. The shock of the cold water woke Krazy straight up from his drunken state.

"What the fuck?" Krazy snapped while looking down at his drenched clothes.

Wink went into a blind rage. He snapped, grabbing Krazy up by the neck and shoving his head hard against the shower wall.

"Wink, what the fuck?" Krazy's words were muffled because Wink was choking the shit out of him. Krazy was too drunk to fight him off, so he did what he could, which was continue to plead for his life.

"You killin' me, Wink." Krazy gasped for air. His eyes rolled to the back of his head, and his grip slowly released from Wink's wrist. "You killin' me. . . ." His voice lowered.

Wink let go of Krazy's neck, sparing him his last breath. He stood up and watched as Krazy held his throat and gagged for oxygen. The love Wink had for Krazy was the only thing that kept him from putting a bullet into his head.

"I'ma fix it!" Krazy yelled from the tub as Wink left the bathroom. "I'ma fix it," Krazy said in a slow, low tone of voice.

Chapter Eighteen

Krazy didn't waste any time keeping his promise to Wink about fixing things between him and Trey. After he sobered up and changed into some dry clothes, he found Wink in the living room stretched across the sofa with his hands behind his head looking up at the ceiling. Krazy could tell by the look on Wink's face that he was more than pissed and didn't want to talk, so instead of offering a bunch of excuses, he turned for the door.

He called a cab from the lobby and went home to suit up. The first thing Krazy did when he got home was buy a slew of guns, everything from handguns to assault rifles and a bulletproof vest. Krazy strapped up with twin black .45s, two extra clips, and his bulletproof vest. He grabbed the keys to his Impala and was out the door. His plan was to get Trey in his office and make him promise that the shit between him and Wink was dead and over with. If not, then he had other plans.

Krazy pulled up to Trey's club and knocked the orange parking cones out of the way so he could park. He cut the car off and got out, but as he climbed the curb, two of Trey's bodyguards stepped from the wall with their hands stretched out.

"The club is closed," one of the men informed Krazy.

"If y'all don't get y'all Panther-lookin' asses outta my way so I can go holla at my man . . ." Krazy tried to step between the two men, but the men closed the gap between them.

"I said the club is closed! What part of 'closed' don't you understand?" The man stared down his wide black nose at Krazy.

Seeing that he was obviously outnumbered, Krazy thought his options over quickly. He chose the last one: to show them two bitch niggas why they called him Krazy. He stole off on the bigger one first, figuring that if he knocked him out, he'd have a fighting chance with his little bull-back partner.

Krazy's first punch didn't knock ol' boy out, but his second and third ones sent him staggering back. Krazy rolled with the punches his partner planted all upside his head. Krazy rushed the man into the wall of the club, then scooped him off his feet. They all ended up on the ground, Krazy on top of ol' boy with his partner on Krazy's back.

"Ahhh!" the man at the bottom of the pile yelled. It was one of those cries only the soul was capable of mustering. Krazy was biting a plug out of his nose.

"Tell 'em to get off me," Krazy said with a mouth full of blood and the man's nose.

"Stop! Get off him!" the man ordered his partner. His voice echoed down Jefferson, and people passing by in their cars were stopping to check out the midday brawl.

Trey saw the scuffle on the surveillance monitor and sent Live and JT out to break it up. Live's big, muscle-bound ass snatched the little bull-back guy off Krazy's back, and then he yanked Krazy up by the back of his shoulders.

"Ahhh," the man at the bottom of the pile roared out in sheer agony when Live yanked Krazy up. He caused the man to lose his nose. All was left of the nose was the bottom portion where the nostrils met. The violent patch on the man's face quickly filled with thick blood.

Krazy spat the nose to the ground and squared off for round two. He rocked back on his heels with both hands up in a boxer position while waiting for an opening so he could tear into Live's ass. He still wanted blood from when Live pulled his gun on him.

But JT stepped forward, offering peace. "Look, dawg, why don't you get in your car and leave?"

"Li'l nigga, stay outta grown folks' business," snapped Krazy.

"T-Money ain't seeing nobody right now," Live said in a deep, challenging voice.

Krazy was about to lift his shirt and air all their asses out, but as soon as he was about to Kurk out, Trey's voice came over the intercom box mounted in the wall of the club. "It's okay, Live, let him in."

Live grudgingly stepped aside, letting Krazy pass. JT and Live stayed outside to help ol' boy find his nose while Krazy stepped inside the club. When Krazy got inside, the ground floor was packed with niggas who he deemed to be off-brand. They all sported black varsity jackets with the letters MS embroidered in red stitching. Krazy mean mugged every one of them as he made his way toward the bar.

"That's far enough."

Krazy stopped and looked up at Trey as he leaned out his office window.

"Fuck you mean that's far enough? Nigga, I'm coming up to holla at you," said Krazy. He took a half step before two muscle-back niggas blocked his path. Krazy looked around and saw that everybody was on point. They all had hands on some type of gun: some pistols, others shotguns. Krazy knew he was in no position to be teeing off in there, so he looked back up at Trey and spoke. "You need to tell ya flunkies to sit down somewhere so I can come up and holla at you."

"We don't have nothing else to holla about, Krazy. Remember what you said? We're not family anymore.

Look around you." Trey waited a few seconds, then continued, "You see the faces around you? This is my family now. I spared yo' life once already by not letting Live kill you. The first one's on me. The next one's on you."

"What, you threatening me, Trey?" Krazy hollered up.

"I'm letting you know that if you want to live, yo' ass need to make this yo' last time stopping through here. Please show this gentleman to the door," Trey told the two WWF-built niggas blocking Krazy.

The men each grabbed Krazy by his arms and turned him around, but Krazy snatched away. "Get the fuck off me," he said, looking over his shoulder at the men. They were on his heels as Krazy kept his stride toward the front door.

"And tell Wink I know he's back in town. I'll be to see him soon!" Trey hollered before the door closed.

The men shoved Krazy in the back, sending him stumbling out of the club. They shut the door and locked it before he could catch his balance.

Krazy clenched both hands into tight fists and stared at the club's door. "Ewww!" he roared, wishing he could get back in that door. He would go in with both guns blazing. Krazy become enraged with anguish. It hurt him to have stood there and let Trey's soft-as-pussy ass get that off on him. It was in total violation of everything he stood for. No one had ever talked to him like that, at least not without having to pay for it.

Krazy smacked his hands together after taking one final look at the club. When he turned around, Live and JT were crossing the street. Krazy waited until they climbed the curb, then started in their direction, tucking both hands under his shirt.

"You still here?" asked JT. His eyes bucked wide at the sight of the twin .45s Krazy had aimed at his face.

Two bright flashes sparked from the barrels, blowing JT's head off. Boom! Boom! Live tried to come out of his pants with his Beretta, but he never made it up because Krazy spun and emptied both clips into his chest and back as he tried to run. When Krazy finished shooting, the thunder from the shots still lingered in the midday air. People were stopping and pointing as he stood over Live with both guns empty and smoking.

"Oh, my God. I think he killed them," a woman standing across the street said.

Krazy snapped out of his trance and started toward his car while reloading his guns. "You ain't seen nothin'!" Krazy yelled at the nosy woman standing in front of the cleaners. She quickly turned her head, hoping that Krazy would please leave and not decide to kill her next.

As Krazy opened his car door, the front door of Trey's club swung open and niggas came running out with their guns. Krazy let off a couple shots, enough to buy himself some time to jump in and pull off. The men scrambled from the sidewalk, running into the middle of the street and firing back on the car as he sped away. Two bullets crashed through the back windshield and another hit the quarter panel as Krazy made a sharp right turn on Woodward Avenue.

Krazy came up from his slouched position and smashed down on the gas while keeping his eyes on the rearview mirror. His adrenaline slowed down, and he started to relax once he made it to the Lodge Expressway. He'd killed two of Trey's men and made it out of there alive. "I'm a warrior!" he roared. "You bitches wanna go to war? I'ma take y'all to war!" Krazy yelled at the road ahead of him. He slammed his hands hard on the steering wheel. "It's wartime."

Chapter Nineteen

Downtown at the federal courthouse, Special Agent Defauw and his partner were briefing Willie on the direction of the investigation. It had been almost two years since Willie got busted and started working for Defauw, and yet he hadn't delivered anything concrete that would bring down an indictment for conspiracy on Wink. They had him on possession and distribution, but they wanted Nina and her people. Trey was another story. Since his connect, Sammy, was dead, and they had more than enough evidence to send him and his crew to prison for life, the Feds were in no rush. It was a package deal. They would round everybody up at once.

"I'ma get 'em. You just gotta give me some more time," Willie pleaded. His ass was on the brink of being hauled off to prison because he hadn't lived up to his end.

"You know what, shithead, you're this close"—Agent Defauw held his index finger and thumb in a pinch position—"this close to me picking up this damn phone and having the Marshals carry your ass over to Wayne County."

"Sir, I swear to you that I'm doing my best. Please give me some time."

Defauw cut Willie off. "I don't want your best! I want indictments!" Defauw paced the floor. His partner, Special Agent Hornberger, was keeping notes as he always did for the debriefing. He set his pen down at the ringing of his desk phone.

"Special Agent Hornberger," he answered on the second ring. He listened intently to the caller, then snapped his fingers at Defauw.

Defauw walked over and took the phone from his partner, but before he put the phone to his ear, he barked at Willie, "You've got one week to get me those indictments, or I will see to it that you're picked up. Now get the hell out." Defauw dismissed Willie, then took his call.

"No, I don't want you to arrest him. You're not to arrest anyone until I give you the okay." Defauw slammed the phone down, then returned to his pacing.

Agent Hornberger tapped the tip of his pen nervously against his notes. He was waiting for Defauw to say something with regard to the call because it seemed urgent. Hornberger thought they should do something. In fact, he believed that they had a lawful duty to do something.

"We've invested a lot of time, resources, and money on this investigation. Too much to see it go down the drain over nothing," Defauw said. "Our asses are on the line here. Washington is calling, and they want convictions."

"Yeah, but what about the two dead bodies we have over at Geno's? Our guys said they've got a tail on the shooter, so why don't we bring him in? He's a killer, for Christ's sake."

Defauw stopped in his tracks and met eyes with Hornberger. "I'm going to tell you why, Frank. First off, that's Detroit homicide's crime scene and their two dead bodies. And so is the shooter. That's all of their concern, and none of ours, unless it's going to help crack these indictments. If not, to hell with those niggers! Let 'em kill each other off for all I care. Lord knows they're making my job that much easier. What we need to be focusing on is where we'll be in the next ten years in our careers. Are you with me, partner?" asked Defauw.

Hornberger caught the extra emphasis that Defauw put on "partner," and he didn't like it because he didn't like breaking the law. But not only was he in a catch twenty-two, he was also terrified of Defauw's violent temper.

"Yeah, of course I'm with you."

"Good. Good," Defauw repeated. His eyes returned to their normal blue, and he backed off Hornberger.

"After these indictments come down, I've got a feeling we'll both be getting a big, fat promotion. Where do you want your new office?" Defauw changed the subject to lighten the mood.

Chapter Twenty

"Yeah, I killed that fat rat bitch. So what? You niggas don't want no problems," Wink said, pretending the empty road ahead of him was Trey. He was thinking about Trey finding out that he killed his connect. Wink would never admit to anything, and he damn sure wasn't about to deny it. It was what it was. That was his attitude. *More so, fuck Trey's soft ass.* Besides, this was the same Trey who let some young punks hog-tie his ass and rob him for everything he had, plus the $250,000 Wink had to put with it so they wouldn't kill his pussy ass. *So yeah, fuck that nigga!*

Wink seriously doubted that Trey really wanted to go that route with him anyway, because he knew the nigga wasn't built like that for real. He was hiding behind those fake, baby gangstas, and if they kept playing, Wink was gonna hit all their heads. Wink tried to push those thoughts out of his head. *I ain't hard to find. If y'all want it, come see me.*

Wink blocked the Feds from his mind as well. He made up his mind that he wasn't about to be looking over his shoulder and living in constant fear. If they had something on him, bring it on and stop with all the pre-show shit. Wink told himself that the very next time he saw some agents following him, he was going to pull over and ask them what the fuck they wanted. He'd let their asses know, *yeah, I know y'all investigating me. You bitches ain't got nothing on me. I know it, and y'all know it*. Wink liked the idea so much that his grimace was replaced with a Colgate smile.

Even if they were calling themselves bunching an investigation on him, they were a day late and a dollar short because Wink had sold all the cocaine he was going to sell. He had the 200 kilos in the storage he just bought from Nina, but he didn't plan on moving them for a while. He was going to sit on them for a minute, then have Willie quickly move them. Then it was game over! And more importantly, fuck the Feds and their investigation. Wink had $15 million tucked away and had no plans to look back. He was going into business with Armeeah's cousin, Bazzi. They were going to expand Bazzi's franchise of strip clubs. That was Wink's exit from the game.

Wink turned his pager and cell off as he pulled into the driveway of his mini mansion. He popped the glove box and tossed both his pager and phone inside, then locked it. He didn't want any disturbances whatsoever. He wanted to surprise his beautiful fiancée. He wanted to hold her in his arms and cover her with kisses and let her know just how much he loved and missed her.

He cut across the lawn and took the stairs three at a time in anticipation of embracing Armeeah. She swung the door open and stepped aside as Wink reached the landing. Wink kissed Armeeah's cheek and waited as she closed the door and put all four locks on, two of which Wink didn't remember being there before he left.

"Baby, what's wrong? Who you see out there?" Wink asked, stepping over to the window. He peeked out the window but didn't see anything. Wink turned Armeeah around by her waist so she faced him. "What's wrong?" he asked, seeing the worry in Armeeah's eyes.

"Wayne, some men came over this morning. They say they're DEA agents, and they want to talk to you."

"Did you let them inside the house?" Wink asked. He became nervous and angry. Nervous because the Feds were now showing themselves. Angry because them slimy sons of bitches knew where he lived, and they had Armeeah all shook up. "Meeah, answer me. Did you let them in the house?"

"No."

"Good. You did good." Wink was relieved a little, because at least he knew they hadn't planted any bugs around his house. "What did they ask you, and what did you tell them? Try to remember everything, Meeah. This is very important." Wink followed Armeeah over to the sofa. He stood while she sat. "Everything, Meeah."

"They didn't ask me anything. They already knew my name and who I am to you. They just said they needed to talk to you and that it would be in your best interest to call them when you got home." Armeeah looked at the card Agent Defauw had given her. Then she set it on the coffee table. "Wayne, what do these people want?"

Wink picked up the card, and without looking at it, he tore it into tiny pieces. "This is what they wanna do to me, and to our lives. They want to have me sitting in prison with my father. That's what they want! So it's very important that you not talk to any of them anymore. Do you hear me?" Wink warned. He dug into his pocket and pulled his lawyer's card from his wallet.

"Here! You give this to their ass the next time they wanna talk. Tell 'em to call Mr. Culpepper if they wanna talk!"

"Wayne, you're scaring me."

Wink realized that he'd been yelling at Armeeah, and she hadn't done anything wrong. He took a deep breath, then took a seat beside her. "I'm sorry, baby." He reached for her hand. He lifted her chin and looked deep into her eyes. "I didn't mean to scream at you. It's just I need you to understand how important this is. Those people are not here to help us. They want to hurt me, and the only way to stop them is for you to do exactly what I told you. Okay, baby?"

"Okay." Armeeah dropped her eyes. Wink pulled her closer and began massaging her temples.

"It's going to be okay," he whispered.

He continued to massage Armeeah's face until she relaxed, and then he planted soft kisses all over her neck and face. Within minutes, he had taken her mind off worrying about the Feds. Wink laid Armeeah across the sofa and slowly undressed her. He kissed her stomach for a bit, thinking about the unborn child. Armeeah put her hands on Wink's head and guided him down to her clit. She gripped both his ears like a steering wheel as she rolled her hips in the same slow circles Wink was making around her clit. Wink licked and sucked Armeeah to three toe-curling orgasms, and then he sat back and allowed her to return the favor. They made love all over the house for hours, finally retiring to their bedroom.

Wink lay on his back with his eyes to the ceiling, while Armeeah made little circles with her finger in his chest hair. "Baby, when are we going to get married?" asked Armeeah. It had been only a couple of weeks since Wink proposed, but she wanted a date.

"Pick a date, baby, and that's the day. Whatever day you choose," Wink said, then kissed the top of Armeeah's head.

"You mean it, baby?" Armeeah sat up, excited.

Wink smiled back at his wife-to-be. "Yes, I mean it, so call your mom and sisters and tell them y'all have a lot of planning to do."

"I love you so much." She stole a kiss and tore the sheets off in a rush for the phone. She stopped just short of the door and spun around. "June third. That's our date," she happily announced.

"It's a date." Wink smiled as he watched Armeeah go off. He put his hands behind his head and thought about how his life had changed for the better, having Armeeah by his side and all. He looked forward to June 3 and the birth of their baby boy. He could feel it was a boy!

For a second, he thought about his mom and what she might be doing. He had been meaning to go see her and hopefully fix things between them. How badly he wanted to, but it wasn't that simple. Wink promised he'd go see her soon, and hopefully she'd accept his invitation to their wedding. Besides, he knew his mom would welcome her grandbaby with open arms. "We'll see."

Wink reached for the remote, hoping to take his mind off everything. He flipped through the channels, looking for an old rerun to watch, but he stopped on the four o'clock Channel 4 News after recognizing the building in the background as Trey's club, Geno's. The top of the screen read, Breaking Story, Live Action.

Wink turned the volume up as the reporter gave her account of what had transpired. Yellow crime scene tape wrapped around the club's entrance, preventing onlookers from crossing the bloodstained sidewalk. Two mug shots flashed across the screen. The reporter described them as the victims of a fatal gun brawl. Wink recognized them immediately as Live and JT. Wink sat up in bed and waited for the reporter to say who was responsible, but she said that police had no solid leads and that witnesses were refusing to cooperate.

Wink cut the TV off and lay back on the pillows. His mind started racing a thousand miles per second. Somehow he knew that Krazy was behind all this. It had his MO all over it. Wink snatched the sheets from his legs and rolled out of bed. He grabbed his clothes scattered about the room and dressed on his way downstairs.

He heard Armeeah in the kitchen talking on the phone, more than likely with her mom or one of her sisters. Wink didn't bother telling her he was leaving, because she would most certainly veto him going. But Wink had business to handle. He went out the front door and quickly got into his car. As he pulled out of the driveway, he pulled his cell from the glove box and called Krazy.

"What up doe?" Krazy answered on the second ring.

"Where are you? We need to talk," said Wink in a dead-serious tone.

"I'm at the crib. I been callin' you all day. Where you at?"

"On my way to see you, so don't leave." Wink hung up the phone, then punched the gas down. He could hear it in Krazy's voice that it was him.

Chapter Twenty-one

Krazy was waiting on the porch when Wink pulled into his driveway and parked. Krazy timidly stepped off the porch, meeting Wink halfway up the walk.

"Back inside," ordered Wink. He brushed past Krazy while looking around the house. Wink had a feeling the Feds were watching them all.

Krazy followed Wink inside the house, making sure to keep his ten-feet distance out of firing range, just in case Wink teed off on him. Wink stopped in front of the stairs. He put both hands to his face and slowly wiped the stress away. Krazy was leaning against the door, looking like a guilty child about to be scolded.

Wink spoke through his hands in a lagging voice. "Tell me you didn't kill Live and JT." Wink knew the answer by the way Krazy started shaking his head like he always did when he was caught dead wrong.

"Fuck them bitch-ass niggas," Krazy said. "You ain't even gon' ask me my side of the story, is you?" Krazy followed Wink into the living room while continuing to plead his case. "You ain't see my windshield. Them niggas was tryin' to kill me. And Trey's bitch ass was the one who gave 'em the green light."

Wink stopped in his tracks. He peered at Krazy, then folded his arms like, "Nigga, I don't believe you."

"You tellin' me Trey was there and he let the shit go down like that?" Wink watched Krazy with an eagle eye for any signs that he was lying. He knew Krazy like a book, and he didn't see any signs.

"I'm tellin' you, Wink, the nigga wouldn't even let me up to his office so I could holla at him. He had these niggas all surround me, and after he finished tellin' me how we wasn't family no more, he had them niggas rush me out the club. And he said that he knows you're back in town, and he'll be to see you soon."

Wink was stewing on the inside because that was the second time Trey had threatened him on some sly shit. Not to mention what he'd done to Krazy, letting them off-brand niggas take shots at him after tossing him out of the club. Yeah, Trey had definitely gotten beside himself. And it was time to put his ass back in its proper place: six feet under.

"What we gon' do, my nigga?" Krazy asked.

"We gon' give 'em what they want. An all-out war. Them li'l bitches ain't ready to die for real. When them thangs go to busting, watch they run and leave Trey's ass to die all by himself." Wink realized the depth of his words as he spoke them. He was really about to kill his best friend. He was tighter with Trey than with Willie or Krazy. They were like brothers for real.

Wink went back to pacing the floor while Krazy rubbed his hands together in anticipation of the coming blood-bath. He left Wink to his thoughts while he rushed to his arsenal of guns in his bedroom. Wink threw himself onto the chaise lounge, frustrated with the decision he had to make. He squeezed his eyes tight and rubbed the sides of his face, wishing that none of this was real.

"Where did we fall off?" Wink asked as if Trey were standing before him. It had only been three years since they'd started hustling, and Wink wondered if they had changed that much, to the point where they now wanted to kill each other. Wink hadn't let the money change him, and he was never one high off of power. But he could see the dark side that the drug game brought into his life with all the murders. And now he had to add Trey to that already-long list of bodies.

"Damn." Wink sighed deeply. He closed his eyes and tried to remember better times. Wink broke into a wide, closed smile as he recalled the time that he and Trey got arrested in Trey's momma's car. They had stolen it to go downtown to the River Rock club. They were only twelve at the time and looked every bit of it, so when the police pulled them over, there wasn't a snowball's chance in hell that the cops would let them go.

The police car pulled up behind them, and Trey saw the flashing lights in his rearview. "Shit," he said.

Wink turned around to look out the back window. "Shit."

"What do I do?"

"I don't know, outrun them?"

"This Ford Fiesta ain't got enough power. I'ma pull over and talk my way out."

Wink didn't say anything. He felt like he had to pee his pants. He could feel his hands shaking.

The police approached the car with hands on their guns, one on either side of the vehicle. The cop on the driver's side told Trey to roll down the window. Trey followed the instructions.

"License and registration," the cop said.

"Funny thing is, Officer, I left my house without my license."

"Step out of the car." The officer took a step away from the car.

The moment Trey and Wink stepped out, the officers laughed. "These two nappy-headed fools," the passenger side officer said.

The cops handcuffed them and sat them on the ground. They made Wink and Trey sit there while they waited for a tow truck to take the car to impound.

Trey cried the whole way over to the youth home because he knew his mom was going to beat a patch out of his ass once she got the call. Wink knew his own mom would be upset too and would most definitely be beating his back in once they got home.

"Wink, you gotta tell my moms it was your idea. She gonna kill me."

Wink looked at Trey. His face was tearstained and his eyes bloodshot. He was crying hard. "What?" Wink said.

"Please. I'm begging you. If my moms thinks it was your idea, she won't go so hard on me. I'ma still get mines, but it won't be certain death."

Seeing how scared Trey was and how hard he was crying, Wink felt sorry for Trey. He was actually surprised at how scared Trey was. Wink figured there was no sense in both of them getting their asses whooped, so he told Trey's mom that he took her car keys and made Trey come along. Wink never forget what she said.

"Yeah, well, he shoulda beat yo' ass like I'm 'bout to beat his." Trey's mom beat his ass all the way out of the youth home and some more once they got home.

Wink's mom wasn't too far behind. She showed up with her murda mask on, looking like she was ready to kill something. When the sheriff signed Wink out and handed him over, that was exactly what she did, half killed him off in there. They both got it the worst and were on punishment damn near the whole summer.

Wink thought, *those were the good ol' days.* His beaming smile vanished as he sat up. Things could never go back to the way they were. Trey had let the money and power go to his head, to a point where he no longer looked at Wink and Krazy as family.

"I'ma show you what I do to niggas who ain't family," Wink said as he stood up.

Krazy walked into the living room looking like he was on his way to Vietnam with all the fatigues and the artillery he had strapped across his chest and legs. Wink looked him up and down like he done lost his rabbit-ass mind.

"Where'd you get all that from?" Wink couldn't help but laugh.

"You never know when it's wartime. I stocked up the day after I was released. Here, take this." Krazy handed Wink a getup similar to his own.

Wink waved the war suit off. "Nah, I'm straight on all that. Nigga, who you think we is, the A-Team?"

"What about these? Take a couple of these." Krazy held the sides of a duffle bag open.

Wink looked inside the bag at the grenades. "Nah, I'm good, my nigga." He chuckled while shaking his head no.

"A'ight. I'm telling you they're here if you need them. So who we hittin' first?" Krazy asked. He couldn't wait to get on his bullshit.

"This ain't 'bout to be no long, drawn-out process. I'ma take care of Trey," Wink said. He gazed out the bay window for a moment, then continued, "You do what you feel is necessary with them Money Squad bitches. Just leave Trey to me, a'ight?"

"I got you, my nigga." Krazy didn't care, so long as he got to kill somebody. He was itching to get started. "You ready?"

"Listen, the Feds are watching us, so be careful out there, and don't be getting into no shootouts in broad daylight. I don't know how you got away with that shit earlier when I know damn well the Feds is watching Trey's club."

"'Cause I'm a beast!" Krazy clenched his jaws and put extra emphasis on the "beast."

"Yeah, well. Don't get caught slippin', and one more thing, Krazy."

"What's up, my nigga?"

"That shit you did, gettin' drunk and tellin' the business. That shit can never happen again," Wink said in a warning voice.

Krazy nodded in agreement. Had it not been for him spilling the beans, none of this would even be going on. But Wink wasn't about to dwell on the past. He meant what he told Krazy. If it ever happened again, he'd be joining Trey in the cemetery.

Chapter Twenty-two

Willie had been blowing up Wink's phone ever since he left the federal building. He had already gotten the word from Trey about what had happened, and he wanted to hurry up and get this indictment on Wink before he and Trey killed each other, leaving him to do all the prison time by himself.

Willie had checked his pager to see if maybe he missed Wink's call, but the only pages he had were two from Agent Defauw putting in their new code, 360, which stood for the amount of time Willie was going to get if he didn't step up his snitch game. He would get 360 months, which broke down to thirty years, and with the Feds, that was considered a life sentence.

Seeing the death code made Willie sit up in his seat. He gripped the wheel with one hand while he pushed redial for the tenth time.

"What up doe," Wink answered on the third ring.

Yes, Willie silently sighed in relief. "Where you at? I need to holla at you," he said, hoping Wink would meet him.

"Meet me at the laundromat on Anglin."

"I'm on my way now. In a minute." Willie hung up and tossed the phone in the passenger seat. He pressed down on the gas in a rush to get over to the laundromat. If anybody was going to be doing 360 months, it was going to be Wink, Trey, and whoever else the Feds wanted before he served a single day.

Willie pulled into the parking lot of Soad's Laundromat on 7 Mile and Anglin. He parked beside Wink's Benz 500 and hurriedly cut the car off and got out. Willie looked inside Wink's car and didn't see him, so he started for the side door, figuring Wink must be inside waiting for him.

Wink was sitting on top of one of the dryers toward the back. He waved Willie over, then slid down from the machine.

"What up doe," Wink said, extending his hand for Willie's. They met with a half hug and ended their embrace with a slap on the back. The laundromat was empty with the exception of the old man serving as the change machine behind the bulletproof glass. Wink looked at the old man and put his arm around Willie, turning him in the opposite direction.

Willie didn't waste any time running down the questions Agent Defauw rehearsed with him. "When you gon' introduce me to the connect so we ain't gotta always be on hold?"

"Whoever said anything about me turning you on to the plug?" Wink tucked his head back at Willie.

"Nah, I'm just saying that it would be a good look for business, because you obviously been too busy to keep up with the shit. I got niggas blowing me up all day and night."

"Let 'em get it from somebody else. Right now we got more serious shit to worry about. I know you heard what happened earlier up at Trey's club."

"Yeah, and I wish you hadn't done that. What you think Trey's gonna do, just sit back and not do anything?"

"That's exactly what he's going to do. Not a mothafuckin' thing!" Wink's voice had raised with anger. He had to pause for a second so he could calm down. He looked over his shoulder into the booth where the old man sat. The man hadn't left his game of solitaire. Wink turned around and continued. His voice returned to its original whisper.

"I called you here 'cause the shit is 'bout to get deep, and I need to know whose side you're on."

"Here you go with this 'whose side' shit."

"Nigga, I told you from day one that you had to make your choice. Ever since Trey went out to Texas and got his own plug, I told you to make your decision."

Willie lowered his eyes to the floor and shook his head no. "So what are you asking me for, Wink, 'cause I know it's bigger than just me saying, 'Yeah, I'm with you.'" Willie looked up and met eyes with Wink.

"Willie, remember that day in my car I told you never to cross me? Remember that day? We was right out there in the parking lot."

"Yeah, I remember." Willie looked away.

"Now I want you to stand there and look me in my eyes, and tell me, do you see a damn fool?" Wink waited until Willie gave him his eyes. 'Nigga, I know what you've been up to out here. What, you thought I wouldn't find out? I been knowing you all your life, nigga."

Willie's heart was thumping like a mothafucka. He was just waiting for Wink to say he knew that he was standing there with a wire taped to his chest, and that the Feds were listening to everything as they spoke. Wink grabbed Willie around the neck and pulled him close enough to kiss him. Willie fought back the sudden urge to take off running for the door. His eyes registered with the amount of fear only a coward staring death in the face could embody.

"I know you've been double hustling for me and Trey. I know you've been running keys down to Mississippi for that nigga. I know you call yourself being a part of his Money Squad Family, Will$." Wink let the "$" ring.

Willie was just relieved he hadn't found him out for being the true-blooded rat he had become. Wink let all of what he knew soak into Willie's brain, then he finished, "I also know that you know where Trey lives now."

"Wink, why you wanna put me in the middle of y'all beef? That's between—"

Wink cut Willie off before he could finish. "You put ya'self in the middle when you started playin' the fifty, nigga, but that shit ends right here, right now." Wink brushed his coat aside, revealing the butt of his woodgrain, nickel-plated three-pound-seven. "You gon' make your mind up today whose side you on: mine if you tell me where Trey's living, or his if you don't."

Being the natural-born coward, scared-to-die-ass nigga he was, Willie picked the winning side. He'd deal with Trey when he crossed that bridge, but right now Wink had him hemmed up, and his only way out was to throw Trey under the bus. "He's at his crib out in St. Clair Shores. I got the address in the car."

Wink released his grip from Willie's neck and took a step back. Looking into Willie's eyes, Wink could see that the game had changed him, too, and he could no longer trust him. Wink knew that eventually he would kill Willie, too.

Willie tried his hand one last time to get Wink to turn him on to the connect. He just needed for Wink to say a name, and he'd have him. "What about the work? You gon' turn me on to the connect or what?" Willie asked, following close behind Wink as they exited the laundromat.

Wink spoke over his shoulder at Willie. "We're done after this run. I got this last two hun'd and we're done."

"What do you mean we're done? I ain't got the type of money you sittin' on. I'm not ready to leave the game. Why don't you turn me on to the plug, give me the number, and I'll make my own moves," said Willie.

"Trust me, my nigga, we have more than enough bread to get out. I wasn't just planning my out, but yours as well," lied Wink. Just as soon as he got done knocking Trey's shit loose, he was coming for Willie. Knowing that he was playing the fifty made it that much easier.

"I wish you'd let me do me," said Willie.

"My peoples ain't tryin'a meet nobody new. If you wanna find your own connect, I got some money for you to do that, but for right now, let me get that address."

Willie accepted the defeat of knowing that Wink wasn't slipping and he wasn't going to introduce him to the connect. Willie dug into his glove box and handed Wink the napkin with Trey's address on it.

Wink looked up at Willie and told him, "Remember whose side you on." Wink said that as if to say, "Nigga, you bet' not warn Trey that I'm coming."

"I got you, my nigga." Willie gave Wink some dap, and they parted ways.

The only thing on Willie's mind was that 360 months. He turned off his pager because he couldn't stand to hear from Agent Defauw at the moment.

Chapter Twenty-three

I wish it would have been another
How long will you mourn me?
How long will they mourn my brother?

The lyrics of Pac muffled the drunken sniffles of the many men gathered around grieving the deaths of Live and JT. The corner house of Charest and Emery looked like a scene from *Colors* there was so much red and white out there. All the Money Squad members put their red and white colors on to honor their fallen brothers. They all had on RIP T-shirts bearing smiling faces amid the mob. They wanted blood and lots of it. But tonight they would mourn their lost and just be together.

Lee-Mac jumped from the curb he'd been silently sharing with Dilla, ran to the middle of the street, and slammed his bottle of Rémy to the ground, shattering it to pieces. "This some bullshit!" he cursed to the sky as if he were face-to-face with God. Lee-Mac lowered his stare and let his legs fold under him. "This some bullshit," he softly cried into the street. Live was all he'd had. They were like brothers.

Dilla set his drink down and walked over to Lee-Mac. He kneeled down and put his arm around Lee-Mac. Dilla felt his pain, because JT was like his brother.

"We gotta be strong, Mac. We all we got now," Dilla said into Lee-Mac's ear. "We gon' get 'em," Dilla assured him. He let Lee-Mac get it all out, then carried him into the house.

Krazy watched the scene from his Lexus truck. He was parked two blocks over, on the corner of Emery and Gallagher, ducked low in his seat with a Gucci bucket hat pulled down over his eyes. He had been parked out there since early in the day when the members first started showing up.

Krazy had enough heat in the truck to launch another war, and that was his every intention, but to run out there with all them niggas standing out there Macked up, it would have been a straight suicide mission. Even Krazy wasn't that crazy. Even if he were to lay a few of them down, when the smoke cleared, he would definitely be among the dead on his way to the morgue. Krazy wasn't ready to die yet, and especially not at the hands of no bitch niggas. He lowered the small set of binoculars from his face and lay back in his seat while keeping his gaze ahead.

"Yeah, I'ma wait you bitches out," he said. Krazy hated how deep they were, because in his world, a coward ain't have no business having no power. Trey had all them niggas running around on some fake gangster shit, when he himself was a full-blooded bitch and a coward at heart. Krazy had his sights set on Dilla and Lee-Mac, seeing as how they were the last two official members of Trey's Money Squad Family. He was going to paint the city red with their blood first, then slaughter whoever else wanted to jump they ass out there.

Krazy had found out from a crackhead named Word Man that the house they were all gathered at belonged to Dilla's momma. *Stupid-ass young nigga. All that money you touching, and you still got yo' momma in the same house.* Krazy couldn't help but chuckle, because he had done the same thing at Dilla's age. "Don't worry about it. I'ma tax that ass."

Now as a white thread fought to peek through the dark clouds, Krazy was sliding out of his Lexus truck. He crossed the street and tucked his hands deep inside the wool pockets of the army fatigue coat he sported. He picked up his stride after locating the butt of a blue steel Ruger. Krazy looked over his shoulder then down a side street off Emery as he neared the alley behind Dilla's house. Not seeing anyone, Krazy cut down the alley and leaped over the rusted back fence into Dilla's yard.

Krazy remained in his crouched position until he was satisfied no one had seen him. Well, almost no one. Dilla's mutt-ass pit bull was staring up at Krazy, looking like he was ready to start barking. "You betta not," Krazy said through clenched teeth. He slowly stood while clutching the trigger, ready to blast the mutt if need be. The dog got the message and retired to his house to let Krazy do his thing.

Krazy didn't have a set plan of how he was going to kill Dilla, other than go up in there and fill his face and chest with nothing less than a clip. He never planned what he was going to do because it took away from the thrill, and besides that, Krazy felt like the Angel of Death himself, because when he came to get you, there was no escaping.

As Krazy climbed the back porch, he could hear the morning news on the television. He quietly twisted the screen door handle and eased in between the back door and the screen door.

"That's a damn shame. Folks need to learn how to raise they kids," Krazy heard a woman say to the television.

Krazy tried turning the doorknob, hoping for the same luck, but it was locked. Just as he stood back to kick the door down, Dilla's momma opened it. She was on her way out with the trash in her hand. She froze at the sight of Krazy.

"Boy, what the hell?" she said.

Krazy gripped her old ass up and forced her back inside the house. He closed the door with his foot and whispered into the woman's ear, "Where is your son?"

Dilla's mom shook her head no, like she would never tell. Krazy tightened his grip around her mouth, then shoved her in the back. "Move around, bitch," he whispered. They cut through the kitchen and farther into the house. Krazy checked the living room and the back rooms. They were all empty, so he shoved the old hag toward the stairs leading up to the master bedroom, but she wasn't going, not willingly. Dilla's mom used the heel of her shoe to stomp down on Krazy's foot, and she was biting a plug out of his arm, trying to free herself from his death grip.

"Ahh. You bitch," Krazy said as he fought the urge to bend down and nurse the stinging pain in his foot. "Where the fuck is you going?" Krazy asked while he fought to contain her.

"Ma, is you a'ight?" Dilla called out. He rolled off his bed and started to come downstairs. He saw Krazy and ran to get his gun.

Boom! Krazy blew her brains out the front of her head after seeing Dilla.

"I'm tired of wrestlin' with yo' ass," Krazy said and looked down at the woman's dead body. He heard Dilla upstairs slamming through drawers, and quickly put his back to the wall.

"Dilla," Krazy called out in a light, ringing voice. "Come out and play, Dilla. I just killed yo' mammy, Dilla boy. What are you gon' do about it, Dilla? I know you hear me." Krazy tried to peek upstairs, but Dilla fired down two shots, missing his face by inches.

"Close, but no cigar!" yelled Krazy. This was what he lived for. He was so geeked his dick got hard. "That's right, fight back, nigga! You can fight all you want, but yo' ass still gon' die." Krazy geeked himself up to go in. "You ready to die, nigga?" he roared. He spun around the corner, gun blazing.

Dilla fired back, but he got the bad end of things because he wasn't wearing a vest. Still he held his ground, taking in the hot slugs and accepting death. After taking seven shells to the chest and stomach, Dilla finally crumbled over with his empty gun in hand.

Krazy cautiously climbed the steps, preserving the last two slugs for Dilla's dome. Krazy stood over Dilla, looking down into his eyes. He could tell that at the very moment, the Angel of Death was pulling at his soul.

"Here, let me help you." Boom! Boom!

Krazy fired his last two shells dead center into Dilla's face, putting him to rest. He tucked the steaming hot Ruger in his coat pocket and started downstairs. He clutched the bite wound Dilla's mom had bestowed upon him. She had bitten through the coat down to the bone. Krazy stopped in the hallway, where she was sprawled out, dead. He cocked his foot back and kicked her square in the ass.

"Bite that, bitch."

Chapter Twenty-four

After hearing Wink say that he was getting out of the game, Agent Defauw was forced to go back to the drawing board because Willie's rat ass wasn't turning up anything solid. Defauw decided he would use what he did have, which was a mean bluff game. He got a warrant signed by Judge Victoria Roberts before her chambers closed, and sent a convoy of federal agents to raid Wink's mansion. Defauw knew Wink wouldn't be stupid enough to have anything in the house, but it was his way of initiating contact between them.

Wink was on his way out the front door when he stopped dead in his tracks, his eyes bucking wide at the sight of all the Suburbans climbing his front lawn.

"Oh, shit!" Wink slammed the door shut and ran through the house, pulling two Glocks from his waist.

"What's wrong, baby?" Armeeah asked, turning the corner out of the kitchen.

"Take these, and put 'em where I showed you. Go!" yelled Wink, looking over his shoulder.

Seconds later, the front door came crashing down, and agents rushed in with their guns drawn. "Get down on the floor. Do it now!" a white DEA agent ordered after spotting Wink in the hall.

Wink raised his hands into the air and slowly got down. The agent signaled for another agent to take Wink. After searching him, the two agents handcuffed Wink and stood him up, then walked him out to the living room.

Armeeah was already on the sofa, cuffed with her hands behind her back. Wink gave her a look like, "What about the guns?" His heart seemed to skip a beat when he followed Armeeah's eyes over to the lampstand where the two Glocks sat with the clips beside them.

Fuck it, Wink thought as the agents sat him on a sofa across from Armeeah. He was on his way out to kill Trey when they'd rushed the house. The guns were clean, so it was just a matter of illegal possession of a firearm. Wink gave Armeeah a stern look to keep her mouth closed and to ask for a lawyer no matter what they said. Armeeah nodded as if she knew the business.

Agent Defauw made his grand entrance like he was J. Edgar Hoover himself. Two agents nodded in the direction of the living room. Defauw sauntered in that direction. "Have you read them their rights?" Defauw looked over his shoulder at the two field agents.

"We were waiting for you, sir."

"Find anything yet?"

"Just the two firearms." The agent showed Defauw the Glocks. "We caught her on the way upstairs, probably trying to hide them. Our agents are still searching."

Defauw turned his attention to Wink and Armeeah.

"My fiancée has nothing to do with this," Wink said, thinking about his unborn child. He couldn't let them haul Armeeah off to jail. He'd never hear the end of it from her dad.

"Maybe she does and maybe she doesn't. That'll depend on your decision whether to help her," said Defauw. He had every intention of taking advantage of the situation. He didn't give a fuck if Armeeah was going into labor, her ass would be delivering the baby downtown at the county jail unless Wink did as he said and help her.

"Look, you got two guns. Let's get this shit over with so I can get my bond," said Wink.

Defauw looked down his crater-filled nose at Wink and smirked. "Trust me, when you take that ride, your ass won't be coming back. Now I'm going to tell you some things, and then I'm going to allow you some time to make your mind up."

"You can tell whatever you gotta say to my lawyer," Wink said, giving "lawyer" about twenty syllables. "His name's Otis Culpepper."

"I know who he is, and let me tell you, he won't be able to save your ass once the indictments come down." Defauw allowed his words to flirt with any possible fear Wink fought not to show. "I know everything about you, Wink: when you eat, sleep, shit, and go visit your father in Leavenworth."

If Wink weren't cuffed, he would have leaped from the sofa and beaten the sleeves off of Defauw. Who was this cracker to be mentioning his father?

"I know your fiancée here is three months pregnant, and unless you help me, she's going to be giving birth from a federal prison cell. And I'ma tell you what else I know. I know that you're buying two hundred kilos a week from the Cuban crime family headed by Franko Guerra. I know that your father is the one responsible for you meeting Franko's people and that he's the one orchestrating your moves."

"Are you finished?" asked Wink.

"Yes, I am."

"Good. Now let me tell you what I know. I know that you're full of shit. You don't know anything, 'cause if you did, we wouldn't be sitting here having this conversation. I know that you're violating my rights as well. I asked for my lawyer, and at that moment all your theories should have ceased." Wink took a deep breath, then looked over at Armeeah and said, "Unless you have anything else on me with all that you know, my fiancée is ready to go to jail so we can get her bond."

Agent Defauw turned beet red. If there weren't a room-
ful of agents there, he would have kicked Wink's teeth out
of his mouth. Defauw snatched Armeeah from the sofa
and handed her off to one of the agents. "I want her ass
booked on illegal possession of a firearm, and make sure
you process the paperwork after four. Let her ass spend
the weekend in Wayne County." Defauw gave Armeeah a
starting nudge, then returned to Wink.

"You are a worthless coward," he said to Wink, with his
finger pointed at Armeeah. "How can you sit there and
watch your pregnant fiancée get hauled off to jail?"

"She's in love with a gansta."

"We'll see how much of a gangster you are when you're
sitting beside your father in Leavenworth."

"I'm actually going to see him next week. I'll be sure
and tell him you said hi."

Agent Defauw was about to blow his top. He couldn't
stand being mocked, especially not by some young black
punk. He ordered the cuffs off of Wink, then stormed out
the front door.

Wink rushed to the window, but the agents already
had shot off with her in one of the Suburbans. "Fuck!"
Wink yelled. He looked around at the remainder of the
agents and what damage they had done to his house. This
was not how he wanted to live the rest of his life, with
these crackers constantly fucking with him.

He rushed over to the cordless phone beside the sofa.
He had Mr. Culpepper's number on speed dial from the
last time they'd stopped by the house.

"It's the weekend, Wayne. Unfortunately, she's going
to have to sit tight 'til Monday. I'll get her out on a writ if
I have to, but it'll be on Monday."

"I guess I don't have no choice but to wait."

"We'll get her. I want you to stop by my office, and we'll
go get her together."

"A'ight, bye." Wink slowly lowered the phone to the receiver. That wasn't what he was hoping to hear, but fuck it. It came with the game.

Wink blamed all of this on Trey, and he was going to pay in blood. Wink couldn't stand being in the presence of the agents anymore. He left them in the house to finish searching, knowing they wouldn't find anything else. He just had to get out of there and try to clear his mind.

As Wink drove, all he could think about was the look Trey would have on his face right before he killed him. It wasn't just personal anymore. Wink had to kill Trey. He figured that was the only way he'd shake the Feds.

Meanwhile, Agent Defauw was busy laying his trap for Wink. He rode shotgun while his partner Agent Hornberger punched the triple-black Suburban. They were tailing Armeeah down to the federal building. "His nigger ass is too smart for his own good. He seems to think he has it all figured out." Defauw glared at the passing traffic for a bit, then continued, "He's planning to take Trey out of the picture because that's who he believes is tying him to the investigation."

Agent Hornberger took his eyes off the road and put them on his partner. He knew exactly where this was going, and he for once was sick of all the unnecessary bloodshed. Enough was enough. "So what are we going to do? We have to bring him in now before another body drops," said Hornberger.

"We are going to do no such thing. We need smart-ass to off his partner. It's our trump card."

Hornberger had the mind to obey the law he'd sworn to uphold and report Defauw to their supervisor just as soon as they reached the federal building. He had the mind, just not the heart. He would continue to do as Defauw ordered, no matter how much blood was lost.

"We'll see how smart your ass is," Defauw said, seeing into the future—Wink's future.

Chapter Twenty-five

"You mean to tell me all them fuckin' guns we got, not one of them has a drop of blood on it? What, y'all niggas scared, or do I need to hire some real guns?" Trey was yelling at the top of his lungs into the speakerphone. He had just gotten the call about Dilla being killed, and yet nothing had happened in return.

"Trey, we're on it. We got everybody from east to west combing the streets," said Lee-Mac.

"Fuck combing! Mothafucka, I want 'em raked, and I want bodies bagged. Don't call my phone with no more sob stories. I don't give a fuck who else dies. Just find those niggas, and get it done!" Trey picked up the receiver, then slammed it down hard in Lee-Mac's ear.

Trey was fuming because his Money Squad Family was losing the war, and they were over 500 strong versus two niggas: Krazy and Wink. Not only was Trey losing the war, he was losing money, because he still hadn't patched things up with Junior abut Sammy's murder. Trey wondered how long he would be able to keep his MS movement going without drugs to generate the money they all quickly had grown accustomed to blowing.

Trey was hiding out at his mansion in St. Clair Shores while he waited for the smoke to clear. He knew just what Krazy was capable of doing, and he didn't want any part of it. He just hoped that when the smoke cleared, his team would be the ones left standing. In the meantime, though, Trey was going to continue doing what he did best, and that was hide.

He kicked his feet up on the cherrywood desk and pulled a stogy from the inside pocket of the burgundy smoking jacket he wore. He set fire to the cigar while pulling in the thick cloud of smoke. He leaned against the headrest of the chair and began blowing rings of smoke to the ceiling. Trey could see Wink being laid to rest, his coffin being lowered into the ground, while he stood beside Wink's mom, consoling her. Trey told himself that was the way it had to be. Things would never be the same again.

"You never could accept the fact that I was my own man, could you? Everything always had to be Wink's way, always!" Trey nodded in agreement with his twisted plot. He took another pull from the stogy, then said, "Yeah, well, let's see if you can't plan your own funeral."

Chapter Twenty-six

"Get the fuck outta here!" snapped Lee-Mac. He was shooing the crowd of onlookers who had come to show their respect to Dilla and his mother, Ms. Campbell. They were placing items on the growing memorial. Lee-Mac pulled his .380 out and fired two shots in the air. Boom! Boom! Thunder ripped through the morning air, causing a stampede of folks trying to get the hell out of dodge. All to be heard following the gunshots were heels hitting the pavement, car doors slamming, and tires peeling against the street.

"Nosy mothafuckas. Dilla ain't even know that many people," Lee-Mac said to the backs of those fleeing the scene.

When the corner cleared up, all that was left were the many teddy bears, candles, and cards folks added as a memorial. Lee-Mac turned up the rest of his Henny, then joined the few members who hadn't fled on the corner.

"What the fuck is wrong with you?" asked Willie. He hadn't come to show his support. He was there to gather information and hopefully save his ass from going to prison.

Lee-Mac stopped in front of Willie, and his first thought was to bust Willie across his face with the empty Hennessy bottle, but instead he raised the .380 to Willie's forehead. "Nigga, you out here why?"

Willie went straight into bitch mode, raising his hands high above his head. "Come on, Mac, you trippin', my nigga. I was just saying you shouldn't have done that to those people."

"Nigga, fuck all that. Answer my question." Mac cocked the hammer back and pressed the barrel hard against Willie's forehead. "What the fuck is you doing out here?"

"I'm family, remember? Money Squad 'til the world blow up," Willie said, trying to talk his way out of whatever Mac was tripping off.

"Nah, you ain't never been family. I don't give a damn what Trey says or how much money you put on the table. You one of them niggas."

"Mac, dawg, I'm standing here with y'all because I'm family," Willie said. He was so scared that he was on the brink of crying. "We fam, Mac."

Lee-Mac looked deep into Willie's eyes and knew that he was lying. He reached to his side and pulled his cell phone from its clip. "Here. Prove it." He handed him the phone. "Call that nigga Krazy and see where he's at."

Willie looked around at the other members and saw that they were all riding with Mac on this. To them he was an outsider, and he'd be dead and stankin' unless he made that call to Krazy. Willie thought while dialing Krazy's cell, *where the fuck is Defauw? I know you're listening*.

"What up doe," Willie said, trying to sound like his normal self.

"Ain't not shit. Where you been hiding at? Niggas need to holla at you 'bout yo' man Trey," said Krazy.

"You know me. I been trying my best to stay outta all that."

Lee-Mac pressed the barrel deeper into Willie's skin like, "Nigga, stop bullshitting!"

"But uh, where you at? I'ma come holla at you."

"Shit, me and Wink at my crib. Fall through and fuck with us. We just chillin'. Wink over here stressing me and him out."

"I'm on my way."

"A'ight, in a minute," said Krazy.

Willie handed Lee-Mac his phone back, hoping that he was free to go. "He's at his crib out in Oak Park."

"Good. You can show us where it is." Mac grabbed Willie by the arm and turned him around. One of the other members opened the back door to Lee-Mac's Yukon for Willie to get in. Lee-Mac climbed in behind Willie and held him at gunpoint for the entire drive.

"Tell 'em where we're going," ordered Mac.

Willie's bitch ass promptly gave the directions to get to Krazy's house. He sat back in his seat as the truck started moving. He was trying to figure out his own escape, because from the look of things, Lee-Mac was going to kill him just as soon as he finished killing Krazy.

Defauw, you need to be sending somebody to get me. An airstrike or something. He couldn't believe the Feds hadn't rushed in to save him like they'd promised they would when he first started snitching for them. Agent Defauw told him that if there'd ever come a time they had to rush in and save him, to get low and wait for an agent to pull him up for cover. Well, now was the time, Willie thought as they crossed 8 Mile heading into Oak Park, Michigan. Help was nowhere in sight. Willie was on his own.

Chapter Twenty-seven

Lee-Mac told the other four carloads of members to wait for him at the Amoco gas station just around the corner of Krazy's house. Mac wanted Willie to point out the house first, and then they would all go back and bomb rush the crib.

"It's coming up on my right," said Willie.

"Slow down," Mac ordered the driver. He sat up in his seat and peered through the tinted window at Krazy's house. "Yeah, that's him." Mac knew the house belonged to Krazy because out front sat Krazy's shot-up Impala.

Mac tapped the driver's headrest and ordered the driver to go back to the station.

"So now you believe me when I tell you I'm on your side? We family, right?" asked Willie. He needed some type of affirmation that Mac wasn't going to kill his ass.

"Yeah, we fam."

Willie didn't believe Mac by his tone of voice and also because he had yet to put the gun away.

When they pulled into the parking lot of the Amoco service station, Willie began scouring for an escape route. He inched his ass toward the door, and before the truck could come to a complete stop, he was up and out the back door.

"Catch that nigga!" yelled Lee-Mac.

Two carloads of niggas packed in and gave chase, but there was no catching Willie. He had been running his whole life, and there was no way in hell he was going to let them niggas catch him so they could kill him. Willie booked across Livernois, feet touching his ass, while hollering the code word. "Help!"

Lee-Mac climbed down from the truck and briefed the other two carloads of his men on how he wanted Krazy killed. "I want his ass dragged out dead or alive. But I want to look him in the eyes to make sure he's dead. Let's go!" Mac clapped his hands together, and they all climbed into their cars. Lee-Mac pulled a fully automatic AK-47 from underneath his seat. He cocked a shell into the chamber and ordered his driver to pull over across the street from Krazy's house.

Lee-Mac slid out the hatch of the Yukon to join his men at the curb. He split the eight men into groups of two. "I want y'all to surround the house, and on my call, we gon' air this bitch out. After we finish, we goin' in. Let's go."

It was broad daylight, and all them niggas were toting something heavy. They were about to turn the quiet suburban street into baby Iraq. Lee-Mac stood in the middle of the front lawn with his AK-47 held waist level at the house. He waited for his men to all take their positions.

"Here, g'on and hit some of this good gan. It'll take ya mind off it," Krazy said as he stood over Wink lying on the sofa.

Wink took the blunt from Krazy without looking at him and took a long pull. Keeping his stare into space, Wink said, "My nigga, they got my woman downtown in that musty-ass county jail, doing who knows what to her. She ain't built like that to be down there with them giddy bitches." Wink was right there with Armeeah. He could feel her pain and how scared she was. He was scared for her.

Krazy sparked up another L, then said, "Shit, we can always go bond her out."

"They ain't gave her no bond yet."

"Nigga, I'm talking 'bout a gangsta's bond," Krazy said, pulling the chrome .45 from his waist. He waved it high in the air. "Nigga, we can run up in that bitch and get her. You know I'm down."

Wink couldn't help but smile, because he knew Krazy was dead-ass serious.

Boom!

"Man, put that shit down. You high and—"

Boom! Boom! Boom! Laaka! Laaka!

Wink rolled off the sofa onto the floor. He'd thought it was Krazy who had let off the shot, but the shots kept coming. Boom! Boom! Laaka!

The bullets were tearing through the windows and walls like a knife cutting through butter. Wink hugged the side of the sofa for dear life. He looked around for Krazy but saw no sign of him. The way those bullets were flying through the house, Wink knew he wasn't going to make it out alive.

Suddenly the shots stopped, and to Wink's surprise, he wasn't dead. He lowered his hands from his head and slowly rose from a crouch. Feathers from the sofa mingled high in the air with drywall dust and broken glass. Just when Wink thought it was all over, the sound of guns being reloaded and cocked came from the front of the house. Wink rose up and saw the shadows of three men on the porch.

Krazy bent the corner carrying two M-16s. He tossed one to Wink and led the way. The front door flew open, and shots filled the room. Wink scrambled to his feet. He caught one of the men coming in from the kitchen and flatlined him dead in his tracks. Wink laid on the trigger, dropping the man's partner a few feet behind the first man. Before Wink could turn around so he could go help Krazy, two more men came running through the back door with guns blazing.

Wink exchanged shots, but he got the worst end. He caught two slugs in the shoulder, causing him to spin and drop his gun. As he lay on the dining room floor, eyes to the ceiling, the only thing Wink could think about was Armeeah and their unborn child. The shots were getting louder and closer. Wink's heart started racing as he tried reaching for his gun. The blood loss was making him weak to the point his eyes became heavy. He fought to keep them open. *I can't die like this. Not now.*

Krazy killed the two men who entered the house first, but Lee-Mac wound up getting away. He saw how his men came flying back out the door with their heads literally knocked off and decided he didn't want any part of that. He thought they would catch Krazy with his drawers down and just run up in there and kill him, but he was the one running. He damn near had Willie beat. Krazy lit the back of the Yukon up as Lee-Mac climbed into the back seat ordering his driver to pull off.

When Krazy got inside the house, two men lay on the porch looking like they belonged in an episode of *Forensics.* That was how bad their wounds were. Krazy smiled at his work, then remembered that Wink was in the house.

He ran through the living room looking all around. He stopped and so did his heart once he saw Wink's gym shoe sticking up. Krazy prepared himself for the worst as he walked over to where Wink was laid out. Krazy let his gun drop to the floor and fell down to his knees. He cradled Wink's limp body in his arms while searching for where the bullet had hit him.

"Get up, Wink. Come on, baby. Don't do this to me," Krazy said frantically. Wink fought to keep his glassy eyes open.

"Fight. Stay with me." Krazy scooped Wink up and carried him through the living room and out of the house. He put Wink in the back seat of his Lexus truck and hurriedly climbed behind the wheel. "Stay with me, my nigga," Krazy said. He looked back at Wink before pulling off.

Chapter Twenty-eight

Willie ignored his pager as it vibrated and slid across the kitchen counter. He knew it couldn't be but one person paging him, Agent Defauw's sheisty ass. Willie finished packing his Louis Vuitton duffle bag with a few hundred thousand dollars he'd managed to stash away. He zipped the bag shut and took a final glance around his apartment. He grabbed the bag from the counter and started for the door, leaving the pager vibrating on the counter.

Willie had made his mind up that it was time to get the fuck out of dodge, because if he stayed in Detroit, only two things were going to end up happening: jail or death. He had no desire for either. The way Defauw left him out to hang with Lee-Mac was a clear sign that the Feds only cared about one thing, which was a conviction. They couldn't care less if Willie turned up dead. Under no circumstances were they going to blow their investigation over a $10 snitch.

Willie reached the ground level of his apartment and cut out the back door. He knew Defauw had some agents tailing him, and just as he suspected, two white agents were parked beside his BMW in a navy blue Lumina. Willie looked over his shoulder at the agents and kept his stride in the opposite direction. He put his hoodie over his head and clutched the duffle bag tight at his side. Willie didn't know where he was going, but with over $200,000, he could just about go anywhere he wanted. And the good part about it was that the Feds didn't know he was leaving.

Willie reached the corner of McDougal and flagged a green Checker cab. He slid into the back seat and handed the driver a twenty. "Take me to the Greyhound station," ordered Willie. He lowered himself in the seat as the cab pulled away from the curb. He prayed that would be the last time he saw Defauw, Lee-Mac, or Wink. He just wanted to go somewhere and start all over and live a normal life.

Chapter Twenty-nine

It took everything Agent Hornberger had in him to keep from jumping up and doing his Super Bowl victory dance and laughing in his partner's face, because he had just received the ass chewing of his career by none other than U.S. Attorney Dennis Archer.

"You have one week, Defauw. Not a second more!" Archer warned before storming out of the office and slamming the door.

Agent Hornberger kept his eyes glued to the empty sheet of notebook paper on his desk. He was still fighting the temptation of rubbing it in, but the glance he stole of Defauw's distraught face was just as priceless. Washington DC had made the call down to Detroit with strict orders to conclude the investigation with Wink and Trey immediately because entirely too much blood had been spilled and no arrests had been made.

Defauw started pacing the floor, trying to let his ass heal before he sat down. "Can you believe this fucking shit?" he started in a whisper. "Since when does Washington give a rat's ass about the body count on niggers? Then again, it is almost election time."

Hornberger thought, *since I made that anonymous call to the inspector general's office.*

"One fucking week before they pull the plug. I'm tired of this department and its constant politics. The direction this office is heading is a complete one-eighty from when I started eighteen years ago. But if that's the way they want to run things, fine. After this investigation is over, I'm putting in for a transfer. Maybe even a desk job." Defauw walked over and snatched his blazer from the coat rack. He slid into the sleeves while continuing his tirade. "I need a cup of coffee. You coming?"

"Yes," answered Hornberger. He pushed away from his desk and stood. He was silently screaming for joy. Finally he would get a new partner. *Am I coming? Why, of course. You think I'd miss a single moment of your defeat?* Agent Hornberger grabbed his coat and tailed Defauw out of their office.

How sweet it was to watch Defauw in his moment of defeat. His reign would soon be over.

Chapter Thirty

"Paging Dr. Hamilton. Please call extension 3427."

The crackling of the intercom shutting off awakened Wink. His eyes fluttered then rolled to the back of his head. A streak of pain shot from his feet up to his neck as he tried to sit up. "Ahh," he groaned. He had no idea that he was in the intensive care unit downtown at Detroit Receiving Hospital, nor did he remember how he got there. He had lost so much blood on the way to the hospital he passed out in the back seat of Krazy's Lexus truck. The doctors successfully completed a blood transfusion, but even then they were doubtful that Wink would pull through.

But they didn't know Wink. He was a fighter. There was no way in hell he was going to allow two slugs to be the end of him. It was going to take a hellava lot more than that to hand in his jersey. Wink had things to do, places he had yet to go, and a beautiful fiancée he was going to marry. There was only one thing stopping him from leaving: he was handcuffed at the wrist to the frame of the bed.

Wink fought through the pain and sat up in bed. He jerked hard at the frame trying to free his arm, but the more he moved, the tighter the cuff got. And it was already bone tight, damn near to the point of no circulation. The first thing that popped in Wink's mind was the dead bodies at Krazy's house. Wink tried to remember how he got to the hospital, and where was Krazy? *I gotta get up outta here*. While he searched the room with his eyes for something to free himself, the door swung wide open, and in stepped his lawyer, Otis Culpepper. *Damn.* Wink couldn't have been happier to see it was "set 'em free" Culpepper.

And that was exactly what Culpepper did. He stopped in the center of the floor looking no less than a cool million in his $5,000 tailor-made suit and small black Mauris. He looked over his shoulder at the two redneck sheriffs, and with the coolest tone, he ordered them to uncuff Wink. He pulled the signed writ from his blazer's inside pocket and fanned the papers loose like, "Not now, but right now!"

"You see the signature on there? Richard P. Hathaway," Culpepper said, giving the judge's name about a hundred syllables.

The two red-faced sheriffs reluctantly unhooked Wink. Culpepper had everything already lined up. He snapped his fingers, and in came his assistant with Wink's change of clothes and wheelchair ready to roll. Culpepper was on point getting Wink out of there fast, because the sheriffs were already making phone calls to try to block the release. All they had was the right to question Wink, and now they were hurriedly seeking a warrant.

"That's okay, Diane. We can get that on him once we get him in the van," said Culpepper. He double locked the wheels on Wink's wheelchair, and then he and Diane lifted Wink from the bed and put him in the chair.

"Ahh," Wink groaned from the aching pain lodged in his left shoulder where he was hit. The doctor had put a few bandages over the wound and put his arm in a sling.

"The doctors haven't released him yet," one of the sheriffs said.

"I'm releasing him. Now if you don't get the hell outta my way, I'll have your badge sitting on Judge Hathaway's desk by noon."

The sheriff knew Culpepper meant business. He hated this smart nigger standing before him, wearing a suit that would cost him three months' salary. Nonetheless, he moved aside and allowed Culpepper to push Wink out of the room.

Within minutes, Culpepper had Wink packed into the back of a conversion van he'd rented, and they were skirting out of the hospital's parking lot with his assistant Diane in tow. Culpepper slowed down once they reached the Chrysler Freeway, but still he kept an eye on all three mirrors and both hands on the steering wheel.

"Let me find out you used to be the getaway driver back in the day," Wink said. He was stretched across the back seat, staring into the empty road ahead.

"I keep trying to tell you not to let this suit fool you. I'm from the ghe*ttoe*. You hear that 'e' on the end?" Culpepper joked as he glanced in the rearview at Wink.

Wink pulled back a hurting smile, and said. "Yeah, I hear you." Everything hurt. It hurt just thinking about trying to sit up.

Culpepper saw how much pain Wink was in and said, "Remind me to stop at the pharmacy so we can pick up some painkillers."

"I'm all right," Wink lied. "Were you able to get Armeeah a bond?"

"I got Judge Hathaway to sign you both over to me on a writ this morning. My assistant is calling Wayne County right now to let them know so they can start her discharge papers."

"Thanks, Pepp." Wink knew that he didn't have to go the lengths he had.

"Well, I want you to lie low for a while. That's how you can thank me, because I can't have no bodies turning up while you're under my name," he said. "I checked into something with your investigation."

"What you find out?"

"A bunch of nothing. They're keeping a tight lid on this one, but my gut tells me that someone close to you is handing you over."

Wink could only think about Trey. It was his flamin' hot ass that had the Feds breathing down his neck. He and his Money Squad bitches. But Wink was about to put an end to their reckless ballin' and an end to the Feds' investigation. Culpepper pulled up to the front entrance of Wayne County Jail and double-parked beside two sheriff cars.

"I'll be right back," he told Wink. He put his hazards on and reached for the door handle.

Wink watched through half-closed eyes as Culpepper and his assistant disappeared inside the double glass doors. Wink tried to suck up the constant pain and hide any sign that he wasn't well. He didn't want Armeeah to be all worried when she saw him. She had been through more than enough already. Wink still couldn't believe he had let the Feds haul her off to jail pregnant and all. They were some dirty, foul-playing mothafuckas who would stop at nothing in their efforts to convert a gangsta into a rat. Wink would never roll over and spread his ass cheeks for the government or anyone else. He sighed and just promised to never let it happen again. He was going legit after this, so he wouldn't have to worry about the Feds ever again.

Wink pulled back a smile as wide as the Detroit River when he saw Armeeah coming out the front door. Culpepper held the door open for her, then quickly ushered her into the van. Armeeah climbed in the back seat and wrapped herself up in Wink's arms. She squeezed her eyes tight and thanked Allah that they were reunited. Wink kissed her hair and face, appreciating every second of their reunion. "I love you," he said between kisses.

"I love you too," Armeeah said, ready to cry.

"I'm sorry, baby, that this happened. It'll never happen again, I swear." Wink held Armeeah tighter for reassurance.

"I'm okay," lied Armeeah. Those seventy-two hours had kicked her ass and nearly killed her. If it weren't for Allah and a few hundred dollars she had given the guards, she would've never made it.

"Did anyone hurt you in there?" Wink sat Armeeah up and took a look at her.

"I'm all right, Wayne. Really." Other than the wrinkles in her jeans and shirt, she was flawless.

Wink smiled, then pulled her back under his arm. *I can never let this happen again.*

"Wayne, I just want to go home," said Armeeah.

Culpepper looked in the rearview as he punched the van down 94. He met eyes with Wink and shook his head no.

"Baby, I think it'll be a good idea if we don't go back there until all this is settled."

Armeeah sat up and separated herself from Wink. She folded her arms, cocked her head into an attitude position, and then gazed into Wink's eyes. "And when is it going to be settled, Wayne? I'm not going to have to make another trip to the county jail, am I?"

"Baby, no. This will all be over soon. I promise. Okay, you believe me, don't you?" Wink said, reaching for Armeeah's hand, but she kept her stare out the window.

Culpepper saw that Wink needed some help, so he chimed in. "Armeeah, I can assure you that those people will never bother you again. I'm going to have the judge sign an order for them not to show up at your residence or seek any further contact."

Armeeah wasn't trying to hear what Culpepper was saying, because she knew he couldn't guarantee her that.

All she wanted was to go home and forget that any of this ever happened. But instead, Culpepper took them to his mansion out in Grosse Pointe. He figured they would be safe there at least until the indictments came down.

"Welcome to my castle," Culpepper said, pulling into the long driveway up to the house. He parked the van and got out to help his assistant unload Wink's wheelchair.

"Stop, Wayne," Armeeah said, snatching her arm away from Wink.

"Meeah, I know this isn't how we planned to live our lives, but I need you with me so we can come outta this."

"What is this, Wayne?" Armeeah turned from the window, cutting Wink off. "I would like to know what this is and why the Feds are investigating you. Is it about drugs? Because you told me you were leaving that stuff alone."

"Meeah, listen!" Wink raised his voice just enough to calm her down and let her know that he was still the man. "Regardless of why they're investigating me, I need you to do as I say, and that's stay here with Mr. Culpepper for a little while. I told you, these people want to destroy me. But I'm not going to let that happen." Wink looked her in the eyes, took Armeeah's hand, and kissed the back of it. "June third. That's our date, remember?"

"Yeah," Armeeah said in a light voice, the voice Wink fell in love with. He kept the kisses and talk of their day coming. "Have you decided where you want to have the wedding?"

Armeeah smiled and looked away. "I'm still trying to decide."

"Well, that's what I want you focusing on, planning our wedding. I want you to have the wedding of your dreams, okay?"

"Okay," Armeeah softly said as she closed her eyes and accepted Wink's tongue.

"Come on, you two lovebirds." Culpepper had Wink's wheelchair locked and ready at his side door.

"Oh, my God. Wayne, what happened to you?" Armeeah asked, looking down at the chair.

"It's nothing. Couple of scrapes but I'll live." Wink bit his bottom lip to keep from hollering out as Culpepper and his assistant hoisted him down from the van. He forced a smile as he looked up at Armeeah, whose eyes were filled with concern. She climbed down quickly and took Culpepper's place at the handles of Wink's chair.

Culpepper led them inside and showed them to the guest quarters. He said that he had to get back to his office, but he already had his personal chef in the kitchen preparing a gourmet meal. "I'll see you when I get back."

"Thanks again, Pepp. I owe you big," Wink said from the comfort of the king-sized bed.

"Yeah, well, you just relax and heal up. Let me do the fighting for right now." Culpepper smiled at Armeeah, then tapped the doorframe before leaving.

Armeeah immediately started pampering Wink, trying to take all his clothes off, fluffing his pillows. "I'm going to start you a bath," she said. She tried to get up from the bed, but Wink grabbed her hand and pulled her on top of him.

"We can take a bath together later. Right now, I just want to lie here and hold you."

"Okay, baby." Armeeah kissed Wink's lips, then lay across his chest. They both were lost in thought. Armeeah gazed into the empty bathroom, hoping that everything would be all right.

Wink was staring up at the ceiling, plotting how he was going to kill Trey. It had to be done right and soon.

Chapter Thirty-one

Trey hadn't left his fort at his mansion since the war had kicked off between him and Wink. He was running out of time on his promise to Junior of having his father's killer caught by the time they met. Today was the day of their meeting, and all Trey had were a bunch of excuses, which he was certain wouldn't interest Junior. He needed blood. That was the only thing that was going to save his own ass and maybe even his drug connect.

Trey was sitting behind his home desk with two of his bodyguards standing behind him and two more guarding the door. Trey was listening to Lee-Mac plead his case as to how he allowed Krazy and Wink to get away.

"I can get 'em, T-Money. I just need more time and some more men. I can have it done by tonight," pleaded Lee-Mac. He didn't realize that he was boxed in by Trey's new muscle-bound bodyguards. They were all just waiting for the nod from Trey, and his ass was good as dead.

"Are you finished?" Trey asked, looking up from the game of tic-tac-toe he'd been playing himself in. "You finished?" he repeated.

"Yeah," Lee-Mac said. He didn't have a good feeling about his predicament.

"Good, 'cause we're outta time. Well, you're out of time, I should say. I gave you more than enough time to handle the business, but you couldn't take two niggas out. Two bitch-ass niggas! You had how many men with you? And yet you're the only one to make it back alive. You

shoulda died with the rest of 'em. What you do, run?"
Trey waved his hand to silence Lee-Mac. "Save that weak
shit. Bottom line is you fucked up not once but twice.
And since I'm outta time, I guess you'll have to do." Trey
gave the nod to his four goons, and they enveloped Lee-
Mac's little ass like a rain cloud.

"We 'posed to be family! Money Squad!" Lee-Mac cried
out as the men dragged him out of the room. He kicked
and clawed like a cornered cat, holding on to the edge of
the doorframe for dear life.

"Y'all know where to take him. Wait for me before y'all
kill him," said Trey. He ignored Lee-Mac's screams for
mercy and picked up the phone on his desk. "Have my
car ready." Click.

Part one of Trey's backup plan was complete. He was
planning on telling Junior that Lee-Mac was the one
who killed his father. Now all he had to do was hope that
Junior bought it. Blood was blood—that was the way Trey
figured it—and if Junior did buy it, then he would have
killed two birds with one stone. Once Trey smoothed
things over with Junior, he was going to reorganize the
ranks of his Money Squad Family. And this time he
would have nothing but killers riding at his side. Then
he could focus on Wink and Krazy.

Even with his plan, Trey wasn't taking any chances
with Junior and their meeting. Trey, being the natural-born coward he was, wasn't going to allow Junior or
anyone else to rock him to sleep. Even if they came to
terms going forward, Trey would travel no fewer than
a hundred deep whenever he went to meet with Junior,
and that was exactly how many Money Squad members
he had on deck just in case.

Trey set up the meeting at his warehouse in downtown Detroit, right off the river. He normally kept his shipments of cocaine in the warehouse, but seeing that it was empty and large enough to hold the meeting, Trey decided it would be the best spot. He had his men all positioned around the outside of the warehouse and some on the roof. He and his closest bodyguards stood inside, gathered in a circle around Lee-Mac, who was tied to a chair and had duct tape over his mouth. Lee-Mac growled with tears in his eyes. He couldn't believe Trey was doing this to him. He tried rattling the chair in hopes of breaking free, but one of the bodyguards backhanded him so hard that he went out.

"A'ight, everybody, be on point. Here they come," said Trey.

Junior's four-limo entourage pulled into the garage halfway and parked right under the sliding door so it couldn't shut and trap them inside. Junior's people weren't slipping either. They were on point and ready to do whatever Junior wanted.

Trey nervously waited. Trey put on the phoniest smile he could muster and held it steady as he met Junior in the center of the floor. Trey had his hand extended like they were long-lost friends, but Junior refused his hand. Instead he looked over Trey's shoulder at Lee-Mac sitting in the chair. There was snot and blood running down Lee-Mac's nose. He was passed out, his head slumped forward.

"Is that the piece of shit?" Junior asked as he rolled up his sleeves.

Trey spun on his heels and smirked. "Yeah, that's him. The man who killed your father." Trey closely followed Junior over to the chair.

"Is he still alive?" Junior asked.

"I saved him just for you," lied Trey. He watched Junior intently as his eyes took on a scary look of possession, his breathing became rapid, and beads of sweat formed all around his fat neck. Junior was so geeked to be face-to-face with his father's killer, he looked like he was about to bust a nut. Trey smiled because part two of his plan was complete. He stepped aside as Junior snapped his fingers, signaling his men to bring his torture kit.

Junior opened the black suitcase and removed a small pair of pliers. He grabbed the back of Lee-Mac's head and forced the pliers inside his mouth, locking on his two top teeth.

Lee-Mac's eyes bucked open at the feeling of the cold steel in his mouth.

"I knew that would wake your ass up," said Junior, still holding his firm grip on the pliers. "When I'm finished with you, your own mother won't be able to recognize you." Junior called Lee-Mac a nigger in Spanish, then snatched his teeth out of his head.

The pain Lee-Mac felt was indescribable. It was beyond pain. It was pure torment. Junior went to work on the remainder of his teeth and sickly had the nerve to bag them up. He grabbed Lee-Mac around his bloody face and laughed down into his eyes. "I am going to make a necklace with those." He leaned back his head in a sinister laugh, then returned to his state of delirium. He reached inside his torture kit and thumbed through many choices. He pulled up a long strand of razor-sharp trip wire.

"Which hand did you use to kill my father with?" Junior waited for Lee-Mac to answer, and when he didn't, he became enraged, not realizing that he had snatched all the man's teeth out of his head. Lee-Mac couldn't have answered him if he wanted to.

"Here, you take this end," Junior said, handing Trey one end of the wire.

Trey's stomach did a backflip at the sight of all that blood. He thought Junior was just going to kill Lee-Mac and be done with it, but he was on some real-life torture chamber shit. And now he wanted Trey to help him saw Lee-Mac's arm off. Junior wrapped the wire under Mac's armpit, then demonstrated to Trey how he wanted it done. "Push and pull. It's going to come right off," said Junior. He took the first pull, to which Trey reluctantly returned his trust. He was on the brink of throwing up and shitting all over himself he was so sick to his stomach.

Ten pushes and pulls and off came Lee-Mac's right arm. He was still alive, but barely. Junior wanted his ass to feel every second leading up to his death.

"Come on. Let's do the other one," ordered Junior.

Trey sucked it up and took his position, and they started on the other arm. Trey wasn't a killer, but he didn't feel the least bit of remorse. It was business.

Chapter Thirty-two

Meanwhile, Krazy was across town tucked low in the back pews of Solomon Temple Church on 7 Mile and Marx Street. Today was Dilla and his mom's funeral service, and Krazy knew that if there was anywhere he was going to find a bunch of Money Squad bitches, it would be at Dilla's funeral. And they were showing up by the hundreds, all wearing their red and white colors.

Stupid mothafuckas, Krazy thought as he watched the church fill up. The hood was funny like that. Niggas would go to war until somebody got killed, and then on the day of the funeral, everybody would get all dressed up like today didn't count. Them niggas were crazy and stupid for thinking they could push pause on beef. The shit wasn't a video game, not with Krazy. He was there to show them niggas that it wasn't beef, but war.

Krazy had dressed in red and white to blend in with the many members, and to keep them from recognizing him, he wore a Rasta hat with a wig full of long dreadlocks. He capped off his disguise with a pair of Locs sunglasses, which he used to scan the church. He wanted Lee-Mac because he didn't like how he got away the other day. He didn't see any sign of Lee-Mac nor Trey. Not that he was expecting to see Trey there. Krazy knew Trey too well to even expect his scary-Jerry ass to show up. It could've been his own funeral, and if it were possible, his terrified ass wouldn't show up to it.

Krazy waited through the viewing of the bodies, eulogies, sad songs, crying out, collapsing, and all the shit black people do at funerals. After two hours of the hootin' and hollerin', the services finally concluded, and still there was no sign of Lee-Mac.

That's all right. I ain't put all this shit on for nothin'. Krazy slid out of his crowded pew and started for the door. As soon as he got outside, he tore the wig and sunglasses off. It was time to lay some shit out. All Krazy could think about while he was leaning on the back hatch of his Lexus truck was Wink lying in ICU and the doctors telling him that he might not make it. "This for you, my nigga." Krazy cocked a round into the chamber of his fully automatic Mack 11 and waited for the front doors to the church to open. He was parked directly across the street from the double entrance doors giving him a clean shot at everything that came out.

Krazy could see the doors getting ready to open, so he came out of his crouched position and stood up between his truck and another car. Two of the church ushers opened the doors, each putting their backs to the wall to hold them open. Krazy zeroed in on the twin pearl white caskets descending the steps of the church. He waited until both Dilla and his mom were out of the church, and then he ran out into the middle of 7 Mile and opened fire on the caskets and the men carrying them. The men were all caught in a hail of gunfire. They dropped the caskets and tried getting their guns, but Krazy was relentless in his onslaught. He stood in the middle of the road and laid on the trigger until the Mack 11 spit its final round. He disappeared behind the thick cloud of gun smoke and into his truck.

Krazy enjoyed the bloody scene from his rearview mirror as he skirted away from the curb. Four of the pallbearers were stretched out on the steps in a pool of blood.

That's enough for one day. But as he made a screeching right turn down Conant, he saw a Buick Lacrosse make the turn with him.

Krazy sat up and fixed his mirror. He could see the heads of two white boys, and one of them was talking into a radio. "That's the fuckin' Feds," Krazy said. He had no idea they were stalking Dilla's funeral.

"You bitches think I'm going back to prison, you got me and life fucked up." Krazy made another tire-screeching turn down Robinwood, and sure enough, the Buick made the turn with him. The passenger put the red siren light on the dashboard, and the driver honked for Krazy to pull over.

"Y'all really want me to pull over?" Krazy asked as he spun the clip on his Mack 11. "Just remember that y'all wanted this." Krazy slammed on his brakes at the intersection of Robinwood and Anglin. He put the truck in park and jumped down with the Mack in hand. "This what you bitches want, huh?" yelled Krazy.

The agent sitting in the passenger seat widened his eyes, and he began slapping his partner's arm to get them out of there. The driver tried backing up and spinning the car around, but it was too late. Krazy was airing their asses out. He shot the driver in the neck then head. His body crashed to the steering wheel, and the car began to slowly roll backward until it hit a telephone pole and came to a stop.

Krazy raised the Mack to his eye, taking dead aim at the agent's backs. He damn near did a frontward flip, the impact of the dum-dum was so violent. Krazy sprinted down the block, where the agent tried desperately to crawl the curb. Krazy had learned his lesson about leaving witnesses. He pressed the barrel into the back of the agent's head and squeezed off two quick shots, leaving nothing but the man's neck and a cut-off piece of vertebra.

Krazy jogged back to his truck after tossing the Mack 11 inside the car with the other dead agent. The Feds wouldn't have to look too far for the murder weapon. Krazy skirted away from the scene feeling like Scarface himself. "You crackers don't want it with me! I told you mothafuckas I'm not going back!" Krazy roared. He was high off the adrenaline rush. He hadn't thought about how hot the city was about to be with federal agents all scouring the streets in search of him. Krazy meant what he said. He wasn't going back to prison. He reached in the back seat for a fresh Mack 11, and he cocked it back and set it on his lap. He cranked up Pac's "Me Against the World" and punched the gas.

Chapter Thirty-three

"Where are you going, baby?" Armeeah asked, waking up from her light sleep. She had been lying across Wink's chest with her arm locked underneath him to make sure he didn't leave her in the middle of the night.

"Meeah, I have to take care of something." Wink sat up and pulled the sheets off his legs. He searched the dimly lit room trying to locate his clothes. He and Armeeah had been sleeping all day, and it was killing Wink because he wanted to find Trey and kill him so they could go back to living a normal life.

Armeeah talked from the bed in a worried voice as Wink slid into his jeans. "Wayne, what is it that has to be done at this hour, and why can't it wait until morning?" Armeeah looked over at the beaming red numbers on the alarm clock. It was 2:45 in the morning.

"Meeah, look where we're living. We're hiding out in my lawyer's guest suite. I can't live like this, and I won't allow us to live like this." After Wink buttoned his shirt, he went and sat on the edge of the bed. He reached for Armeeah's hand and pulled her to him. Wink wrapped her hair around her ear, then caressed her face with the back of his hand. "I need you to trust me. After tonight we'll be back living in our home and living a normal life. I promise, okay?" Wink said softly, and then he kissed Armeeah's hand. Before she could answer, he had her engulfed in kisses.

When Armeeah opened her eyes, Wink was gone. She reached for one of the throw pillows and squeezed it tight between her legs. Tears quickly welled in her eyes and began pouring over. Armeeah wanted so badly to get up and run after Wink because she had a feeling that something bad was going to happen. "Be careful," she squealed, then buried her face in the pillow.

Wink had taken the keys to Culpepper's Jag from their hook in the kitchen. He was driving the royal blue coupe down Jefferson on his way to his apartment so he could suit up. Wink tried calling Krazy on his way, but his phone kept going straight to voicemail. Wink still hadn't remembered how he got to the hospital or if Krazy made it out alive. The thought made Wink's blood boil, and he floored the Jag the rest of the way.

He pulled into the valet section of his apartment building. The valet booth was closed, so he put his hazards on and quickly entered the building. On the way up in the elevator, Wink popped a few dry Motrins to kill off the throbbing pain that stubbornly rested in his shoulder. He still had on the sling from the hospital and the bandages they'd patched him up with, but all that was coming off just as soon as Wink got inside the apartment. He was in no shape to be going out on a mission, but he knew that time wasn't on his side. The Feds could move in any day now, and he wanted to be ready when they did.

The elevator stopped on Wink's floor, and he quickly made his way off, power walking the short distance around to his apartment. He stuck the lone key inside the lock and let himself in. He felt around the kitchen wall for the light switch, and nearly shit himself when he saw somebody's feet dangling over the arm of the sofa out in the living room.

Wink snatched a butcher knife from the knife kit on the counter and slowly started for the living room. Wink lowered the knife to his side after seeing that it was only Krazy. He set the knife on the table beside the sofa, then walked around.

"Krazy, get up." Wink snatched Krazy's foot off the sofa. "Get up!" he ordered.

"What up doe," Krazy said in an irritated voice.

"Nigga, how did you get in here?" demanded Wink.

"I let myself in." Krazy sat up and wiped the crust from his face. "I couldn't go home, so I came here."

"Why can't you go home?"

"You ain't seen the news? I had to stretch two of them DEA bitches."

"You did what?" Wink asked, reaching for the remote on the coffee table. He turned on the TV and flipped through the channels. Sure enough, the story was being run on Channel 7 Action News. The screen read, **Two DEA agents slain on Detroit's east side after a high-speed chase.** The news said nothing about having a suspect. They just asked for viewers to call the hotline if they had any information. A $50,000 reward was being offered. Wink cut the TV off and tossed the remote on the sofa.

Krazy watched from the sofa as Wink went to pacing the floor. "I had to murk they ass, Wink. They jumped behind me after I finished airing them niggas out at Dilla's funeral. I couldn't let 'em take me back to prison."

"Nah, you did what you had to do. I'm not tripping on that. I just want to make sure they don't know who you are. What car was you in?" Wink stopped to face Krazy.

"I was in the Lexus."

"You still got the temp tags on there, right?"

"Yeah."

"Good," Wink said, then went back to pacing the floor. "The news didn't say anything about you. Trust me, if they knew who you were, your picture would be on every station twenty-four seven."

"Yeah, you right." Krazy was a little relieved. He was waiting for Wink to give the next call.

"Look, shit is getting too hot for us to be out here trying to kill up the whole city. We need to be focused on staying outta jail, and the only way we gon' do that is if we kill Trey."

Krazy nodded his agreement. "I'm with you, my nigga. When is we moving out?"

"Right now. And as soon as we get Trey done"—Wink waited a long moment because he didn't know how Krazy was going to feel about his next move—"we gotta kill Willie too. I no longer trust him."

"Shit, I was gon' kill his bitch ass anyway because he right with Trey like a nigga don't know what time it is."

Wink pulled back a smile and stuck out his fist. He hit rocks with Krazy, then said, "It's just us now. We gotta take care of each other."

"Don't be getting all sentimental on me, nigga," Krazy said, lightening the mood. He followed Wink into the bedroom and took a seat on the bed while Wink dug around in the closet. "Them cracker-ass doctors said that you weren't gonna make it. That's why I got the fuck out!" Krazy shouted from the bedroom.

"Yeah, well, them crackers don't know that niggas like us don't quit." Wink came out of the closet carrying two army-issue AR-15s, both equipped with hundred-round drums packed with armor-piercing .223s.

Krazy was high just off the feeling of the rifle. "Can you imagine being hit with one of these?" Krazy asked, looking over the cooling system.

"Nah, but I can imagine hitting Trey's bitch ass with it."

"You tryin'a do the nigga dirty."

Wink cocked his AR-15 back and slid into his hoodie. "Yeah, that's why I bought 'em." He grabbed the two extra clips and headed for the door. "Come on. Let's get this nigga done."

They took Krazy's Lexus truck and headed out to Trey's mansion in St. Clair Shores. "You think he's there?" Krazy asked, looking over at Wink.

"If he is, you already know his scary ass got a bunch of bodyguards watching the house. Shit, we gon' just lay down everything moving. But make sure we get Trey," Wink said, glaring into the road ahead.

"You ain't gotta tell me but once." Krazy sat up all geeked and ready to kill. He couldn't wait!

When they reached the address Wink had scribbled onto a napkin, Krazy slowed down as they passed the mansion. "Yeah, that's his Benz right there," advised Krazy.

"A'ight." Wink was taking in every angle of the crib. "Circle the block and park near the corner," ordered Wink. He got busy gearing up and checking his guns.

Krazy parked on the opposite side of Trey's street. He peered through the small binoculars that he kept tucked under his seat.

"Where'd you get those from?"

"You gotta always be prepared." Krazy said, lowering the binoculars from his face.

"Yeah, a'ight, Rambo. What you see?"

"Nothin'. I don't think the nigga is there, but then again it is early, so he might be asleep."

"Well, let's wake that ass up." Wink pulled on the door handle and slid out of the truck. He and Krazy crossed the street and speed walked down to Trey's driveway.

"Remember. Lay everything out." Wink led the way to the side of the house.

Krazy jerked the patio screen door open and quietly slid it back. They searched the bottom floor, and it was empty. Wink pointed to the upstairs. He led the way up the spiral stairs through the dark hall leading to the bedrooms. Wink stopped at the last room and peeked in through the cracked door. He didn't see Trey, but what he did see was the thickness of a woman's body lying in bed.

"What you see?" Krazy whispered from behind. He had just finished searching the other four rooms.

Wink stepped aside for Krazy to get a look.

"Damn, she thick."

"Go get that bitch up," ordered Wink.

"With pleasure." Krazy pushed the door wide open and charged into the room. He snatched the sheets off of ol' girl and dragged her to the edge of the bed by her ankles.

"What the hell are you doing? Get yo' hands off me."

"Bitch, shut up," Krazy hissed as he looked the girl's naked body over.

"Where is T-Money?"

"Dead, bitch. And unless you wanna join him, you gon' do exactly what I tell you. Now get yo' ass up," snapped Krazy.

Wink stepped forward and looked at the girl. "Where is Trey?" he demanded.

"I don't know. Why are y'all doing this?" The girl started crying because she thought they were there to rape her.

"What you want me to do with her?" asked Krazy.

"Take her downstairs and tie her ass up."

Krazy snatched her up by the arm and led her out of the room. Wink looked over at the bed and thought, *I'll be here when you get home.*

Chapter Thirty-four

Trey was back riding high with his cocaine connect, Junior. They let the blood of Lee-Mac wash away their differences. Hell, Trey didn't give a damn so long as he was back in with the Mexican Mafia. It was all he cared about. And Junior seemed to be happy, so everybody was happy. They opened Trey's club, Geno's, back up and partied until the sun came up. Trey went all out to make sure Junior had a good time. He had the most exotic strippers he could find on deck, and the bar flowed with champagne like a water fountain. They got so high and drunk that everyone was on the brink of passing out.

The party ended at around seven in the morning. When Trey and Junior stumbled out of the club, the morning sun nearly blinded them. Junior caught his balance, put his arm around Trey's shoulder, and slurred into his ear, "My friend." He sounded like a motorbike that wouldn't start, dragging the "d."

"I am glad we killed that fucker, because I really like you." Junior paused to finish off the fifth of Dom P he'd been holding.

"I like you too," Trey said with a smile as they both staggered for the curb where Junior's limo sat idling.

Junior set the empty bottle down on the sidewalk, then reached his short arms up to Trey's shoulders. He looked deep into Trey's eyes as to say, "Nigger, I'm not that drunk and I'm not stupid neither!"

"Our debt is settled, but we can never allow anything like this to happen again." Junior squeezed tighter on Trey's shoulders to make sure he got his drift.

"I understand, Junior. Business as usual." Trey knew the meaning in Junior's words. He was telling him that he knew Lee-Mac didn't kill Sammy, but he accepted the nigger's blood as a sacrifice. Junior had his reasons for going along with Trey's lie. Junior wanted the power his father had, and that included the family cocaine business.

"Business as usual. And remember—"

Trey finished his sentence. "I know. This can never happen again."

Junior patted Trey on the back. "Good. Good." He climbed into the back of his limo, and Trey watched nervously from the curb as the black convoy faded into the distance of Woodward Avenue.

"T-Money!" Trey's new bodyguard, Bullet, called out from across the street. He waved Trey to come on because he had the car ready.

Trey crossed the street and sank into the back seat of his triple-black bulletproof Benz 500. He leaned his head against the soft leather and returned to his deep contemplation about Junior. They both were thirsty for each other's business, and Trey knew that if Junior really wanted to, he could have had him killed a long time ago. Trey began to relax at the thought of everything being back to normal. Well, almost everything. He still had to find Krazy and Wink. Once they were dead and in the grave, then and only then would things be back to normal.

When Trey made it to his mansion, he sent all his bodyguards home and told them to take the day off because they were going to need all the rest they could get. They were about to turn up the heat on finding Krazy and Wink, and then it was back to the Money Squad getting money.

"A'ight, y'all niggas be ready," Trey said, closing the back door of the Benz. He walked up the driveway to the side door and let himself in. Trey wondered if his "new bitch," as he called her, was awake. He didn't care. If she wasn't, he was about to wake her ass up to some hard dick. Trey had it all planned out. He was about to take a quick shower, slide in the pussy, bust a nut, then go to sleep.

He entered through the kitchen and trekked the dark halls around the solid oak staircase. Trey began unbuttoning his shirt and unbuckling his jeans as he neared the master bedroom. He could see Eva lying in bed on her side, sound asleep, as he entered the room. *I'll wake that ass up in a few minutes,* Trey thought, staring through the darkness at Eva's curvy silhouette underneath the satin sheets. Trey set his gun on the nightstand, then stripped down to his boxers. He walked into the bathroom and started a shower, not knowing what awaited him.

Trey sang his rendition of the Isley Brothers' "For the Love of You." He made up the notes he didn't know and hummed the melody as he ended his five-minute shower. He hummed all the way to the bedroom as he dried off. He dropped the towel to the floor and walked over to the bed, pulled the sheets back, then climbed in.

Trey scooted close up to Eva and let his hand slide down her muscular, strong . . . He jumped up, realizing that wasn't Eva lying beside him. Trey clicked on the lamp and reached for his Glock on the nightstand, but it was gone.

"You lookin' for this?" Wink asked as he rolled off the side of the bed. He had Trey's Glock pointed dead at his forehead.

"Wink, what up doe, my nigga. You ain't get none of my messages?" Trey asked, stumbling backward and nearly knocking the lamp over.

"Yeah, I got your message. You talkin' 'bout them li'l niggas you sent at me and Krazy? Yeah, I got it."

"Wink, that wasn't my call. Those young bastards did that on their own. But I already took care of all they asses, I swear."

"Look at you." Wink gave Trey a look of disgust. "You gon' be a bitch all your life, huh? All the way to your grave."

"My nigga, it ain't gotta end like this. I don't care about you killin' my connect. Fuck them taco-eating motha-fuckas. We can go back to being a family. You, me, Krazy, and Willie. Remember how it used to be?"

Wink clenched the gun tight as he tried to keep it together. He had to kill Trey. "It can never go back to the way it was. You changed on me, Trey. I changed, we all changed, and for what? Some money. Nigga, I would have died for you!" Wink raised his voice while backing Trey into the corner of the room.

"Come on, Wink. Please, my nigga. If it's about the money, I'll leave the city and never come back. You can have this shit. Just don't kill me, please."

"You think that's why I'm here, to kill you 'bout some money? Nigga, who paid two hundred and fifty stacks to get yo' bitch ass back when them li'l niggas snatched you up, huh? Me, that's who, and did I ask you for a single dime back? I was the one who brought you into this shit. I made you chop that goofy-ass high-top fade off and park yo' momma's Honda. If it weren't for me, you would still be somewhere break dancin'. So fuck nah, it ain't 'bout no money. I'm about to hang both our jerseys." Wink could see Trey's soul through his eyes. He was stuck and about to die.

"I love you, my nigga," Trey said in a last, desperate attempt.

Wink closed his eyes and squeezed the trigger. Boom!

The hard slump of Trey's body rode the ringing waves of the shotgun. Wink couldn't even open his eyes. He couldn't stand to see Trey lying there dead. It wasn't supposed to be this hard.

"I love you too."

Krazy heard the shot and came flying upstairs to check on Wink. "You a'ight in . . ." Krazy let his words fade as he stepped into the room. He saw Wink standing over Trey's body with his face buried into his arm, crying his eyes out.

Krazy gave Wink a moment to himself, then calmly approached him. "We gotta go, my nigga. It's over," Krazy said, wrapping his arm around Wink. "It's over," he repeated, then started for the door.

Tears continued to freely flow down Wink's face. He felt like a part of him died back there. But as Krazy said, it was over.

"Hold on for a second. I gotta take care of something." Krazy stopped Wink at the front door. He flipped his AR-15 around from his back to the front and stepped into the living room, where he had Eva tied to a chair.

Her eyes filled with tears as Krazy raised the rifle, taking aim at her pretty face. "Hmmm!" Eva fought to voice her last words from behind the torn T-shirt wrapped around her mouth.

"Let's not make this harder than it is. You knew I was going to kill you." Laaka! Laaka! Laaka!

Krazy enjoyed watching the three wolf heads tear patches out of Eva's face. He took a lasting look at the gruesome scene, then stepped back into the foyer with Wink.

"I'm ready now," Krazy said, opening the door for Wink.

They power walked the short distance up the street to Krazy's truck and quickly got in, still clutching their AR-15 rifles in case the police decided they wanted to show up.

"Keep the lights off," Wink said as he leaned his seat back so the nosy neighbors who were now standing on their lawns couldn't see him.

Krazy made it to the end of the block and gunned the engine. He hit the lights once they made it to the intersection of Mound Road, thinking they were in the clear, but a St. Clair Shores police cruiser had bent the corner heading in the opposite direction. Krazy and the officer driving locked eyes for all of five seconds until the cruiser was at the rear of the truck.

"Come on," Krazy grumbled at the two slow-driving cars preventing him from making a turn.

"Just be cool," Wink said in a calm voice while playing the side mirror. He saw the tail lights on the cruiser come on.

"They 'bout to hit a U-ie." Krazy punched the gas, barreling his way through the two cars. Krazy sideswiped the entire passenger side of a Corolla, taking off the mirror and front bumper. He was trying to shake the blue and red lights flickering in his rearview.

"Damn, they on us," Wink said, turning around to check the distance between them. The cruiser had closed the gap between them. They were only about two cars behind.

Krazy gripped the wheel with one hand and massaged the stock of his AR-15 with the other hand. The empty road ahead was about to end as they sped toward 22 Mile Road and Mound. The only out Krazy saw was the rifle lying across his lap. He looked over at Wink and thought, *damn*. He didn't want Wink to go down with him.

"My nigga, I'ma blow through this intersection. That should give us enough distance for you to jump out and run."

"What? I'm not getting out." Wink looked at Krazy like he was really crazy.

"Wink, they didn't see you when they passed by, and ain't no sense in both us going to jail. Just get out when I make this turn." Krazy grabbed the wheel with both hands and checked his mirrors one last time, then punched the gas harder.

The traffic at the intersection of Mound and 22 Mile was heading in the crossing direction. Krazy blew past an idling van waiting at the light and headed into traffic.

Wink squeezed his eyes closed and prepared for the impact of the oncoming Explorer. Bom! Bom! The horns of dozens of cars filled the air as Krazy somehow made it through. Wink opened his eyes, not believing they had escaped death. He made up his mind that he wasn't leaving Krazy. They were going out together.

"A'ight, my nigga, I'm 'bout to make this turn, so be ready."

"I'm ready," Wink said, cocking his AR-15 back and sending a round into the chamber. "Two guns are better than one, right?" Wink asked, holding his AR straight up.

Krazy looked over like, "Let's do this then." He made a screeching right turn on Toledo Street and hurriedly pulled over to the curb. The cops had fought through the congestion and would be bending the corner in a matter of seconds.

Neither Krazy or Wink spoke another word. They simultaneously reached for their door handles and stood at the rear of the truck with their guns pointed for the corner. As soon as the nose of the cruiser peeked around the corner, they opened fire, knocking out all the windows and tires, leaving the two officers stranded.

Krazy and Wink started walking for the dismantled and smoking squad car, guns still blazing. The passenger tried to jump out and run, but they equally lit his ass up, nailing him to the side of the car in a hail of bullets. His body slowly slid down the car and crashed against the cement face-first. His partner was already dead, but Krazy was still giving it to him.

"That's enough. Let's get the fuck up outta here," Wink said, holding his arm out for Krazy to stop shooting. More sirens could be heard in the distance, and Wink didn't want to be there when they arrived.

Wink grabbed Krazy by the arm, turned him around, and started running for the truck. This time Wink took the wheel because he wanted to make sure they made it home alive.

Chapter Thirty-five

"I want you to take this hot-ass truck somewhere and burn it down to the frame," Wink said as they pulled into the back of his apartment building. He put the truck in park and started wiping his prints off the steering wheel.

Krazy hadn't said anything. He was lost in a deep thought of regret. He felt like he could have done a better job killing the police.

"You hear what I said, nigga?"

"Oh, what's up?"

"I said to burn this bitch. Not tomorrow or the next day, but right now. I'ma get you another one," Wink said, still wiping at the door panels and dashboard.

"Yeah, I'ma do that, but what we gon' do now? I know you ready to lock the city down and get this money, right?"

"You ain't been listening to nothing I been saying, have you? Nigga, I'm done. It's a wrap. Time to get on something new." Wink thought about the chain of strip clubs he was going to open with Bazzi.

"Oh, yeah, like what? Enlighten me, 'cause I'm tryin'a figure out where it is I come into play on all this."

"What do you wanna do, Krazy?"

"Shit, ball out and get this money. Body some niggas if they get in the way. You know, everything y'all was out here doing when I was upstate."

Wink thought about the 200 keys sitting in storage. He had planned on letting Willie move them, but since he was MIA, Wink didn't have any need for them. He didn't need the money. He was just thankful to be alive and still free after all the bullshit he'd been through. He dug in his pocket and started twisting the storage key off his ring. "Here," he said, handing Krazy the lone brass key.

"What's this for?"

"It's yo' blessing. You know where E-Z Storage is at?" asked Wink.

"Yeah, it's off Telegraph Road."

"Exactly. The garage number is on the key. That's yo' blessing." Wink reached for the door handle using his shirt. "Get rid of this truck today," he said, shutting the door behind him.

"I'm 'bout to right now," Krazy said while climbing over to the driver seat. He stuck his hand out to give Wink a play.

"We gon' get up in about a week or so. I need some time to clear my head and put things in motion," said Wink.

Krazy knew just what Wink meant. "I feel you, my nigga. You let me worry 'bout Willie's bitch ass. You take as much time as you need, then get up with me."

"A'ight. Be safe," Wink said. He waited as Krazy skirted off with the music blasting.

Wink crossed the lot to Culpepper's Jag. He got in and just sat there with his hands on the wheel, staring out into the moving traffic on Jefferson Avenue. Wink could see Trey's face right before he killed him, and he could hear the loud thump of his body slamming to the floor. Wink closed his eyes and sucked in all the air his lungs could stand, then slowly let it go. "It's over." He opened up his eyes and put the key in the ignition. He started the car and pulled out of the empty lot.

Wink reached for the radio and turned the dial to 94.5, the Oldies but Goodies station. Earth, Wind & Fire's "September" was on. Wink turned the volume up and tapped his fingers to the music. He broke back a smile at the thought of winning the game that so many other niggas had lost their lives playing, to either jail or the graveyard. He rejoiced in the fact that he wasn't in either. The only place he was going was to the top.

Wink sat up and stomped the gas to the floor. He had a pregnant fiancée to get home to.

Chapter Thirty-six

"I owe you my life, Pepp," Wink said as he closed the trunk of the Jaguar. He had just finished packing Armeeah and their belongings into the car. Wink stood beside Culpepper in the driveway and continued to express his gratitude. "I owe you big," he said.

"No, what you owe me is fifty thousand dollars, and I need it by Monday," joked Culpepper. He tapped Wink on the shoulder. "No, seriously, you take it easy out there, because you got to know that those lifeless bastards are still watching and waiting for you to slip up. So go straight and don't look back," Culpepper said sternly. He had really taken a liking to Wink and not just his money. He had seen so many cats on the bad end of the stick that he didn't want to see Wink added to that long list. Because he had a chance to get out and ahead.

"Thanks, Pepp, and you ain't got to worry about me lookin' back. Hell, maybe next time you represent me, it'll be in a civil case dealing with some millions of corporate money."

"That's what I'm talking about. Don't be afraid to dream. And never stop thinking. I'd love that. You got any ideas on what you're going into?"

"I have this strip club venture lined up. You think you can help me put the deal together? I need somebody to make sure all the ink is correct before it dries."

"Whenever you're ready, just get me the paperwork."

"A'ight. I'ma get on outta here. I'll get the car back to you along with that money I owe you."

Culpepper waved his hand like, "Take your time." He turned Wink around by the shoulders and stood behind him. He spoke into Wink's ear. "You see that beautiful woman sitting right there?" he asked about Armeeah. "Spend some time with her. I'll see you when I see you."

Wink smiled as Armeeah looked their way with that innocence she embodied.

"I got you, Pepp. And thanks again."

Culpepper opened the door for Wink and said goodbye to Armeeah.

"Bye, Mr. Culpepper." Armeeah smiled.

"Let's go home, baby," Wink said, starting the car. He pulled out of the driveway and reached over for Armeeah's hand. "You know I love you, right?" he asked before kissing the back of her hand.

"I know, and I love you too, baby." Armeeah still had a worried look in her eyes because too much was going on in their lives and she needed to know that it was over. "Wayne," she said softly.

"Yeah, baby."

"Is it over?"

Wink kissed her hand again, and in a settled voice he answered, "Yes, it's over." Thoughts of Trey filled his mind. No matter how badly he wanted to block Trey out, Wink knew deep down that it was impossible. He'd be living with that haunting thump of Trey's body hitting the floor for the rest of his life.

"Good, I'm glad that it's all over with," said Armeeah. She linked her fingers with Wink's and leaned against his shoulder while he drove them home.

The Feds were sitting in a black Chevy Lumina parked down the street from Wink's house. Wink looked them dead in their faces as he drove by slowly. The driver made his finger into a gun like, "I'm going to get you."

Wink looked down at Armeeah. She was still curled up under him. She hadn't seen the two agents, and that was exactly the way Wink wanted to keep it. He was going to call Culpepper as soon as they got in the house to let him know the Feds were still harassing him. When he looked in the rearview, the Lumina was gone.

"We're home, baby," Wink said, pulling up the driveway and around to the door. Armeeah sat up and smiled, glad to be home. Wink popped the trunk and got their bags. When they walked through the front door, Armeeah was stuck with her hands to her face and tears in her eyes. "Wayne, look what they did to our home," she said, taking a step into the living room. She stopped and turned around.

The Feds had left the house in shambles. They punched holes through the walls and broke all the glass tables and lamps, pretending they were looking for drugs and money, but really they were mad because Wink wouldn't cooperate. They'd torn holes in all the sofas and pulled up the carpet in the living room.

"Why would they do this?" cried Armeeah.

Wink buried her in his chest and rubbed her hair, trying to console her. "It's going to be all right, Meeah. Baby, I promise we'll fix everything. It's only stuff. We can replace it."

"I know, but it's our home."

"I know, baby. I know." It sure didn't feel like home anymore. The Feds had demolished nearly everything. It was going to take a while before it could feel like home again.

Chapter Thirty-seven

Wink thought it would be best if he sent Armeeah to stay with her parents while the contractors repaired the house. He wanted her to come home to a fresh house and not what the Feds had left. Maybe then she'd start smiling and be able to relax and forget all about what had happened.

"Why don't we just stay at your apartment?" Armeeah asked as they drove to her parents' house.

"My lease is up," Wink lied. He didn't want them staying there because he knew the Feds were still crawling around there, and he didn't need them popping up and spooking Armeeah.

"So where will you stay?"

"I'll get a room."

"Then that's where I want to be. I want to be with you, baby."

"Meeah, me too. But I need you to listen to me. Spend some time with your mom and sisters. Plan our wedding, do some shopping, whatever. Just relax and unwind. Can you do that for me?"

"Yes, I can do that," she said, reaching for Wink's hand. "But what about you? What are you going to be doing?"

"I'm going to get with your cousin Bazzi, and we're going to look at some clubs to open up."

"I'm proud of you, baby. You kept your word by leaving that stuff all behind you."

"Thank you. But you gotta know that you're the main reason I'm doing this. If we had never met and weren't about to get married, I'd still be out there. I love you, Meeah."

"I love you too."

They got caught at a red light, so Armeeah used the short time to show Wink how much she loved him by leaning over and giving him a wet, passionate kiss. Bom! Bom! The light had turned green, and the other drivers were laying on their horns for Wink to get moving. He looked up in the rearview, then mashed down on the gas. He couldn't wait to get everything all ironed out with Bazzi and get married, then have their baby! It was like a second chance at life, because Wink knew that he had dodged a bullet with the Feds. He would never do anything to get back in their palms.

They pulled into Armeeah's parents' driveway and parked. Wink stopped Armeeah before she got out of the car.

"What's wrong?" she turned and asked.

"Not a word of this to your parents or sisters. I don't want them worrying about us, okay?"

"Okay, baby."

"June third," Wink said, then parted a smile.

They looked up, and Armeeah's mom was standing on the porch smiling from ear to ear. She waved her arm for them to get out of the car and come inside.

"Remember, not a word." Wink popped the trunk and grabbed Armeeah's two suitcases.

Her mom's smile vanished at the sight of the cases. "What is this?" she asked, pointing.

"Ma, our house is being remodeled, so I'll be staying here until it's done."

"Oh, *Alhumadillaha!* I thought that you were about to tell me that the wedding was off. I have over two hundred guests coming, you know."

"Well, you can tell them all to wear their best, 'cause we're going to have the most beautiful wedding of the summer. How are you, Ma?" Wink said, kissing his future mother-in-law on the cheek.

"Better now that you guys are here. Let's go inside, and get you all settled."

Armeeah hugged and kissed her sisters and cousins, who were all in the front room, saving her father for last. "Hi, Dad," she said, kissing his forehead.

He didn't say anything, never did. He just sat there in his recliner, clutching a can of beer, with his eyes fixed on Wink.

"How are you, sir?"

"I'd be better if you get the hell out of my house and never come back." That was what he said with his cold stare.

"Ay, Wink. I didn't know you were out here. How long have you been here?" Bazzi asked, coming out of the kitchen.

"We just got here a few minutes ago. What's up, how are you?"

"You know me, man, business as usual. Say, when do you think you're going to be ready? I got some good prospects."

"I'm ready now. That's why I came to holla at you."

"You feel like taking a ride?"

"Let's do it."

"Let me tell the fellas in the basement I'm leaving, and then we can go."

Wink tried to relax while he waited in the living room with Armeeah's dad. He hadn't broken his stare yet. "You and Bazzi going into business?"

Wink couldn't believe his ears. The old monk had broken his silence. "Yes, sir. We're going to expand his business with more clubs."

"That's what this family is about: business."

Wink thought the old fart was warming up to him and that he would keep talking, but just like that, he shut down. He took a swig from his beer and glued his eyes to the world news.

Wink thought about what he had said. *This family is about business.* Was that his way of saying that he accepted Wink into their family?

"You ready?" asked Bazzi. He grabbed his coat, then kissed the old man on his forehead. "Later, Poppa."

Wink nodded on his way out.

"Let me ask you something, Bazzi," Wink said as they walked to the curb where Bazzi's Benz 500 was parked.

"Anything."

"Will he ever accept me into the family?"

Bazzi laughed, then popped the locks.

Wink climbed in behind him and said, "No, I'm serious. 'Cause every time I come around, we never speak, and it's like that's the way he wants to keep it."

"Wink, you Muslim now, and that's all that matters. Armeeah could be getting ready to marry the prince of Saudi Arabia, and my uncle still wouldn't out and say, 'Yes, you have my blessing to marry my daughter.'" Bazzi started the car while looking over at Wink. "But we accept you with open arms, cousin."

"Thanks, Bazzi." Wink smiled. That's all he needed to hear. As long as everyone else accepted him, he could put up with ol' Poppa.

"So have you decided how much you're looking to invest?" asked Bazzi.

"I'ma say two million. What do you think you can do with that?"

Bazzi sat up and pressed down on the gas. "We can do a whole lot with them kind of numbers. First, I'm going to show you what one of our running clubs looks like, and then I'll take you past a few prospective sites."

They pulled into the parking lot of Bazzi's club over on Michigan Avenue. Right off the bat, Wink was sold on the idea of owning one of these spots. The club looked like it belonged out in Miami or Cali.

"You built these from the ground up?" asked Wink as Bazzi pulled around to the valet.

"You would think, right?" Bazzi smiled.

The entrance of the club was set off with large pillars, mammoth marble facades, and lush landscaping. "It's actually a renovated job. Not bad, huh?" Bazzi said on the way in. "Come on, let me show you the inside." Bazzi wrapped his arm around Wink's shoulder and let him inside the club.

The bar featured rows of flat-screen televisions, chandeliers, and a thunderous sound system. Bazzi and Wink stood under the EXIT sign while Bazzi pointed everything out.

"Let me show you the rest of the club," he said, leading the way.

"Hey, Bazzi," a few early working dancers and shot girls said as they crossed the bar.

"How are you lovely ladies doing? Say hi to my cousin Wink."

"Hi, Wink."

"Come on, before we both get into some trouble," Bazzi said, shaking his head.

Wink was loving the attention of the strippers. He could see himself coming in for work every day being greeted by a flock of bad chicks, all of them just throwing the pussy at him.

Bazzi finished showing Wink the rest of the club, which consisted of two VIP rooms and a split-level "Ballers Only" upstairs equipped with another fully stocked bar. They retired to Bazzi's plush office with two bottles of Moët.

"So what do you think?" Bazzi asked as he popped the cork on his bottle.

"I think it's the best club I've been in. But why did you choose the name Starvin' Marvin's?" asked Wink.

"Well, my brother's real name is Marvin. So that's where Marvin comes in, and the starving represents our hunger. We're going to take over the business, Wink. It's a $200-million-a-year industry."

"Don't forget about me now," Wink said, popping his cork.

"With two million dollars, we can open five of these, and they'll all be yours with me as your manager and front man," said Bazzi.

"And how much does one of these clubs take in each month?"

"I took in over two hundred thousand dollars last month alone, and that's after paying everything. It's called profit. In a matter of two years tops, you'll have your two million back and a steady cash flow for the rest of your life."

Wink liked the sound of that. He was already set financially, but now he could go legit and never have to look back. "I'm ready. When can we get started?"

Bazzi turned up his Moët for a long swallow, then slammed the bottle on his desk. "Let's take another ride. I want to show you how one of these places looks before we renovate it. You're not going to believe it."

Chapter Thirty-eight

Bazzi showed Wink two dilapidated clubs off Livernois and Central. "I can get the owner to ink an agreement with zero down. All we'd need is money to cover renovations, and we need to agree to manage the clubs."

Wink's eyes lit up.

"I told you it's a solid moneymaker. It's how me and my brother got started," Bazzi said.

"That's what I'm talkin' 'bout," Wink said.

"You know it. This is a solid business venture. But you know it's just as competitive as the streets."

Bazzi threw out all the rules and played by his own. Whatever it took to get to the top! He had gone so far as to shut down one of his main competitors, Tycoons, when he planted a 14-year-old girl to pose as a stripper, then tipped the police off and brought the Channel 4 News out, making the city padlock the club indefinitely.

"You vicious," Wink said. He wasn't with no shit like that, because that was some borderline rat shit.

"It's called winning," Bazzi told him. "You have to bring the streets to the boardroom because no one else is playing fair."

They were going to open both clubs up at the same time. The one off Livernois was a little bigger than the one on Central. Wink wanted his office in the Livernois club, and something similar to how Bazzi had his laid out. Wink was going to let Bazzi work his hand on bringing the club to life, but he still wanted to be hands-on, even if it was helping the contractors out. When it was all done and the clubs were up and running, Wink wanted to be able to look at them and know that he was a part of their birth. Plus, it would give him something to do since he wasn't in the game anymore.

Bazzi didn't waste any time getting the ball rolling. He had the contractors on standby while he waited for Wink to look over their contracts and sign them. Wink told him to give it a couple of days so he could have his lawyer look everything over, and if things were on the up-and-up, they had a deal.

Wink called Mr. Culpepper at his office and asked if he could stop by so they could go over the contracts.

"Sure. Meet me for lunch at Fish Bones."

"Okay, what time?"

"I'm on my way now. My stomach is touching my back," said Culpepper.

"A'ight. In a minute."

Wink had been lounging in the club on Livernois daydreaming about the opening: who he would invite, what he'd wear, and what the place would look like when completed. He could see it all: naked strippers prancing around the club, working the ballers out of their pockets, and all the while he'd be getting filthy rich.

The clubs were set to go under renovation just as soon as Wink put his signature on the contracts, and they were scheduled to open by June. Wink smiled as he turned the lights off in the club and locked the doors. June was going to be a good month for him: first his wedding, and then the grand openings of his two clubs. He couldn't wait to share the news with his father. Wink knew he'd be happy to see him leave the game.

Wink found Mr. Culpepper stuffing his fat face with the crab leg lunch special. Culpepper waved Wink over and stood for him to sit.

"Thanks for meeting me on such short notice," said Wink.

"It's okay. You're paying, and besides, we need to talk anyway."

Wink's stomach turned a little. He sat up in his seat and braced himself for the news. "About?"

"The DEA wants to do a sit-down with you and, of course, me."

"Did you tell them I said to suck my daddy's dick and that I'd run through hell first with gasoline drawers on before I ever sell my soul?"

Culpepper nodded as he cracked open another crab leg. "That's exactly what I told them. But you know, as your lawyer, I had to let you know their interest."

"Well, I'm not interested in their interest."

"I know you're not a rat. You forget or something? You know I have never represented a snitch, and I'm not about to start. I don't know what they want, but I have a good feeling they'll be back."

"Back with what?"

"They will be back with more questions and definitely more pressure. But I don't want you getting all worked up. Let me do some digging around and see what I can't turn up. In the meantime, let's look at these contracts of yours."

Wink pulled the two contracts from the manila envelope and placed them on the table.

"Go on and order while I look these over," said Culpepper. He put his glasses on and read with one hand while feeding his face with the other.

Wink had lost his appetite at the mention of the Feds. Why wouldn't them bitches just die somewhere and let him move on with his life? He had beaten the system, won the game, and it was over! So Wink thought. It was never over with the Feds. They were more relentless than a baby momma fighting for child support. They weren't stopping until they got their man or until you rolled over and snitched.

"Everything seems to be in order," said Culpepper as he flipped through the pages. "Simple, standard three-page contract," he said, squinting at the fine print at the bottom.

"What do you think? Is everything straight?"

"I would say yes. Just make sure you get copies, and I'm going to sign as your witness." Culpepper pulled a pen from his shirt and signed both contracts as Wink's witness.

"So when are these clubs of yours set to open?"

"Late June. Don't worry, you'll be front and center when the doors open."

"Of course. I wouldn't miss it for the world."

"I bet you wouldn't, you old freak," laughed Wink. He added his signature to both contracts, then put them back in the manila envelope.

"Aren't you going to order?" asked Culpepper. He caught Wink staring blankly out the window.

"Nah, I lost my appetite at the sound of the Feds."

"I told you, let me dig around and see all I can turn up. But in the meantime, you keep your hands clean and stay out of those damn streets. Focus on your clubs. Hey, I'm proud of you, and I know your old man will be proud too."

Wink sat with Culpepper while he finished his lunch. He was taking heed of everything he said, and he had no intention of looking back. Wink just wished the Feds would leave him alone and for good.

Chapter Thirty-nine

Krazy didn't know what to do when he went to the storage unit and found the 200 kilos that Wink had called his blessing.

"I'm breaking all you bitches down to nickels," he said, excited, as he loaded the keys into the back of his Lexus truck. He was so geeked and anxious to see what Wink had had for him at the storage unit that he hadn't done what Wink told him to do, which was to burn that truck.

Krazy packed all the keys inside the truck, then raced home to switch cars. He stashed all the bricks except five of them. He grabbed some fresh guns, changed clothes, and was out the door, leaving the Lexus in the driveway. He pulled up on Charest Street where he and Wink grew up. Krazy's plan was to take over his hood, then branch out. But he was going to start with the young'uns all out on the block sweatin' his Benz.

Krazy parked and got out, then walked over to the abandoned house where all the young'uns were posted trying to sell their little stones, while others tried doubling their re-up money in a crap game.

"What's up, Krazy? Man, I ain't seen you in a minute," said Murf.

"That's 'cause when I was out here, y'all li'l niggas was still on the porch playin' tag and shit. But I see y'all all grown up now." Krazy was looking at all the faces. Every last one of them were jitterbugs before he caught that case out in Ohio.

"What's good, though? You just stopped through to fuck with us?" asked Murf. He was going on 16 and was the leader of the pack of thirsty young'uns.

"Yeah, come on over and get in this dice game so we can break yo' old ass," said Zeek, Murf's brother.

"Y'all go ahead. I don't wanna break up ya li'l two and few game." Krazy turned his attention to Murf and those posted on the porch. "Who y'all out here workin' for?" he asked.

"We ain't workin' for nobody. We workin' with Rome," said Murf.

Krazy laughed, then said, "That's what he told you." He laughed again, thinking back to J-Bo. "That's funny, 'cause I don't see that nigga Rome nowhere out here. He's workin' you all right."

Someone else said, "Shit, at least we eatin'. Ain't nobody else puttin' nothing in our hands."

Krazy squinted at the little, frail red nigga, and asked, "And who the fuck is you?"

"Teddy," the li'l nigga snapped like Krazy should have known.

"Well, Teddy Ruxpin, I'm about to put more work in y'all hands than a temp service. Question is, can you handle it?" asked Krazy.

"Rome ain't going for that, you coming and settin' up shop," said Murf.

"Murf, what's my name?"

"Krazy."

"And how long have you've known me?"

"All my life," said Murf.

"Okay, then you should know I ain't stuntin' Rome's bitch ass."

"Oh, no? Well, here he comes now." Teddy nodded to the end of the block.

Rome was pulling up in his doo-doo brown Caddy. He parked across the street and hit the horn twice for li'l Murf to come there.

"Fall back," Krazy said, holding his arm out as Murf tried to stand up. "Let me holla at him." Krazy tucked his hands inside the slide pocket of his hoodie and crossed the street.

Rome sat leaned back with his phone pressed to his ear. He hadn't seen Krazy cross the street and walk around to the passenger side. Krazy opened the door, then slid in.

"Nigga, what the fuck you doing?" Rome snapped. He tried to sit up, but Krazy smacked him hard across the face with the barrel of his .380.

"Ahh, shit," Rome cried out in agony. He held the gushing cut under his eye while trying to curl up against the driver's door. "What do you want?" he asked.

"That's a lot better," said Krazy, still holding Rome at gunpoint. "You see those little niggas all out on the porch? I want you to call them over and tell them that they no longer work for you."

"And who do they work for?"

"Me, nigga. Now roll down ya window and call 'em over." Krazy pressed the barrel into Rome's flabby gut and watched as he rolled the window down.

"Ay, Murf, y'all let me holla at all y'all for a minute." Rome's voice quivered with fear because he had heard that Krazy was home and on his bullshit. Rome wasn't trying to fall victim to Krazy's rampage.

"What's up?" Murf asked as he and his crew all gathered around the car.

"Tell 'em," warned Krazy. He pressed a little harder with the barrel into Rome's side.

"Today is going to be the last day of y'all workin' for me," Rome said, stuttering.

"Who we gon' be workin' for?" asked Zeek.

"Krazy will be taking over," said Rome.

"What about all the sack money?" asked Murf.

"Y'all g'on and keep it." Rome was so scared that he had piss running down his leg.

"Y'all go wait for me on the porch," hollered Krazy. When they all turned to leave, Krazy raised the gun and put it to the side of Rome's head. "Look, bitch, if I ever see you on this block again, it's lights out. You understand, bitch?"

"Yeah, man. I don't want no problems. It's yours. I just wanna go home to my wife and kids."

"Good, and that's where yo' ass betta stay." Krazy reached over and started the car. "Now get yo' ass off my block," he said, reaching for the door handle.

Rome peeled away from the curb like a bat out of hell. Murf and Teddy met Krazy in the middle of the street, laughing as they stared into the exhaust smoke Rome left trying to get away.

"What did you do to him?" asked Teddy, still laughing.

"What you're 'posed to do to a bitch nigga. I took his shit. Come on over here to the porch. I wanna talk to all y'all for a minute." Krazy pulled Zeek and the rest of them away from their dice game and made everybody sit on the porch while he stood on the grass and gave them his come-up speech.

He preached to them that he would get them high on money, jewelry, and clothes if they worked for him. He promised to make them millionaires. And for the ones who didn't want to be down, they were no longer welcome on the block. Krazy lifted his shirt to show traitors what lay in store for them.

But not one of them was thinking about betraying him, and they forgot about ol' Rome no sooner than he fled for his life. They were sold on the dreams Krazy was selling about being rich and driving fancy cars.

"Just give me six months, and I'll have every last one of you in a Vette with money to blow and the respect of the city. All we need is six months," Krazy repeated. He took a moment to see his words sink in. For a second, he could see himself along with Wink, Willie, and Trey sitting on the porch, listening to ol' J-Bo sell them his come-up dream. That was the name of the game though. The only person who would be coming up was Krazy.

"If ya ass ain't tryin'a be a part of this, g'on and get outta here now, 'cause once we start, ain't no stopping."

They all looked at each other to see who was going to leave, but everyone stayed put.

"Good," said Krazy. "For now on, we're going to be known as Cash Flow."

Krazy went on to break down their new operation. He told them to trash all the dope Rome left behind. He said if they were caught selling that garbage out on the block, they would be violated, which consisted of a pumpkin-head-style beat down. He said that they would be selling nothing but nickel sacks of the best crack in the city.

"Do as I say, and we'll all get rich. Do anything other than that, and you'll pay," Krazy warned. He used Murf's house to cook up one of the bricks and immediately put them to work.

Chapter Forty

Wink celebrated with Bazzi and a few strippers at his new club on Livernois. They were enjoying lap dances in wooden chairs where the stage would soon sit.

Bazzi turned up his bottle of Dom P for a long swallow, then let out a roaring burp in the face of one of the dancers. "I'm sorry, baby," he said, smiling.

"You's a fool with it," laughed Wink. He too was draped with a fine yellow bone.

"Call me what you want. Just don't call me broke. Ain't that right, baby?" Bazzi pulled the girl closer to him, palming her thick ass cheeks. She nodded in agreement.

"Just think, Wink, in a matter of a few months, you'll be able to come here and kick back every day."

"This is the life, right?" Wink smiled up at the lovely C-cups just inches away from his lips. They were indeed tempting, but Wink wasn't stuntin' ol' girl. He was just having a good time and celebrating the fact that he was now legit. In two years or so, he could have enough legal money to launch his own chain of strips clubs and whatever else he wanted to get into. But in the meantime, he was going to enjoy the present.

The strippers took a breather from dancing. They had danced ten songs straight and needed something to drink. Bazzi watched their asses intently as they swayed over to the bar. Without breaking his stare, he said, "Wink, don't you do like me and let these places ruin your marriage, because there's a lot for a man to say no to in this business."

"I didn't know you and your wife was having problems," said Wink.

"Yeah, we have for some time now. I keep thinking one day when I get home she's going to be gone." Bazzi lowered his eyes to the rim of his bottle. He traced the hole with his finger, then continued, "I couldn't blame her if she did leave."

Wink got the message Bazzi was trying to send, that there was an evil side to the business. Wink thought about Armeeah, and he couldn't fathom the thought of her ever leaving him.

"All I'm saying is be careful." He tapped Wink on the knee, then stood up and walked over to join the dancers at the bar.

Wink turned up the rest of his champagne and began staring blankly into the distance of the club. He thought about everything his life had become. Although he had many reasons to be thankful, he couldn't forget what he'd lost along the way. He'd lost his father to the game, his best friend Trey over money and power, even somewhat of his soul to the many murders.

Wink knew that he couldn't fix any of it and that he would have to learn to live with regret. But there was one thing that he could fix and wanted to, which was the loving relationship with his mom. Wink wondered what she was doing and how she was making it. He could still see the look of devastation on her face when he blew Gary's brains all over the kitchen. Wink closed his eyes. "I'm sorry, Momma."

I gotta go see her. He wanted to tell his mom how much he loved her and how much he missed her. He wanted to wrap her into his arms and kiss her forehead like he used to. Most importantly, he wanted to forget all about the past and just love his mom again.

"Ay yo, Bazzi. I'ma holla at you tomorrow," said Wink.

"What, you outta here?" Bazzi asked from the bar.

"Yeah, I gotta take care of something."

"All right. Well, you know we start renovating in the morning."

Wink managed a smile. "I wouldn't miss it for the world." Wink waved bye to the strippers on his way out of the club.

He got behind the wheel of his Benz and asked himself before starting the car if he was ready to face all the built-up pain and strife he'd been harboring. Wink took a deep breath, then started the car. He drove deliberately slowly while thinking of what he would say when his mom opened the door and saw him standing there. Nothing seemed appropriate, yet he kept on.

When Wink turned down Charest, he could see his grandmother's gold Cadillac peeking from the end of the driveway. He knew she would have a mouthful to say, rather curse. He parked across the street and cut the car off. For a few minutes he sat there looking at the house, knowing that the only thing keeping him from his mom was him.

He saw the curtains pull back and his mom peer out at his car. He wondered if she knew it was him. *Does she want to see me?* Wink fought the temptation to leave and willed himself to pull the door handle and get out of the car. He locked eyes with his mom as he crossed the street, and her eyes seemed to widen with disbelief that it was in fact her son. She disappeared from the curtain as Wink climbed the steps up to the porch. He was a nervous wreck standing there. *Is she going to open the door?* he thought as the seconds turned long. *Damn,* Wink thought, looking at the door. *Why did I come here?* He didn't want to cause his mother any more pain than she must have already been going through. He swallowed hard and nodded slightly, as if to say he understood.

As he turned to leave, he heard the locks clicking, and then the door slowly opened. It was his grandmother standing with her hands on her hips.

"Hi, Grandma." Wink had to clear his throat because he was on the verge of breaking down.

"Wayne, you've got a helluva lot of nerve coming here," said Grandma. She felt no sympathy for the tears welling in Wink's eyes.

"I know. I just . . ." Wink's voice cracked.

"It's okay, Momma," Wink's mom told his grandmother as she stepped to the door. She put her hands on Grandma's shoulders and moved her aside. "I'll be fine, Ma."

"Okay, but if you need me, I'll be right in the living room." Grandma gave Wink the evil eye as she left them to talk.

Wink's mom gave her an assuring nod that she was all right, then watched her go off.

A lone tear streamed down the side of Wink's face as he looked his mom over. He saw the stress he'd put her through in the lines around her eyes that hadn't been there before and the gray strands flowing through her hair. He knew that he'd put every last one of them there.

"Ma, I'm sorry," Wink managed to say before breaking down. Tears were pouring down his face as he stood there crying his soul out.

"It's okay, Wayne," his mom said, taking him into her arms. She let his head rest on her shoulder while she rubbed his head.

"I'm sorry," Wink cried.

"Let it out, baby. Just let it out." She patted Wink on his back and dropped some tears of her own.

Wink knew he had to be strong for his mom, so he tried pulling himself together. He stood up straight and wiped the streaming tears from his mother's face, but they kept flowing, as did his. He looked deep into her eyes and wished that he could take all her hurt away and endure it himself.

Wink wrapped her hair around her ear just how he used to. "Momma, I still love you."

"Momma loves you too, baby."

There was a slight pause as Wink fought for more words, but instead he allowed his heart to speak. "Ma, I need you to know that I never stopped loving you. What happened should have never happened. Not like the way it did. I'm not here asking for forgiveness, because I know that it may be too soon. I just needed to see you and know that you're all right."

"Wayne, I'll always be your momma, and I will always love you regardless of what happened. I think that we need to forgive each other. You're not the only one at fault. We all are. Momma should have sat you down long ago and tried explaining the situation with your father. Lord knows I should have. It just wasn't easy, baby."

"It's okay, Ma. Don't cry anymore."

"No, it's not okay. I need us to forgive each other. I don't want to go on with you hating me for what happened to your father."

"I could never hate you, Momma. I will always love you. I am trying to forgive us." Wink couldn't help but think about his dad stretched out with two natural-life sentences.

"Me too, baby. Me too. But we must forgive ourselves before we can forgive one another."

"I agree," Wink said dryly.

"Why don't you come inside and stay awhile?" Wink's mom didn't want to see him leave, because she was afraid it might be the last time she'd see him.

Wink squeezed his mom's hand as she turned for the door.

"What's the matter, Wayne?" she asked as Wink stared into the house.

He wasn't ready to set foot in that house just yet, and perhaps never. The vivid scene of Gary lying dead on the kitchen floor and his mom screaming played through his mind. "I can't stay, Ma," Wink finally said.

"Well, baby, when am I going to see you again?" she nervously asked.

"Tomorrow." Wink smiled. "I have someone I'd really like you to meet," Wink said.

Wink's mom smiled too. "Who is she?" she asked.

"Someone very special. But she'll always be number two." Wink stole a kiss from his mom's forehead, then said, "Tomorrow I want to treat you both to dinner, so pull out your best."

"I'll be ready, Wayne, and please be careful. You are still all I have."

"I love you too." Wink kissed his mom again, then turned to leave.

She stood on the porch with tears in her eyes. It hurt her to watch him go, but she was thanking God for their reunion.

Wink waved bye to both his mom and his grandmother, who was occupying the curtain. As he drove to his apartment, he tried to relive every emotion he felt while talking to his mom. He questioned whether he seemed sincere, and if she really forgave him. What hadn't he said that he should have said?

Wink told himself that the first thing he was going to do was move his mom out of the house, because she shouldn't have to live there, constantly being reminded that her son killed her fiancé in the kitchen. Besides, he didn't know if he'd ever be able to set foot in that house again after what happened. It would be good for them both.

Wink tried thinking about something that would take his mind off the stress between him and his mom. He knew Armeeah would be happy to finally meet her. She'd only been asking forever, it seemed. He called her at her parents' house and told her he had a surprise and to be ready because he was on his way to get her. He wanted everything to be perfect when Armeeah met his mom. It would be a start to rebuilding their loving relationship.

Chapter Forty-one

The clock was winding down for Agent Defauw to start making arrests on the sixty-eight-person indictment handed down by a grand jury in the Eastern District of Michigan six days prior. Defauw had been hoping to catch Wink in the act of making a drug buy so he could tie him to a conspiracy with Nina and Franko, but he had nothing. What he had were twenty-four hours remaining before he was taken off the case and reassigned.

Defauw, along with Hornberger, held a roll-call meeting on the tenth floor of the federal building with other field agents and units from the Detroit Police task force to discuss the roundup of those listed in the indictment. Trey had been number one, but since he was now dead, Wink was named number one.

Defauw passed around pictures of Wink and Willie. He advised that Willie was an informant who had fled. He stressed the need to bring Willie in alive because he was the glue to make everything stick. Last but not least, Defauw passed a prison mug shot of Krazy around the room.

"This man is considered to be armed at all times and very dangerous. We have reason to believe he's responsible for the killings of Special Agents Murray and Byers, so proceed with caution. But by all means we want him off the street. Are there any questions?" Defauw asked, looking around the room.

Everyone seemed to understand their positions and what was expected of them.

"All right then, I want everyone to be geared up and ready to go by zero eight hundred hours tomorrow. We'll hold a brief roll call, then move out." Defauw clapped his hands, dismissing the meeting. He was still upset that Washington had interfered with his investigation. Defauw wanted Franko's organization, but it seemed he managed to elude the long arm of the law once again.

Frustrated, Defauw looked at Hornberger and said, "I'm putting in for a transfer just as soon as this is over."

He just didn't know that Hornberger was jumping for joy inside. *Yes!*

Chapter Forty-two

The contractors finished repairing Wink's house sooner than expected. It was perfect timing, because now he could have dinner with his mom and Armeeah in the comfort of their home. He sent Armeeah out to get some new china for the evening while he made sure everything around the house was just right. His mom and grandmother would be arriving in less than an hour.

Wink was dry mopping the kitchen floor when his cell phone rang. He looked around trying to find the phone and followed the ringing into the living room, where his phone sat on the fireplace mantle. He flipped the phone open and pressed it to his ear. "Hello."

"Wayne, listen to me. I need for you to meet me at my office. It's urgent." It was Mr. Culpepper.

Wink could hear the concern in Culpepper's voice, and it made him uneasy. "Pepp, what's going on?"

"In person," Culpepper said flatly.

"Can it wait until morning? I'm about to have dinner with my mom."

"I need to see you tonight!" Culpepper put emphasis on "tonight."

"I'll stop by your place around eight."

"See you then." Click.

Wink lowered the phone to his side and pushed the END button with his thumb while gazing nervously through the house. Whatever Mr. Culpepper needed to tell him couldn't be good news. Wink could hear the worry in his voice.

Suddenly what seemed to be a good day had taken a turn for the worse. *Please just let it be about the clubs.* He didn't even want to hear the word "Feds" anymore. He set his phone back on the mantle and finished getting ready for his mom and grandmother. He took a quick shower, then dressed in the slacks and button-down Armeeah had set out for him. She was back from buying the china and downstairs setting the table. She looked up and smiled as Wink walked into the dining room.

"What do you think?" She stepped back, waving her hand for Wink to see.

"It looks nice," Wink said in a distant voice.

"Honey, is everything all right?" Armeeah could see the distraught expression on Wink's face.

"Yeah. Just a little nervous about you meeting my mom," lied Wink.

"Here, let me." Armeeah finished buttoning Wink's shirt, and then she stood on her tiptoes for a kiss. "It'll be fine," she assured him.

The doorbell sounded twice. "That's them."

"How do I look?" Armeeah asked, brushing down the sides of her dress.

"Like my wife. Come on." Wink led her by the hand to the front door. His mom and Grams were standing on the front porch, each with minks draped over their backs.

"Come in." Wink kissed them both and allowed them to step inside. He closed the door and took their minks, then introduced Armeeah, who was a nervous wreck.

"Wayne, you didn't tell me she was so beautiful," his mom said of Armeeah.

"You did teach me to have good taste."

"Hmph," ol' Grams grunted. She kept her nose in the air.

"How are you paying for this place, and how much it cost?" Ol' Grams didn't hold her tongue either, and she was nosy as a mothafucka.

"Ma," Wink's mom said in fear of Grams cranking up.

"Don't you be 'ma'ing me. You need to be tryin'a figure out how he can put you up in a house like this."

"That's already in the works," Wink said, hanging their coats. "Ladies, shall we?" He waved to the foyer. He led them through the living room and into the dining room.

"After dinner, I will be happy to give you all a tour of the house," said Armeeah.

"I would love that," said Ma Dukes.

"In the meantime, y'all have a seat while we get dinner ready." Wink pulled their seats out, then kissed his mom on the cheek before helping Armeeah in the kitchen.

"Does she like me?" Armeeah whispered as she pulled the shrimp scampi from the warmer.

"Yes. She's going to love you. So just relax." Wink grabbed the platter of boiled lobsters and carried them out. He placed one on each of their plates, then returned to the kitchen for a bottle of wine.

Armeeah laid out all the sides dishes: baked potatoes, shrimp scampi, broccoli, and buttermilk biscuits. They sat, and ol' Grandma said for everyone to bow their heads so she could bless the food.

"What's wrong, baby?" Wink's mom asked after seeing the looks on Wink's and Armeeah's faces.

"Ma, I hadn't told you, but I'm Muslim," said Wink.

"Lord, Jesus," Grams cranked up. "I didn't raise no damn Muslims. I raised you up as a Christian."

"Grandma, I know that. But I am a grown man now, and I have chosen Islam as my faith." Wink reached over for Armeeah's hand. "We're Muslims," he said.

"Baby, you don't owe us or anybody else an explanation. I'm just happy you have accepted God into your life," Ma Dukes said, smiling. She looked across the table at her mother, to which Grams rolled her eyes and grunted.

Wink blessed the meal by saying, "*Bismillallah,*" which means "in the name of Allah" in Arabic.

"I was going to wait until we finished eating dinner to tell you ladies this, but I have to make a quick run when we're done." Wink paused for a moment.

His mom wiped her mouth of the scampi, and asked, "What is it, Wayne?"

"Armeeah and I are engaged to be married."

"Really!" Ma Dukes said, excited. "When are you guys getting married?" she asked.

"June third," said Armeeah.

"That's not all," said Wink.

"Oh Lord," said Grams.

"We're pregnant, too. So, Ma, you're going to be a grandma, and well, Grandma, you'll be a great-grandma."

"I can't believe this! When is the baby due, and what are we having?" asked Ma Dukes.

"Well, I have a surprise of my own. I haven't yet told Wayne this, but we're having a boy," said Armeeah.

"A boy?" Wink asked, excited.

Armeeah nodded, smiling. "I'm due September tenth."

"You have to let me throw the baby shower," pleaded Ma Dukes.

"I would be honored," said Armeeah.

They finished eating dinner, and Armeeah went to show off their home in detail. Wink kissed his mom and Grams bye and said that he'd see them soon and that it was urgent he left.

"Be careful," Armeeah said, then kissed Wink.

Wink couldn't stop thinking about how nervous Mr. Culpepper had sounded earlier. It was almost as if he were scared for Wink. *What can he possibly need to speak with me about that's so urgent?* Wink thought as he punched his Benz 500 down the expressway in a rush to get over to Mr. Culpepper's house.

Wink made it to Culpepper's and killed his lights as he pulled into the driveway, parking behind Culpepper's Jaguar. Wink got out of the car with his cell phone pressed to his ear. "I'm on the porch," he said after Culpepper answered.

A few minutes later, Culpepper emerged from the side of the house. He waved Wink from the porch to come around back.

"My bad, did I wake you?" Wink asked, following Culpepper into the house. He was wearing his housecoat and slippers.

"No, I was catching up on some cases. Let's go into my office."

"You know how much I hate surprises, Pepp man. So just give it to me," said Wink as they entered Culpepper's office. Wink opted to stand with his back to the door and waited as Culpepper situated himself behind his desk.

"I told you they would be back."

"What is it this time? What do they want?"

"Blood. Yours, to be exact." Culpepper slapped the indictment on his desk and watched Wink's eyes dread its existence.

Wink stepped from the wall and picked the papers up. He read, "U.S. Grand Jury Indictment, Eastern District of Michigan." Wink's heart sank to see his name listed as number one on the indictment. The charges were distribution of cocaine exceeding 500 kilograms, conspiracy, and tax evasion.

"This is bullshit! How can they indict me when they don't have anything?"

"Obviously they do."

"I'm certain they have shit!" Wink raised his voice. He knew the Feds didn't have anything. Trey was dead.

"Listen, Wayne. I've been doing this for a long time, and trust me, your name would not be on there without

the government having something on you. What they
have, I have no idea as of yet. But you being number one
tells me that it's strong."

"Well, you need to find out what it is they think they
have on me so we can clear my name."

"And I will do that." Culpepper paused for a moment.

"Don't tell me there's more," said Wink.

"They're making a sweep first thing in the morning.
Every name on that list will be rounded up at the Wayne
County jail by lunch. So I suggest you get low."

"I'm not running. They don't have nothing on me. Plus,
we'll bond out."

"Dammit, Wayne!" Culpepper slammed both hands
on his desk, then stood up and leaned forward, glaring
at Wink. "This is not the State of Michigan we're dealing
with here. They're not going to give your ass a bond.
They'll convince the judge that you are a danger to the
community and a flight risk. You'll be denied bond, and
you'll sit in the county for two or three years while we
fight for your life!"

"Life?" repeated Wink.

"Yes, life. And then some. Wayne, you need to go home
and get your fiancée, pack some money, and get the hell
out of Detroit before the sun comes up, 'cause tomorrow
will be too late. They're coming!"

Wink lowered his eyes to the Oriental rug on
Culpepper's floor. He couldn't fathom the Feds giving
him life. For what? They had nothing, Wink was certain
of it. But still, Culpepper had never been wrong before,
and he had no reason to lie. *Damn. What am I going to
do?*

"Right now, you need to be doing some of your best
hiding until I can sort things out and perhaps save your
life. But you're of no value sitting in prison."

"Where will I go?" asked Wink. His world seemed to be
growing smaller by the second.

Culpepper slid open his desk drawer and handed Wink two plane tickets, a fake ID, and a key ring. He walked around the desk and put his hand on Wink's shoulder. "I never told you this before, Wayne, but I love you like a son. Always have. I don't want to see you lose. These are two tickets to Vegas. I own a timeshare down there, and this is the key. You and Armeeah can stay down there while I work this thing out. Your flight leaves at ten thirty."

Wink looked at the tickets, then closed his eyes and breathed in deeply. "How long do we have to stay down there?"

"Just don't be in any rush to come back. And do not call anyone!"

"Thanks, Pepp," Wink finally said.

"You can thank me later. But for now get out of here."

Wink hugged ol' Culpepper for a minute, then with tears in his eyes, he left.

Why now? was all Wink could ask himself during the drive home. He fought back the tears, because crying wasn't going to change anything. The only thing that was going to save him was getting on that plane and leaving.

Wink squeezed the wheel tight with both hands. He had a good mind to just stay and kill whoever had him still linked to the Feds. At this point, he didn't care who it was: agent, prosecutor, judge, whoever.

Wink fought the temptation to be hardheaded. There was just too much at stake. He decided to let Culpepper work his hand while he and Armeeah lay low. Wink prayed that everything would be settled before June third and the birth of their son in September.

Chapter Forty-three

Wink kept trying to call Krazy to put him on point, but he wasn't answering his phone. *I'll try later,* Wink told himself as he pulled into the driveway of his house. He was relieved to see that his mom and grandmother were gone, because he didn't want to have to explain things right now. Wink knew that Armeeah was going to flip all out because he'd told her it was over with the Feds. "Think." Wink stared at the front door to the house. He was having difficulty thinking of the best way to break the news. *Fuck it. I'ma tell her half the truth.*

When Wink got inside, he found Armeeah cuddled up asleep on the sofa with their little pooch in her arms. Wink didn't want to wake her she looked so peaceful. He sat on the edge of the sofa and stared over at the clock mounted in the foyer. It was almost nine o'clock. There was no time for playing. He woke Armeeah up with a soft kiss on her lips. She smiled and slowly sat up.

"You're home," she said, setting the dog down on the floor.

"How'd things go with my mom?"

"I really like your mother. She's a sweet person. We're going to do some shopping tomorrow."

Wink's soul paused at the thought of tomorrow and what lay ahead. "Well, you're going to have to reschedule, because we're going on vacation."

"You never said anything about a vacation!" Armeeah got excited. "Where?"

"It's a surprise, and our plane leaves in an hour, so let's go."

"An hour? But we need to pack."

"The only thing we're packing is money. We'll do all the shopping you want when we get there. Now go and get ready." Wink kissed her again, this time more passionately. He watched Armeeah jump from the sofa and sprint through the house. It was half the truth. They were going on vacation. Question was, for how long?

Wink went down to the basement behind the bar and dug up the floor tiles where he kept one of his safes. He cracked it open and hurriedly removed the entire $250,000. He knew that he and Armeeah wouldn't be able to carry all the cash through the airport. "Think, think," he told himself before scooping all the loot up and putting the tiles back in place. *I know what I'ma do.* Wink carried the money upstairs to their bedroom along with a roll of gray duct tape. He found Armeeah in her closet rummaging through her clothes.

"Baby, what are you doing? I told you we'd go shopping when the plane lands," Wink said.

"I have to pack something."

"Come out here." Wink led her by the hand to the bedroom and pointed at the money spread across the bed. "That's all we're taking." He began undressing her.

"Our plane leaves in less than an hour," Meeah said, thinking Wink wanted sex.

He stripped her down to her thong and bra, then grabbed the roll of tape and two stacks of hundreds.

"What are you doing?" asked Meeah.

"Designing you a dress. I call it money. Just flow with me, baby." Wink stole a kiss, then finished strapping Armeeah up with as many stacks as her frame could stand.

"Now what I need you to do is grab two of your girdles." Wink had Armeeah strap the rest of the money to him, and then they both slipped into her girdles and got dressed.

"I don't know where you're taking me, but I can't wait to get there," said Armeeah.

Yeah. Just be prepared to stay there for a while.

Wink took one long look at the living room before they left. For some reason, he knew it would be the last time he would ever see his house again.

"You ready, baby?" Armeeah bent the corner wearing a full-length gray fur. Wink smiled at his beautiful fiancée and nodded yes.

He opened the door and looked around once more, then closed the door. He didn't even bother locking it because the Feds would be there by sun up anyway. They wouldn't have to kick the door in at least. Wink helped Armeeah into the car, then walked around to his side and got in.

Within minutes, they were at Metro Airport in Romulus, Michigan. Wink parked the Benz and helped Armeeah out of the car. On their way inside the terminal, Wink handed Armeeah her ticket. She opened it up and her eyes widened with excitement. "Vegas!"

"Yep," said Wink as he reached the double sliding door. He just wished it were on better terms.

Wink handed the agent his ticket and fake ID. He could feel his palms get sweaty. His mind was telling him to stay calm as he watched the agent look at the picture on his ID then up at Wink. Wink smiled. The agent kept a blank look on his face, looked back down at the ID, then scanned it. The scanner beeped and blinked red. The agent took the ID out and turned it over to inspect it. He squinted, tilted his head in confusion, and reinserted it into the scanner. Wink's heart was about to beat out of his chest, and he was sure the Feds were about to swarm. The scanner blinked red and then beeped and turned green.

"That was weird. Never seen that before." The agent handed Wink his ID and boarding pass. "Have a great trip," he said. Wink nodded. He was so stressed he was unable to speak. Armeeah breezed through security without incident.

They boarded the plane early because Ol' Culpepper had laid them out with first-class seats.

"May I get you two anything?" asked one of the flight attendants as she stood in the aisle close to Armeeah.

"Something to drink will be fine," ordered Meeah.

"How does champagne sound?"

"That would be great." Armeeah turned her smile to face Wink, who was nervously staring out the window. Armeeah raised Wink's arm and curled up under him. "Is something wrong, Wayne?"

"No, baby. Everything's fine," lied Wink. He kept his stare out the window while running his fingers through her hair. He told himself that once they settled in down in Vegas, he would sit her down and try to explain things.

Chapter Forty-four

At eight o'clock the following morning, the DEA, along with Detroit's own task force, set the city on fire. They had twelve units set up so they could simultaneously conduct each raid and round up everyone named in the indictment.

Agent Defauw and his unit hit Wink's house while Agent Hornberger raided the apartment downtown in the Jeffersonians. Defauw smiled to himself after realizing that Wink had fled. He rejoiced in the fact for two reasons of his own: because Washington had interfered with his investigation, and also because so long as Wink was still out there, he had a chance of catching Wink in a deal with Franko's Cuban cartel.

Agent Hornberger called Defauw from the Jeffersonians on his cellular phone to let him know that he had nothing.

"Same here."

Agent Hornberger could hear Defauw smiling through the phone. He knew what this meant as well. Defauw wouldn't be putting in for that transfer anytime soon.

"What now?" asked Hornberger.

"Finish rounding 'em up." Click. "That's right. Run, nigger, run. When I catch you it will be on my account," Defauw said to himself as he stood in the center of Wink's living room.

"All right. Pack it up. We've got a couple more. Let's go." Defauw clapped his hands while bearing a victorious smirk. He wanted to hurry up and leave before one of the agents miraculously hollered that they'd found Wink hiding in the attic or something. With Wink still on the loose, Defauw's investigation was still alive.

Chapter Forty-five

Meanwhile, two units from the DEA and Detroit task force had hit Krazy's home in Oak Park. They found fifty kilos of cocaine stamped with Franko's Cuban flag in the center of each key. They also found an arsenal of weapons upstairs in the closet. But they focused on the bullet-riddled Lexus truck parked in the driveway. It was confirmed that Krazy was their man in the death of the two DEA agents.

Krazy wasn't home during the raid, but the Feds put an APB out and a reward for his arrest. They released his picture along with Wink's to all the local news stations and the local radio stations. They put up $10,000 for the both of them. As soon as Krazy's mug shot flashed across the TV, people started calling in with sightings. For $10,000, people in Detroit would turn their own momma in, so Krazy didn't stand a chance.

Somebody called in a tip that Krazy was on Charest Street shooting dice. The Feds were following up on all leads, so when the call came through, they sent a unit out to the location. They had strict instructions from Washington to give one warning, then shoot to kill.

Krazy and about twenty of his Cash Flow niggas were gathered in a circle shooting dice in the driveway of their house on Charest. It was payday, and Krazy was trying to break everybody out of their sack money. He stood in the center of the circle with his shirt off, gun at his waist, and a mountainous pile of money on the ground.

Sweating and out of breath, Krazy shook the dice high above his head, waiting for everybody to place their bets. "All bets down," he said before rolling the dice. "Four hoes and meee," Krazy said as the dice spun. "Five!"

Everybody dropped their heads in disbelief because Krazy had made his point. He fell to his knees and hugged all the money into his existing pile. "If ya ass is broke, ain't no sense in standing around sweating and swallowing bets. Get that ass to work, and I'll see ya next week."

The only one who was smart enough not to fuck with Krazy was Murf. He was sitting on the porch clowning all his niggas. "I got loans. Two for ones!" yelled Murf.

Krazy stood up and stuffed all the money in his pockets, then joined Murf on the porch. "Why you ain't get in the game? Shit, yo' li'l money spend too," said Krazy.

"I'm not no damn fool. I peeped game how you was cheatin', switchin' the dice," whispered Murf.

"Cheatin' is the only way to keep the cheat off of you." Krazy laughed and hit rocks with his li'l underboss Murf. Krazy had the hood on lock. He had two crack houses in the middle of the block and two houses directly across the street: one a stash house for the money, and the other for cooking up the crack. He had lookouts posted at every corner and a couple of cars circling the hood with police scanners. In just two days, Krazy and his Cash Flow niggas had run through four keys, and the word was steadily spreading about the good quality of the crack. People were coming from all over the city and even from the suburbs.

"We keep this up, Murf, and we'll be rich in no time," said Krazy. He dug into his pocket and broke bread with Murf on some of his winnings. Krazy thought back to how ol' J-Bo used to play them when he was first coming up in the game. *Gotta keep 'em broke and hungry,* he thought with a smirk. As he counted his winnings, a caravan of agents turned the corner.

"Krazy!" Murf tapped Krazy's leg. He pointed down the street at the four triple-black vans speeding their way.

Krazy jumped from the porch and started to make a run for it, but two more vans were coming from the opposite direction. The vans bypassed everyone else standing out on the block, including all the crack houses and stash houses. Krazy took off running through the vacant lot beside the abandon house they'd been shooting dice at. He could hear tires screeching and then car doors opening.

"He's cutting through the side!" Krazy heard one of the agents yell.

His heart sank realizing that they had come for him. Krazy hit the back gate into the alley and was about to hit the next gate leading to Gallagher Street when a blue Ford Taurus slammed on its brakes at the end of the driveway. Krazy locked eyes with the white man behind the wheel, then looked over his shoulder. Two DEA agents were running through the yard he had just jumped out of.

"Get down on the ground!" one of the agents ordered.

Krazy pulled out his .44 Bulldog and dumped two dum dums into the face of the first agent as he tried to leap the gate. The agent flew back into his partner, knocking him to the ground. Krazy let off another shot at the agent in the Taurus, then took off running down the alley.

Krazy's whole life flashed before his eyes. He was back sitting in his cell at the Ohio State penitentiary reformatory. *I'm not going back,* he thought, gripping the chrome .44 for dear life. He jumped the back fence into a woman's yard. She was unloading laundry baskets from the trunk of her car when Krazy snatched her by the back of her neck and put his hand over her mouth.

"Shhh," he whispered into her ear. He shoved her into the side door of the house and walked her into the living room. "Look, bitch, I'm not going to hurt you so long as you do as I say." Krazy released his hand from her mouth, then put his finger to his mouth. "Who else is in the house?"

"Just me," the woman said in a light voice. She was absolutely terrified. She thought Krazy was going to rape her.

"Turn the news on, then have a seat," ordered Krazy. He walked over to the curtains and peeked out at the street. Cars were flying up and down the street, and Krazy could hear a ghetto bird looming over the area.

"Shit," Krazy said, letting go of the curtain. He realized that he was trapped. It would be a matter of minutes before the Feds had the house surrounded once they used a K-9 unit to track Krazy's scent.

The woman he held hostage had to be in her fifties. She sat on the edge of the sofa watching Krazy pace the floor while talking to himself.

"Bitch! Ain't no need in watching me. What the news talking 'bout?"

The woman used the remote to turn up the volume. The Channel 7 News was broadcasting live from the ghetto bird. They showed an aerial view of Krazy's neighborhood, and then a mug shot of Krazy flashed across the screen. The woman nearly shit herself after seeing what Krazy was wanted for.

"They're lying," he said calmly.

The camera from the chopper zoomed in on the K-9 unit as a pack of DEA agents tailed the German shepherd down the alley where Krazy had killed the agent.

"Come here, get up!" Krazy rag dolled the woman to her feet and led her over to the bay window in the living room. Using her as a shield, Krazy peeked through the curtains. His heart sank at the sight of the vans and cars pulling up to the house. Agents and the Detroit task force jumped out of their vehicles with their guns drawn, positioning themselves behind car doors, parked cars, and trees.

"Please let me go. I have two kids to look after," the woman pleaded with tears in her eyes.

"We gon' die together, bitch," said Krazy. He knew it was over for him, and there was no way he was going to let them take him alive!

One of the agents got on the bullhorn loud speaker and ordered Krazy out. "We know you're in there. We have the house surrounded. This is your one and final warning to come out with your hands up in the air!"

Krazy pushed the woman in her back toward the front door. "Open it up!" he ordered. Krazy held his .44 to the woman's temple as they stepped out onto the small porch.

"Put the gun down!" ordered the agent calling the shots. All that could be heard were the other agents racking their guns and taking aim at Krazy. The lead agent waved them to stand down. He didn't want to have an innocent woman killed.

"Y'all wanted me! Well, here I am!" yelled Krazy. "We holdin' court right here!"

"Son, please put the gun down. We can talk about this," pleaded the agent.

"So now you wanna talk. Just a minute ago you was giving me a final warning. Fuck that, we ain't got shit to talk about. I'm not going back!" Krazy pressed the barrel deep against the woman's temple, then squeezed the trigger. Blaw! Her brains splattered all over Krazy's face, and before the blood could ooze down, he turned the gun on himself and blew his own brains out. Blaw!

Krazy kept true to his word. They'd never take him alive.

Chapter Forty-six

Wink and Armeeah settled in at Caesar's where Culpepper had the timeshare. Wink carried all of Armeeah's bags back to their condo after a four-hour shopping spree. Armeeah bought a whole new wardrobe, along with shoes and handbags. Little did she know, she was going to need it.

"Thank you, baby," she said, wrapping her arms around Wink's neck and pulling him close to her for a kiss.

"You're welcome," Wink said, sounding distant.

"Wayne, what is wrong? You've been in your own world since we got on the plane. And then you didn't even buy yourself any clothes. Talk to me. What's wrong?"

Wink took a deep breath and reached for Armeeah's hands. He led her over to the bed and sat her down. "Meeah, I got something to tell you, and I want you to listen and try to stay calm."

"Okay, Wayne, what is it?"

"Mr. Culpepper told me that the Feds have indicted me along with some others."

Armeeah let go of Wink's hand. She folded her arms and went into attitude mode. "So this isn't a vacation? We're hiding out?" she asked, raising her voice.

"We're not hiding. I'm just waiting to hear from Culpepper that everything is cool."

"And if it's not?"

"Meeah, it's going to be all right," Wink said, sounding unsure. He could only hope for the best.

Armeeah stood up, saying, "I can't believe you would drag me here. You lied to me, and you're still not telling me everything. What is going on, Wayne?"

Wink closed his eyes and lay back on the bed. "Not now, Meeah."

"Then when, Wayne? When?" she shouted.

Wink sprang from the bed and grabbed Armeeah up by the collar of her shirt. With rage in his eyes, he spoke through clenched teeth. "You act like I wanted this. You act as if I haven't done everything I could to prevent this. I'm not out there in the streets. Every night, where am I? In bed, lying beside you. And when I'm not home, I'm at the clubs trying to get things straight for our future. I don't know what the Feds want with me. But like I said, we're gonna wait for Mr. Culpepper to say it's cool to come back."

Armeeah was balled up with her arm blocking her face. She was in fear that Wink might hit her, because she had never seen him nut up like this before.

He released his grip from her collar, then walked over to the patio window. Wink slid the glass door open and stepped out onto the balcony. The sun had just set, but the night air was still warm. Wink leaned over the metal railing and gazed out into the distance of the desert behind the hotel. "Why now?" he asked God. "Why now, after I left the game alone?" Wink knew the answer. It was always like that. There weren't but two ways to leave the game: in either handcuffs or a casket. There was no such thing as gangster retirement.

Armeeah gave Wink a few minutes to calm down before following him out onto the balcony. She walked up behind him and wrapped her arms around his chest, burying her face into his back. "I'm sorry," she said after a long moment.

Wink kissed the back of her hands, then turned around to face her. "No, I'm sorry. I should have never taken this out on you," Wink said while caressing Armeeah's hair.

Her eyes fell to the floor, and still, uncertainty filled her mind.

"Meeah, I know this isn't easy, but I need you to be strong with me. That's the only way we'll make it through this, if we stay strong together."

Armeeah nodded in agreement. Her mind was racing with thoughts of their wedding, their son, their life. Would they even have a life together after this? She wanted to ask Wink a lot of things, like exactly what the government was charging him with and how much time he was facing. But she didn't want to further upset him. She could tell that Wink didn't want to think about it either.

Wink pulled Armeeah into his arms, and together they turned to face the desert. "We'll make it through this. I promise," Wink said, looking out on the horizon. He needed Armeeah to believe it so that maybe he could start to believe it as well. He had no idea that the Feds had caught Krazy and that he'd killed himself. For the first time since he'd gotten on the plane and left, Wink thought about Krazy. He had been so concerned with getting Armeeah out of Detroit that he'd forgotten about Krazy. He was supposed to call him again before they left to put him on point about the roundup the Feds had planned for the morning. All Wink could do now was hope that Krazy was okay. Knowing him, he was straight.

Wink tried to convince himself that Krazy was all right, because he didn't need that on his conscience. He was already dealing with more than enough stress. Wink lay in bed staring at the ceiling. Armeeah was fast asleep beside him. It was 1:30 in the morning. He decided that in the morning he'd call Culpepper and see what the word was. See if things were as bad as they seemed. He rolled onto his side and wrapped his arm around Armeeah's waist. Wink closed his eyes and tried to find peace. *Maybe when I wake up, it'll all have been a dream.*

The next morning Wink woke up and Armeeah was gone. He frantically searched around the condo for her. He ran down to the casino lobby, but there was no sign of her.

Wink rushed over to the front desk and asked the receptionist if she'd seen Armeeah.

"I'm sorry, sir."

Wink slammed both his hands on the counter, and then turned to face the casino. "Thank you," he told the woman without looking back. He walked back to the elevators and rode up to the twenty-ninth floor. "She wouldn't leave me. Not like this," Wink told himself. The elevator stopped on his floor. He power walked back to his condo, praying, wishing, and hoping Armeeah would be there when he opened up the door.

"Meeah! Baby, are you in here?" Wink called out. His voice was full of hurt and pain. His eyes watered from the disbelief that she was really gone. Wink took a seat on the sofa in the living room. He buried his face in his hands. *It's too much for her. She's pregnant.*

"Fuck!" Wink roared as he jumped from the sofa. He raised his foot high in the air and stomped down on the glass coffee table, shattering it to pieces. He grabbed a vase from the mantle and crashed it against the balcony window, busting glass everywhere. "Ahhh!" Wink growled as he threw hurling punches at the air. He had snapped. There was no reason good enough to leave him, not like this.

Wink took deep breaths to calm himself. He sat down and closed his eyes and focused on his breathing. When he reached for the phone, he saw a note Armeeah had left on a little pink sticky pad. It was stuck to the wall next to the phone.

> *Wayne,*
> *I am so sorry, but I just can't deal with this right now. I can't live a life on the run with our son. I love you, but I can't. I will be at my parents' house.*
> *Love,*
> *Armeeah*

Wink snatched the note from the wall and tore it into pieces. "This is all I'm worth, a fuckin' note?" he asked, looking down at the torn pieces of paper. He snatched the phone from the hook and dialed Culpepper's office number. "Put me through to Otis Culpepper."

"One moment, please," said the secretary.

A few moments later Culpepper took the call. "Otis Culpepper here."

"Give it to me," Wink said. He was twirling the phone cord around his finger nervously, anticipating the worst.

"Well," Culpepper sighed, "they made all their round-ups yesterday morning with the exception of you. I'm looking at a bench warrant on my desk right now signed by Judge Rosen for your arrest."

"What am I looking at, Pepp?" Wink cut him short of the BS.

"At least life."

That four-letter word hit Wink like a ton of bricks. He slumped over and rubbed his face. "Life!" he repeated. "For what? I ain't killed nobody. How they gon' give me life?"

"Now you calm down. You know as long as I'm breathing and able to fight, I'm not going to let that happen. Do you hear me?" Culpepper yelled in a father's tone of voice. He knew Wink needed that reassurance.

"Yeah, I hear you," Wink said in a low, not-so-sure tone.

"That's what you're facing right now. I'm never going to lie to you, but if you give me some time, I can get things sorted out to where they need to be. I have to first get all your discovery and see what the government has against you."

"How long will that take?"

"At least four months, if not longer, but with you not in custody the government won't divulge any information. In time I'll be able to get it."

"That's too long," said Wink.

"No, I'm going to tell you what's too long. Life! And I'm talking about all capitals. You keep your ass put and allow me to fight!"

There was a long pause. It was as if Culpepper knew exactly what Wink was thinking. He knew him like a father knew his own son. He could tell Wink was itching to get back to Detroit and take matters into his own hands.

"How's Armeeah? Did you explain everything to her?" asked Culpepper.

"Yeah. And when I woke up this morning she was gone."

"Gone where?"

"Back home to her parents' house."

"Wayne, I'm sorry." Culpepper could hear the defeat in Wink's voice. "You listen. I don't want you doing anything ridiculous, like trying to go after her. Let me talk to her. She's just scared, that's all."

"Pepp, I can't do no life sentence."

"And you won't. Just sit tight, and let me do some digging. I'll stop by her parents' house and talk to her. In the meantime, stay put. How are you on cash? You need anything?"

"I'm all right."

"Good. Let me make some calls. I'll check back with you in a couple hours."

"All right. In a minute." Click.

Wink had no intention of sitting in some condo thousands of miles away while everyone else tried to sort through his life. The only reason he had even gone to Vegas was on the strength of Armeeah and their unborn son. But now that she was gone, he couldn't see himself hiding in a rathole while some crackers sat around downtown at the federal building plotting out his fate. It wouldn't happen.

Wink grabbed up the duffle bag with the money and started strapping all he could to his legs and chest. The rest he would wire to Culpepper. Wink called the front desk and ordered a cab to take him to the Greyhound bus station. He figured if the indictments had already come down, a bus would be safer than the airport even with the fake ID that Culpepper had given him.

He arrived at the bus station and bought a one-way ticket back to Detroit. As he boarded the bus, his gut told him that he was making a mistake and that he should stay. But his pride kept him on the bus. He reclined in his chair and closed his eyes as the bus began filling up. Within minutes they were leaving the terminal.

Chapter Forty-seven

When Wink made it back to Detroit, the first thing he did was buy a copy of the *Detroit Free Press*. He tucked the paper under his arm as he walked through the downtown Greyhound bus station. He slid into the back of a yellow Checker cab and passed the driver a twenty.

"Where to?" asked the driver.

"Just drive. I'll let you know," said Wink.

The cab pulled away from the curb, and Wink unfolded the newspaper. They had a picture of him blown up from the night of Krazy's homecoming party. Wink didn't bother worrying about how they got the photo. He wanted the rundown. The paper read:

> $10,000 REWARD SET FOR KINGPIN.
> *The government is offering a $10,000 reward for information leading to the arrest of Wayne "Wink" Fisher.*

"Who the hell is Fisher?" They had his name wrong.

> *Fisher is accused of conspiracy to distribute cocaine into the streets of Detroit, among other major cities. He's also facing tax evasion charges. Detroit Police are now saying that Fisher may be connected to the slaying of two police officers and the infamous drug lord "T-Money," who was found murdered in his St. Clair Shores home.*

Special Agent Robert J. Defauw of the Detroit DEA office says that it is imperative Fisher is taken off the streets. "Anyone with information about the fugitive should contact either my office at 313-555-7290 or the narcotic units of the Detroit Police at 313-555-4323," Defauw said. "I will personally see to it that the identity of persons giving information will be kept secret."

Wink turned to the next page to where the story continued. He sank low in his seat with his mouth agape and tears welling in his eyes. There was a photo of Krazy and beside it, the caption read, "Gunman kills hostage, then turns gun on himself, committing suicide."

That was the blow of all blows. Wink immediately started blaming himself for not taking Krazy to Vegas with him.

The stubby Arab tapped the meter as it neared $20. "Where to, my friend?" he asked.

Wink gave him a hundred to calm his nerves, along with the directions to Culpepper's office. Wink sat back and glared out the window with pure hatred in his eyes. *These crackers are trying to take everything away from me.*

When they arrived, Wink told the cab to wait and keep the meter going. He got out and walked inside the Penobscot Building in downtown Detroit. He went unnoticed as he made his way through the lobby and over to the elevators. He rode the elevator up to the eighth floor and stormed inside the law offices of Lustic, Zimser & Culpepper.

"Sir, sir, you cannot go in there. Mr. Culpepper is in a meeting," the secretary lied. Wink barged past her desk and straight into Culpepper's office.

"It's okay, Sue," said Mr. Culpepper.

"Are you sure? I can call security."

"Sue, I said it's okay. Now close the door please."

Sue rolled her eyes behind her thick bifocals as she closed the door. As soon as the door caught, Culpepper snapped, "Goddamn you, Wayne! What are you doing here?"

"Fuck all that!" Wink snapped back. He threw the newspaper across Culpepper's desk. It was folded to the story about Krazy. "And don't stand there and tell me you didn't know," said Wink. He had tears in his eyes.

Culpepper looked at the paper, then set it back down. "Yeah, of course I knew," he said.

"Then why didn't you say something?"

"Because I knew you'd do exactly what you're doing right now. Worrying about everyone else except you! Do you want to end up like your friend? Do you?" yelled Culpepper.

"No."

"Then I suggest you find your way back to Las Vegas, because right now these cops are thirsty for your blood. They want revenge for their partners, and I don't want to see them kill you, Wayne."

"I'm not going back to Vegas."

"Dammit. You're just like your father, bullheaded as all get-out."

"You leave my father out of this. Now what I need from you are the names and addresses of whoever's linking me to this bullshit conspiracy."

"What are you going to do?"

"You know the answer to that. What do you think, I'm going to crawl under a rock and hide while these crackers build a case on me? Fuck no. Niggas need to start dying and fast!"

"You want the names?" Culpepper slammed open a file cabinet behind him and started digging through some files. "You want the names, huh?" he asked again, pulling some papers from an accordion file. He slapped them down for Wink to read. "I just got those right after I got off the phone with you. That's the only name they'll need to convict you."

Wink fell into one of the chairs in front of Culpepper's desk. It couldn't get any worse than this. Wink was holding thirty-two pages of wiretaps, statements, and debriefings made by his best friend Willie. Wink read each and every word of the wiretaps in total disbelief. It was like he and Willie were sitting face-to-face having a conversation.

"He's been snitching for years," Culpepper said as he walked over to the minibar beneath another row of file cabinets. He poured brandy for them both, then continued, "He got caught moving some coke through Memphis, and he's been cooperating ever since."

"Where is he now?" asked Wink.

"Willie is in protective custody over at Wayne County. He went on the run for a while, but they caught him yesterday down in Mississippi. Him and his cousin."

Ball, Wink thought.

"And yes, he's cooperating, too. They have you distributing over five hundred kilograms of cocaine over a five-year span. And I'm sure they'll tack on more as time goes on and with the more people who agree to testify against you."

"This is too much," said Wink. He set Willie's statements on the desk and leaned back in his chair. "You mean to tell me the government can know I'm selling drugs, catch me in the act, but don't arrest me?"

"They make the laws to break the law. But that's where I come in. Right now people and police are screaming for blood. It's called politics. You need to give it some time. Allow someone else to become public enemy number one. Then and only then will I be able to start negotiating."

"Negotiating what? I hope you don't think I'm going to prison, Pepp. They haven't caught me with a gram."

"You and over a hundred thousand others who are spread over the federal system serving time. I'm going to keep it honest with you, Wayne, you're going to go to prison, but for how long depends on you."

Wink didn't want to believe it. He didn't want to believe any of it, that Krazy was dead and Willie was a rat. But it was real, and it wasn't going away.

"Just give me some time to work it all out."

"All right, I'ma give you two weeks to work it out. Then I'ma work it out," Wink said.

"Two weeks? You can't be serious."

"Two weeks." Wink let the door slam on his way out.

"You have yourself a nice day," the secretary said to Wink's back as he stormed out of the office.

Wink told his cab to drive him to the club on Livernois. He knew that Bazzi would be either there or at the club on Central, hard at work. Wink couldn't believe it was Willie. All this time he'd been thinking it was Trey who had him caught up with the Feds. That was the main reason Wink had killed Trey, because he was making things hot. Willie's rat ass was right where he needed to be: in protective custody. And that's where he'd better stay, because if Wink got hold of him, God wouldn't be able to save him.

Just as Wink thought, Bazzi was working on the renovations at the club on Livernois. Wink told the cab to park beside Bazzi's Benz and to wait while he ran inside. Wink found Bazzi sanding the top of the old bar counter. He had his back to the door, so he didn't see Wink walk in.

"You act like you know what you're doing," Wink said, walking around the bar.

Bazzi set the sander down and tore off his mask, then rushed over to hug Wink. He hugged Wink like they were long-lost brothers. "I saw the news. Are you okay?"

"Yeah, I'm good."

"Come on, let's go in the office," said Bazzi. "Cash, how much you need?" he said as he closed the office door.

"I'm straight. But thanks. Have you seen Armeeah?"

"Yeah."

"How is she?"

"A nervous wreck. She's worried that you're going to get life and your baby will grow up without a father."

"I can't allow that to happen, Bazzi."

"So what are you going to do? You know the Feds are crawling all around looking for you."

"Yeah, I know. I'm going to wait and see what my lawyer can do, and then I don't know," Wink said.

"Well, you need a place to stay. You can't be out here in the streets. Here." Bazzi tossed Wink his keys. "You remember where I live, right?"

"Yeah."

"Those are my house keys. It's all yours for as long as you need it."

"What about your wife and kids?"

"She left me, took the kids and the dog too."

"Man, I'm sorry," said Wink.

"No, I'm all right, it's you I'm worried about. Lie low until your lawyer can work his hand. I'll stop by in the morning to check on you."

"Can you—"

Bazzi raised his hand, cutting Wink off. "I'll pick her up in the morning and bring her with me. Now go on and get out of here."

"Thanks, Bazzi."

"You can thank me later. Just be careful."

Chapter Forty-eight

Wink spent the night at Bazzi's home in Dearborn. He slept out in the living room on the floor because he wanted to be right there when Armeeah walked through the door in the morning. He wanted to wrap her up into his arms and hold her until she knew that everything was going to be all right.

Wink woke up early and caught the Channel 4 Action News. Agent Defauw had held a press conference in front of the federal building the day before. He vowed to catch Wink.

"Fuck you, cracker. You gon' have to catch me," Wink said as he flipped through the channels. He stopped on an old rerun of *What's Happening!!* As soon as he started to get into the show, there was a knock at the door. Wink jumped from the floor and raced over to the front door. He was excited thinking that it was Armeeah. Wink looked through the peephole at a middle-aged white man who was wearing a Comcast jacket and hat. He was jotting something down on his clipboard.

Bazzi ain't say nothing about no cable man. He looked past the man at the Comcast van parked in the driveway. The van was definitely the real McCoy, but still Wink was hesitant. The man looked up from his clipboard and knocked again, this time harder and longer.

Wink unlocked the door and opened it, leaving the screen between them.

"Sorry if I woke you. I'm here to take a look at your box," the man said, smiling.

"Nah, you didn't wake me. I was in the kitchen," Wink lied. He opened the screen door.

"Well, I'm glad you're home, because I would have hated to have to reschedule." The man stepped inside the house. He pointed to the fifty-five-inch TV and asked, "Is this your main box?"

Wink followed the man close. "I believe so."

In midstride the man spun around with his gun to Wink's face. "DEA! Get down on the ground now!" the man yelled. He was shaking with the gun gripped tight by both hands.

Wink was stuck. *This can't be happening. How did they find me?* Wink didn't know whether to try to run or try his hand with ol' boy.

"I'm warning you, get down." The man was calmer this time. He had this look in his eyes that said he wanted Wink to resist so he could kill him.

Wink reluctantly bent at the knee and slowly raised his hands high above his head. The front door came crashing down, and in came more agents, all with their guns drawn. One of them kicked Wink hard in his back, sending him to the floor face-first. They cuffed him up, then sat him on the sofa. They took turns slapping fire out of his face.

"You lucky if we don't kill your ass," one of the agents hissed in Wink's ear.

Those agents wanted nothing more than to kill Wink as revenge for their fellow DEA agents who Krazy murdered in cold blood. Wink sat there dazed from being slapped to death. He was kind of wishing now that they would off him so he wouldn't have to deal with the consequences. Wink could see his father stranded at Leavenworth USP serving two life sentences. He dreaded the thought of it being him.

As the agents sat around trying to geek one another up to kill Wink, the front door opened and Agent Hornberger, along with U.S. Attorney Gillman, stepped inside. "Stand him up!" ordered Gillman.

Two agents snatched Wink to his feet and held him by the arm while Gillman got nose to nose with him. "I'm giving you one chance to help yourself," Gillman said.

Wink hawked spit in Gillman's face and cracked a wide smirk as the spit oozed down the side of Gillman's face.

Agent Hornberger had to grab Gillman to keep him from getting to Wink. "Get him out of here!" Hornberger yelled at the agents.

"Gladly," one of the agents said. They rushed Wink out-side and into the back of a waiting black van. Wink was thrown into the van head-first, and then the van, along with a caravan of agents, raced Wink over to the federal court building in downtown Detroit.

Agent Defauw, along with a slew of reporters, waited for Wink at the curb in front of the courthouse. The van pulled up and stopped right in front of the reporters.

"You ready, shit face?" one of the agents asked as he got out and walked around to open Wink's door. "It's show time!" said the agent. He and his partner snatched Wink out of the van and held him there for the cameras.

The reporters were firing questions at Wink.

"Sir, is it true you're the infamous Wink?"

"Did you kill street boss T-Money?"

"Will you cooperate with authorities?"

Agent Defauw gave a nod for the agents to take Wink inside. Still, they walked extra slowly for the cameras. They wanted the world to know that they had caught the man connected to the murders of their partners.

Once inside the courthouse, Wink was taken to the sixth floor, where the U.S. Marshals were stationed. He was fingerprinted, had his picture taken, and was put in one of the ice-cold holding tanks.

"Get comfortable, 'cause you'll be here for a long time," said the Marshal. He jerked the bars to make sure the gate was locked. Wink had a feeling he was talking about prison altogether. He could never get comfortable in a place like that. He hated jail. He heard the door at the end of the hall slam shut. It sounded like the end of the world to Wink. He was left all alone. Wink started shivering. The air conditioning was on full blast.

Wink looked up at the air vent, then tucked his arms in his sleeves. He began pacing the floor while racking his brain on how he could beat this. Wink thought of Culpepper. *Where the hell are you?* He knew that Culpepper had heard the news and that he should be down to see him any minute. He thought about what Culpepper had told him yesterday at his office, how the government would only bargain if Wink had his freedom as a chip, turning himself in for a specific deal, but that was all out the window now.

Wink heard the door at the end of the hall click open then close. He could hear the taps from someone's shoes grow louder as the person neared the holding cell.

"Open four!" Agent Defauw hollered back at the Marshal working inside the control booth. The gate buzzed then clicked open. Defauw pushed the gate open, stepped inside, then closed the gate behind him. He walked to the middle of the floor and stopped. He stood with his arms folded high across his chest. He smirked as he stared Wink in his eyes.

"That took some balls, you spitting in Gillman's face. Hell, I've been meaning to do so myself. Guess I never got around to it." Defauw's smile relaxed, and he took on his normal hard-nosed look.

"What do you people want from me?" Wink growled. He took his arms out of his sleeves.

"I told you what I wanted. Franko and his Cuban cartel family."

Wink turned and walked to the back of the cell, then back to where Defauw stood. "I'm not a snitch," said Wink. He glared into Defauw's black eyes, searching for any sign of leniency. But he saw only the dark soul of a heartless cracker.

"If you're not a snitch, then what are you?" asked Defauw.

"What?" Wink asked.

"If you're not a snitch, then what are you?" Defauw was playing word games with Wink. "You're thinking about it. Right now you're considering cooperating, but you're afraid of what everyone will think."

Wink stared at the floor as if what Defauw was saying had some effect on him.

Defauw took a few steps closer and spoke directly into Wink's ear. "Picture your father, Wink, and ask yourself, do you want that to be you? You're not a snitch, and I understand that. I know where you come from and the code of honor you were brought up under. But let me tell you, Wink, that stuff means nothing now. It's every man for himself, and you have to save yourself while you still have the chance. Don't worry about Gillman. I'll smooth things over with him if you're willing to help us. There are a lot of men in federal prison right now who wished they had helped themselves when they were first offered the chance. But now it's too late. The government has turned its back on them. I know you don't believe this, but your father is one of those men."

Wink looked up from the floor into Defauw's eyes. "What do you want me to do?"

"Help me nab Franko. I've wanted him forever, and if you can help me, I would personally see to it that you won't serve a day over five years. You'll be somewhere lying back in the sun under the Marshal's witness protection program. All I need from you is a statement and for you to testify at the grand jury. I'm telling you, Wink," Defauw said, putting his hand on Wink's shoulder, "five years, and not a day more."

Wink waited until Defauw was done selling his snitch pitch, then snatched his hand from his shoulder. "I can never do that, but what you can do is call my attorney Otis W. Culpepper and let him know that his client is requesting a legal call."

Defauw turned beet red. He couldn't get his words out. "You . . . you . . ." He gave up in his effort, then stormed over to the gate for the Marshal to buzz him out. He slammed the gate shut and stormed down the hall, allowing the door to slam behind him.

Wink curled up on one of the benches with his arms tucked into his sleeves. He lay there wondering how much time he'd get if he went to trial and lost. The only thing they were interested in was snitching, and for Wink that wasn't an option. He had promised his dad that when that day came, he would hold his own. Wink had not the slightest bit of regret because it all came with the game. The only thing to do now was fight.

A half hour later, the Marshal hollered from the end of the hall, "You have a legal visit!" The gate buzzed and Wink stepped out. He power walked down the long hall past the Marshal and into the small attorney-client booth where Mr. Culpepper was waiting. Wink let the door slam hard.

"What took you so long?" he asked.

"Oh, no you don't. Had you listened to me, you wouldn't be in this mess. So don't you go trying to shift blame on me." Culpepper was heated. It was going to be even harder fighting with Wink already in jail. He needed the extra leverage. "Have a seat."

"I'll stand." Wink's stomach was in too many knots to sit down. He paced the small booth while occasionally giving Culpepper a glance as he spoke.

"We're not going to cry over spilled milk. What's done is done. We're just going to have to prepare our fight, because they're going to pull out all the tricks now that you're in custody."

"What about a bond?"

"You'll be denied at your arraignment, which is in about a half hour. Be prepared to sit awhile."

"And what's awhile, Pepp?"

"At least a few months while we work this thing out."

Wink dropped his head in defeat. "And then what?" he asked, dreading the answer.

"At least twenty if not thirty years. That's if I can get them to agree to such a deal."

"Fuck that. We might as well go to trial."

"One thing at a time. Don't be in any rush, and let me work my end." Culpepper started gathering his papers into his briefcase. He stood up after closing the latches and peered through the small holes of the visiting screen. "I might as well tell you this now."

"What is it?"

"It was your business partner on the clubs who turned you in. Besides the reward, I imagine he wanted you out of the way so he could beat you out of your end of things." Culpepper watched the disbelief and hurt register in Wink's face. He had seen the look a thousand times in his clients' faces whenever they found out a close friend or family member had crossed them. Culpepper leaned against the door and said with tears in his eyes, "I'll see you upstairs in a few."

Wink collapsed into the plastic chair. How could Bazzi play him like that? It wasn't even about the money, because if he needed something, all he had to do was ask. Wink was starting to see that Bazzi and the rest of Armeeah's family didn't care anything about his black ass. He could get life for all they cared. He was starting to question Armeeah's loyalty. He understood that she was scared, but fuck that! She was supposed to be there when nobody else was. This was the part of the game nobody wanted to deal with: the flip side.

Just as Culpepper said, the magistrate denied Wink any possibility of receiving a bond. The hearing was all rigged up, and it didn't last but five minutes. The government told the court that Wink was a potential flight risk and a danger to the community. He didn't stand a chance.

As the Marshals ushered Wink out of the courtroom, Culpepper hollered, "I'll see you over at the jail."

Damn, jail, Wink thought on his way out of the courtroom. *This shit is real.* Not a soul was there to support Wink. The gallery behind the defense table was vacant. Not Armeeah, his mom, nobody was there on Wink's behalf. And that hurt more than going to jail itself.

The Marshals shoved Wink into the back seat of a tinted silver van beneath the courthouse, and within minutes they were pulling into the parking garage at the Wayne County jail.

"Home sweet home," the driver said, killing the engine.

Wink looked around at the filthy place, and his stomach turned. The Marshals escorted him inside and passed him off to one of the deputies working registry. Wink was placed in a dick-to-booty-packed, musty holding cell. He stayed for hours waiting to be printed and processed.

Wink stood with his back inches away from the wall because he didn't want to catch anything. He creased his top lip to his nose in an effort to ward off the stench rising from some of the guys in the cell. He looked around, shaking his head. He closed his eyes and prayed that when he opened them, he'd wake up from this nightmare.

Chapter Forty-nine

By the time Wink finally made it upstairs to a quarantine block, it was going on midnight. He rushed for the phone, letting his bedroll drop to the floor along the way. "Damn," he mumbled. He pressed the receiver down repeatedly, searching for a dial tone. He ran his fingers across the buttons, but nothing.

"Phone is off until the morning."

Wink hung the phone up and turned around. He nodded at the older black man who sat propped up on the first bottom bunk. The man watched Wink as he scanned the block, looking for a place to get situated. All the bunks were occupied with either dopefiends detoxing or niggas who couldn't make bond.

"You gon' have to pull out one of them tubs," said the man, pointing to the long blue plastic tubs underneath the bunks. They were actually trays used at the morgue to transport dead bodies, but Wayne County was using them as beds whenever the jail was overcrowded.

"Nah, I'm straight," Wink said, looking at the filthy tubs. He took a seat on one of the stainless-steel tables, facing the old man.

"You look familiar. Weren't you in the paper the other day?"

Wink looked at the old man and shook his head no.

"Sure looked like you, anyway. I'm Mr. Rank, but everybody calls me Pops. If you need anything, don't hesitate to ask, and if you wanna shower, my shower shoes are right under the bed. I'ma lay my old bones down. See ya in the morning."

"Thank you," Wink said with a nod. But looking at the crust caked up at the heels of his feet, Wink knew he'd pass on them shower shoes. Everybody on the block was asleep. They all looked so peaceful, like they were right at home, especially ol' Pops.

Wink wondered what they all had done to get there. Whatever it was, he was almost certain none of them were facing life sentences. For a moment, Wink wished he were one of those dopefiends lying there shaking, any one of them.

Wink sat up all night until breakfast. He told ol' Pops that he could have his due: milk, orange juice, cereal, and pastry.

"It'll be right here when you get hungry," said Pops. He put Wink's food to the side for him because he knew that was Wink in the newspaper, and he knew that Wink wasn't going anywhere anytime soon. Eventually his stomach would start touching his back.

Wink clutched the phone, waiting for the deputy working control to turn the phones on. Finally, Wink got a dial tone. The first person he called was Mr. Culpepper.

"Hello," Culpepper said in a groggy tone. He rolled over and looked at the clock while the county's phone went through the automated system. "Do you know what time it is?" Culpepper asked after he pushed 5 to accept the call.

"Yeah, time to get up and start fighting to get me out of here," Wink said as he muffled the phone with his hand and talked real low.

"Wayne, you've only been in there not even twenty-four hours."

"And how much time have you done?"

"I have never broken the law."

"You mean you've never been caught."

"Same thing. Anyhow, listen, I'm about to get up now and head down to my office. I'm going to make some calls. You'll be all right before the day's out, trust me."

"What, you plan on getting me out of here?"

"I wouldn't go so far as to say that, but you'll at least be comfortable. I will be to see you tomorrow after I leave court."

"Pepp, don't leave me in here, man. I will pay you double if you drop all your other cases and focus just on me."

"I can't do that, but you know that I'm going to fight my damnedest anyway for you."

"I'll throw in a Bentley."

Culpepper could see himself cruising to the office, pulling up in a cocaine white Bentley. The greed was settling in.

"Any color," Wink said.

"I'll be to see you." Culpepper didn't want to talk over the phone.

"All right, but before you go, try this number for me." Wink gave Culpepper the number of Armeeah's cell phone and waited as he tried on the three-way.

"They're not answering. I'll try again later when I get to the office. Is there anything you want me to specifically say?"

"Uh, nah, that's all right. We'll try again later on," Wink said.

"Hey, don't let it stress you. It gets better with time, you hear me?"

"Yeah," Wink said, sounding defeated.

"All right, let me get out of here. Talk to you soon."

"Bye." Click.

Wink hung up the phone, reluctantly returning to reality. Wink thought of Armeeah. *Why are you not answering your phone?* She should have been waiting by the phone night and day until he called. He sat on top of the table and watched ol' Pops and a few young'uns play dominoes made out of State soap and Kool-Shot fruit punch drink containers. Those Kool-Shots were so strong they could die a shirt pink, so you knew what they'd do to your insides.

"You got next, young blood?" asked Pops.

"Nah, y'all go 'head. I'ma watch," said Wink. He spent the rest of the day stressing about the streets. He kept calling Culpepper at the office, using his secretary to make three-way calls to Armeeah, but she still wasn't answering.

"We can keep trying if you want," the secretary said. She felt sorry for Wink because she knew what he was going through.

"Nah, that's okay, but thank you. I have to go. They're calling my name," said Wink.

"All right, but if you need anything, make sure you call me. Mr. Culpepper told me to take all your calls and handle anything you may need taken care of."

"I will, and thank you. Bye." Click.

"Young blood, they calling us to go to a rock. Pack up your bedroll," said Pops.

"What's a rock?" asked Wink.

"It's a floor where they got TV and niggas is jailin'. Come on, hurry up, 'cause they're waiting for us."

The slider of the door opened. Wink grabbed his bedroll from the table and followed Pops out to the hall. A deputy checked their floor cards, then escorted them over to the annex.

"You gon' like it over here," ol' Pops said as they walked through the tunnel and onto the elevator. They were assigned to the third floor on the same rock. When they stepped off the elevator, Deputy Wallace took their floor cards. He put Wink in a holding tank and escorted Pops over to the rock.

Wallace was one of the cooler deps. He was on what they called "man time." He treated men as men and cowards as cowards. When dudes got on the gate and started selling wolf tickets to each other or bar fighting, Wallace would wait until night after count, then bring the dude off his rock so y'all could get it in. The only catch was the loser went to the hole. Wallace was also good friends with Culpepper. He got the word that Wink was official and to bless him while he was down there.

"You Wink, right?" Wallace asked.

"What's up?" Wink was reluctant because he didn't know who Wallace was.

"Culpepper called me last night and told me you were here. He's an old friend of mine, and I'll do anything for him. I got you a package here." Wallace held up two stuffed pillowcases. "Just when you run out, let me know, and I'll get you straight."

"Good lookin' out," said Wink.

"A'ight, well, let's get you over to the rock." Wallace let Wink out of the holding cell and handed him the two heavy pillowcases.

"You hungry?" asked Wallace.

"Hell, yeah." Wink's stomach was on E. He hadn't eaten in damn near two days.

"I'ma bring you something back when I go out for lunch." Wallace stood at the control gate and let Wink onto his rock.

The rock was a ten-man unit with five bunk beds out in the open area. It was cool though, because there were only four people on the rock, including Wink.

"I see you know some people," ol' Pops said. His bunk was right next to Wink's.

"Yeah," said Wink. He emptied one of the cases onto his bed. Wallace had laced him with everything from Newports to Doritos. Wink opened the other case, and right at the top was a brand-new cell phone. He looked over at Pops, then hurried up and tucked the phone into his waistband. Wink left the rest of the stuff sprawled out across the bunk while he rushed over to the bathroom stall. He put the makeshift curtain up, then kneeled down beside the toilet.

Wink turned the water on so no one could hear him on the phone. He tried calling Armeeah's cell number again, but she still wasn't answering. He called information and got her parents' home number. His stomach turned as the phone rang.

"Hello," a little girl answered.

"Daaimah, is that you?" Wink smiled, thinking of Armeeah's little sister.

"Yes. Who is this?"

"It's me, Wayne. Is Armeeah there with you?"

There was a long pause of silence.

"Daaimah, are you there?"

The phone went dead. It sounded like someone pressed their finger down on the receiver. Wink dropped his head and slowly lowered the phone to his side. *She doesn't want to talk to me.* He had no one else to call besides his mom, and he didn't want to stress her out any more than what she was already. Armeeah was all he had. All he could do was hope she'd come around. He knew that she loved him and that it had to be her family in her ear, telling her to leave him.

He stood up and turned the water off, then walked back over to his bunk. He shoved everything back into the pillowcase, then lay down. He hadn't slept in damn near two days.

Pops had been observing Wink since they met in quarantine. He could see the stress in Wink's face, and he knew the feeling. Pops had been doing time his whole life. The first bid was always the hardest, but it all came with the game.

"Let me say something to you, young blood." Pops swung around on his bunk so he was facing Wink.

Wink stayed on his back, staring up at the top bunk. "What's up, Pops?"

"Is this your first time in jail?"

"Yeah."

"Well, son, I'ma give you the jewels that was given to me forty years ago. You can't let this time do you, 'cause it'll swallow you up if you let it. You have to leave the streets where they at, which is out there. You have to get into a bid, your bid."

"What do you mean?"

"Whatever makes your time pass without you stressing all day. Some people watch TV, others play tabletops. You might like to work out. The object is to bide your time. Occupy yourself with something other than worrying about them damn streets. I'ma let you get some rest, but when you get up, the old man gon' learn you on some Spades."

"A'ight, Pops." Wink smiled at the OG. He was right. Wink had to bide his time and accept that he was in jail and it was definitely going to be a minute.

Chapter Fifty

Ol' Pops was holding Wink down and helping him keep his mind off the streets. They played Spades, dominoes, cut-throat, tunk, Cassino, and some more shit. Pops, of course, beat the brakes off Wink in all the games. As he'd said, he was "learning" him.

But more importantly, Pops taught Wink the importance of hitting the law library. He taught him how to look up cases, Shepardize for cross-references, and even how to file pro se motions.

"Never put your faith in man. Teach yourself these white-folks' laws so when you get out, you'll do better next time. You have to know the law in order to defend yourself. No one is going to fight for you better than you." Pops was an expert on jailin'. He'd been to Jackson State Penitentiary, federal, and everywhere in between. He was what they called a jailhouse lawyer.

Wink found his bid in the law library. For the past week, all he'd done was play in the library, pulling up cases similar to his to see how the government proceeded in conspiracies. Wink learned that the Feds had a 97 percent conviction rate. It was nearly impossible to beat them at trial. When the Feds came and got you, nine times out of ten, they had you nailed to the cross. Wink was set on being part of the 3 percent who did beat the government at trial. He knew that in order to do so, he'd have to get Willie to change his statement, because without Willie, the government didn't have a case.

Wink hollered at Wallace and told him that he needed a big favor and that it would save his life.

"Name it," Wallace said with no hesitation.

"I have a codefendant over on the protective custody rock. Man, I really need to holla at him. Not on no hands or nothing like that, but just to try to talk some sense into the nigga."

"Say no more. Tonight when the lights go out, I got you."

"Good lookin', Wallace. Man, I owe you."

"I told you, Culpepper is my man, so if there's anything I can do to see you straight, it's done."

Wink couldn't wait to see the look on Willie's face when he walked through that gate with no handcuffs on and no deputies there to save him. He could see him already, scared to death.

Later on that night after count, Wallace sneaked Wink off his rock. Together they got on the elevator and took it down to the second floor, where they kept all the protective custody inmates, homosexuals, and snitches.

"You got ten minutes to do your thang," Wallace said before opening the gate to Willie's rock.

Willie was asleep when Wink silently slid his cell door open. Wink stepped into the cell and stood over Willie as his fat face snored. Wink slapped the shit out of Willie, then choked him. Willie's eyes popped wide open, registering with terror at the sight of Wink. Willie tried kicking and squirming, but to no avail. Wink had his elbows pressed deep into Willie's chest while he choked the life out of him.

"You killin' me," Willie gasped. His eyes rolled to the back of his head, and he stopped resisting.

Wink reluctantly released his death grip and stood up. Had it not been for Wallace, he would have killed Willie in there. Then he definitely wouldn't have to worry about him coming to court and testifying against him.

Willie held his neck, still struggling to breathe. As he hacked and coughed, Wink snatched him out of bed and rammed him into the back wall. "What happened to family, Willie?" Wink had tears in his eyes because he couldn't believe that Willie would actually turn on him.

"They made me do it, Wink. Man, I swear."

"How can they make you cross me? We're supposed to be brothers. How can they ever make you forget that, huh?"

Wink let Willie go, then walked to the back of the cell. He stopped back in front of Willie. "Nigga, look at me," Wink said because Willie was staring at the floor nervously. "You've been working with them people for years. Do you know how much time they're gonna give me if you go in there on me? Life, nigga."

"Wink, I'm sorry, man," Willie cried.

"Fuck being sorry, nigga. What are you gonna do when those crackers call you to testify? Tell me now. Is it going to be my life or yours?"

"Wink, I never agreed to testify on you. That's why I ran. They're holding me now 'cause of the case I caught."

"Willie, I saw yo' statements. The wiretaps, all that shit."

"Yeah, but I never said I would take the stand on you. They wanted your connect and still do. Why don't we just give up them beans-and-rice-eatin' mothafuckas? If the shoe were on the other foot, they would burn our black asses up," said Willie.

"Yeah, maybe, but that's the difference between you and me. I'm not a rat." Wink grabbed Willie up by his shirt, then growled, "I'ma send my lawyer over to holla at you. He's gon' take a statement from you so he can squash all this shit. Don't play no games, nigga. When he comes to see you, sign that statement," Wink warned.

"Man, when this is all over, we can go back to being a family. Trey's dead, and they made Krazy kill himself. It's just us. Tell me we can be a family again," said Willie.

"Of course, nigga. We gon' always be fam. That's why we can't let those crackers divide us. I love you, my nigga."

"I love you too," Willie cried.

Wink gave Willie a hug. While they hugged, Wink said into his ear, "Let's just get this behind us."

"Time up, Wink! I gotta get you back upstairs," said Wallace.

Wink ended their embrace by wiping Willie's tears from his face. "Remember, it's us against them," said Wink.

Willie nodded as the tears continued to flow down his face. Wink patted him on the shoulder, then left. Wallace closed the gate behind Wink, locking Willie in.

"You get things worked out?" asked Wallace.

"Yeah. I think he understands now." Wink felt that Willie would do the right thing by changing his statement. But Wink already had it in his mind that when the day came, he was going to kill Willie.

Chapter Fifty-one

"Have you lost your fucking mind?" snapped Culpepper as Wink walked into the small visitor booth at the county jail.

"What are you talking about?" Wink took a seat across from Culpepper.

"Tell me you didn't go over to Willie's cell last night and threaten him?"

"Nah, he says that he's willing to sign a new statement. I told him you'd be to see him."

"Well, he called the prosecutor and told him that you threatened him last night in his cell. There's a thing called witness tampering, and it carries another ten years. Now I am not even going to ask you who took you over there, but I have a pretty good feeling as to who it was. As of right now, the government hasn't made any mention of filing charges. Let's just hope it stays that way."

"What about the new statement?"

"Don't you get it? He's not changing his statement. The Marshals moved him into one of their Honeycomb Hideouts this morning. We're going to have to fight or plea out."

"Well, what have you dug up? I know you didn't come down here just to cuss me out. And I'm not pleading out."

"No. I came to tell you that I might be able to work out a deal. You have to be reasonable here, Wayne."

"What kind of deal? I hope it's not no crazy numbers."

"That's why I wanted to give you this." Culpepper reached inside his briefcase and handed Wink a letter from his father.

"Read it once you get back. I have to get going. I have court in an hour. But I will see you in a couple of days to let you know the specifics. You think you can stay out of trouble until then?"

Wink was looking at his dad's handwriting on the envelope. "Yeah, I can do that."

Culpepper stood up and pressed the buzzer for the deputy to let him out. "Hold your head up, and call me if you need something," Culpepper said on his way out.

The deputy let Culpepper onto the visitor elevator, then came back to escort Wink to his rock.

Wink tore at the seal of the envelope and sat on the edge of his bunk while he read his dad's letter.

Dear Son,

Words can't begin to express the hurt and pain that I am going through knowing where you are. Insha Allah we'll get through this together, because, son, I love you. I know that I've never told you that before, but I do love you. Always have and always will.

Wayne, I need you to listen to me, and I mean listen good. You're up against the world right now. The deck is stacking against you with everybody trying to save themselves. I don't want to see you end up like me, in here with two life sentences and all appeals shot. Son, I am never coming home. I am going to die in here. My release date says, "Deceased!" What you're going through is real, and these people are playing for keeps. When I caught my case twenty-two years ago, they offered me a deal for twenty years with no chance at early

*parole. I didn't take it. I thought that they had
nothing on me and that I would beat them at trial.
I lost, and now look at me. I would have been home
two years ago. Instead, I'm serving a sentence that
I'll never complete.*

*Son, listen to me. Don't make the same mistake
I made. If they offer you twenty years, take it and
be done with it. I know it's a hard pill to swallow.
Trust me, I know. But life means life. Please, son. I
love you and Insha Allah. I'll talk to you soon.*

Peace and Blessings.

Love,

"Big Wayne"

Wink felt where his dad was coming from, and he
knew that his dad didn't want to see anything happen to
him. But it was always easy for a person to say what they
wished they had done after the fact. Wink couldn't even
begin to think about swallowing twenty years in prison.

Wink thought about how his life would be twenty years
later, how old he would be, whether his mom would still
be living. And damn, his son would be 20 years old by
the time Wink got out. History was about to repeat itself
all over again. When Wink was born, his father was in
prison already. It was too much to think about. Wink
folded the letter back into the envelope, then lay down.

"I see you're back on that trip, stressing. What's the
matter, young blood?" asked Pops. He was sitting on his
bunk across from Wink.

Wink passed Pops the letter and closed his eyes. After
Pops finished reading the letter, he told Wink exactly
what he didn't want to hear.

"Listen to your father, 'cause he knows best. I am going
to tell you the same thing after reading your case over
and seeing all the people set to testify against you. It

doesn't look good, young blood. It never does for us men. We die while the worms live. But you know what, that's the cost of being a stand-up guy. Listen to your father. If they offer you a deal, take your lumps, and move on with your life. You hear me?"

"Yeah," Wink answered dryly. He was hearing ol' Pops, and deep down he knew that he was right. But still it was easier said than done. It was like the world had turned its back on Wink, and the few who were on his side all wanted him to throw in the towel and take twenty years on the chin.

Wink didn't know what to do. *Like the old, wise saying goes, "Damned if you do and damned if you don't."* Twenty years or life: those were his options.

Chapter Fifty-two

The government sent Wink its one and final offer by way of his attorney. They were offering twenty-two years and not a day less. U.S. Attorney Gillman was still pissed about Wink spitting in his face. He would have considered maybe a flat twenty-year sentence, but he wanted Wink to pay for the assault.

Culpepper took a copy of the Rule 11 plea agreement over to the county jail so Wink could look it over. "Can't you get it any lower than that?" Wink thumbed through the plea bargain.

Culpepper shook his head no. "Trust me, they didn't want to offer you that, but Gillman and my partner Lustic go way back. He's doing this strictly as a favor to Lustic. Wayne, they want to give you life." Culpepper paused for a moment. "As your lawyer, I must give you my honest opinion about the case and not just what you want to hear. Wayne, if we take this thing to trial, I believe we'll lose."

Wink set the plea bargain down on the table and began rubbing his temples. "It's not like you to quit, Pepp," said Wink.

"And I'm not. Hell, we can go in there and line 'em up and fight to the bitter end. You know how much I like to fight. But as your lawyer and as your friend, I'm not sure if I want to take that gamble with your life, because when it's all said and done, I get to go home. All I'm telling you is what's best. Take the deal, Wayne. For me, your father, your unborn child, and for yourself. Don't regret this twenty-two years from now."

"How long do we have to make a decision?" asked Wink.

"One week and then trial, unless we file motions."

Wink sighed deeply. He rubbed his face with his hands. "Let's do it," he said through the cracks between his fingers. "Let's just get it done. The sooner the better."

Culpepper reached across and rubbed Wink on the shoulder. "You're doing the right thing, Wayne." Culpepper showed Wink where to sign his life away. He packed the plea back into his briefcase, then stood up for his coat.

"I'll try to arrange with the judge a plea hearing soon and see if we can conduct sentencing all on that day." Culpepper hit the buzzer for the deputy. "It's going to be all right."

Wink nodded with his eyes closed. He couldn't believe he'd just signed away twenty-two years of his life.

The deputy came back for Wink, then escorted him to his rock. Pops was waiting for him by their bunks. "Well, what he say?" asked Pops.

Wink curled up under his blanket. "I just signed a plea for twenty-two clocks," said Wink. "With no possibility of an early release."

"I know you don't want to hear this right now, but you did the right thing. G'on and put this behind you. I'm proud of you, too, 'cause these young niggas in this day and age aren't doing no time. They're telling like ninety going north. I know your old man will be proud of you too." Pops left Wink to his thoughts because he knew exactly what he was going through, and the best thing to do was let him be alone.

Chapter Fifty-three

Two weeks after Wink signed his plea bargain, he was standing before U.S. District Court Judge Rosen, a straight racist who firmly believed that blacks should still be slaves, which was why he took his seat on the bench so that he could lock as many blacks away as he possibly could.

Rosen often said that he would die on the bench. It had been a long time coming, and he showed no signs of slowing down yet. Today, Wink's fate he would decide. Rosen sat high on his bench while thumbing through the sixteen pages of the government's Rule 11 plea agreement. Occasionally he would grunt, then look over his specs at Wink. Rosen was determining whether he'd accept the conditions of the plea. If Rosen rejected the plea, or any part of it, Wink reserved the right to withdraw his guilty plea and proceed with trial.

Finally, Judge Rosen was ready. He took off his specs, then leaned back in his seat, looking Wink over. He wanted to see him sweat. "I have every reason to deny your guilty plea here today. Twenty-two years is not enough relief for society with the amount of damage you've caused. Prison was conceived with you in mind," said Rosen.

Wink stood beside Culpepper with his chin up and his arms folded high across his chest like he was back out on the block. He didn't care either way if Rosen accepted the plea. Wink wasn't about to beg his old ass for a twenty-two-year sentence. He kept his stare on Rosen as he went on and on about why the court should send the case to trial. Rosen wanted Wink to plead out for at least a thirty-year sentence, and even that was considered lenient in his book. He was known for giving out life sentences.

Rosen called a recess and made U.S. Attorney Gillman and Mr. Culpepper join him in his chambers. He wanted to talk over the plea with them. Culpepper whispered to Wink, "This is where he wants us to kiss his ass. Don't worry, he'll accept the plea."

Wink was surrounded by Marshals during the short recess. He took a seat at the defense table and swung around in his chair to face the gallery. The only two people who came to show their support were Wink's mom and his grandmother. *Just like the old saying goes, "When it all falls down, you can always count on Momma." Everyone else is sure to fail you.*

Wink forced a smile at the two. He was happy they came, because at least it meant that somebody loved him. But Wink was hurting at the same time, because he'd never imagined in a million years that Armeeah would just leave him how she had. She'd cut all ties it seemed. Wink hadn't heard from her since they were last together in Vegas. Here his life was on the line, and she was nowhere to be found. *And to think I was going to marry you.* Wink wondered if he'd ever meet his son.

Judge Rosen was followed back into the courtroom by Gillman and Culpepper. Together they managed to convince the old fart that accepting Wink's guilty plea was beneficial to all parties, including tax payers, because it cost money to hold a trial.

Rosen settled into his seat, then cleared his throat. "This court will be reluctantly accepting the defendant's guilty plea adopting the conditions set forth. The defendant will receive a sentence of no more than 264 months, with no chance of early release or parole. The defendant understands that by this court accepting his guilty plea, he will have waived any right to appeal his conviction or attack the validity of any part of the sentence or direct appeal. Would the government like to add anything to the record before the court proceeds?" Rosen asked Gillman.

"Yes, Your Honor. The government would like to address just one issue, that the defendant is not to receive any sentence reductions after sentencing. He has not assisted the government in any investigations, and that's the way both parties intend to keep it. Nothing further."

"And would the defendant at this time wish to say anything before sentencing is imposed?" asked Rosen.

Culpepper led Wink over to the lectern and stood by his side. "Go ahead," said Culpepper.

Wink was no longer nervous, because he knew it was over. The worst was behind him. As he stood at the lectern, Wink thought back to everything he'd been through: coming up in the game under J-Bo, driving Benzes, making his first million dollars, and living in a mansion before his twenty-first birthday. *Those were the good times*. Wink grinned.

But then, of course, came the bad times. Wink closed his eyes and flashed back to killing his best friend Trey. His jaws clenched at the sound of Trey's body slumping to the floor. More pain filled Wink's heart as he thought of Krazy committing suicide. It wasn't supposed to end like this.

Hate overwhelmed him as the cause of all their downfalls crossed his mind: Willie's snitch ass.

"Would the defendant like to say something?" Rosen asked, breaking Wink from his trance.

Wink looked up at Rosen and said, "Yeah. It's a cold game, but it's fair."

Epilogue

Two days later, the Marshals picked Wink up from the Wayne County jail and drove him out to a private airport in Ann Arbor, Michigan.

"Where am I going?" Wink asked one of the Marshals as they sat waiting for the plane to land.

"To start your sentence," the Marshal seated in the passenger seat said over his shoulder.

Smart mothafucka, Wink thought. He sat back and tried to relax, but the anticipation was killing him. Here these crackers were about to put him on a plane and take him to God knows where.

"There she goes," the Marshal said, looking up at the white jet the government used to transport its inmates all around the country.

Wink sat up and watched as the plane landed and skidded down the runway. Like clockwork, the Marshals unloaded Wink from the van. Marshals working aboard the plane stood guard with their double-action shotguns. They passed Wink to the Air Marshal in exchange for some other inmates who were getting off the plane and going back to court for various reasons.

"Enjoy the next twenty-two years," the sarcastic Marshal told Wink as he climbed the steps up the plane.

Wink was afraid he might fall because the shackles around his ankles were too tight. Every step Wink took, they bit into his skin. He made it onto the plane and was ushered to a window seat by one of the Marshals.

Wink sat down, then took a look around the plane. There had to be close to 200 prisoners on the plane, all shackled at their feet and waists. Wink wondered where they could all be going. He leaned his head back and closed his eyes. *I didn't sign up for this shit.*

Within minutes, the plane was roaring down the runway and pulling back up into the air. Wink looked out the window down at the moving cars. He knew that would be the last time he'd see his home state for a long time.

The plane landed in Kansas first, at another one of the Feds' private airfields. There were a number of buses waiting to take prisoners to their designated prisons.

Wink's name was called toward the end of the list, and he was pointed to a bus after being searched by one of the Marshals. Wink boarded the semi-packed bus and took his seat. He wanted to ask one of the guys where they were going, but he didn't want to seem like he was scared. Wink did as all the other men were doing, which was staring out the window.

After the plane cleared the runway, all the buses departed the airfield, heading in different directions. Wink saw a sign that read, WELCOME TO LEAVENWORTH, KANSAS. His heart skipped a beat because he had passed that same sign several times on his way to visit his father.

The bus drove down the same back roads Wink used to get to Leavenworth USP. And sure enough, that was his destination. Wink looked at the old dungeon and shook his head. There was no doubt in his mind that the government had him sent there specifically to prove a point. They wanted him and his father to be trapped together.

"All right, everyone off the bus. When I call your name, step up and give me your register number." One of the full-blooded rednecks from the prison was standing at the front of the bus calling names. Again, Wink's was called last. He walked to the front of the bus and ran off his federal number.

"All right, welcome to Leavenworth." The CO escorted the men into R&D, where they removed the shackles and belly chains.

After the intake screening, each man was assigned to a unit and handed a sack lunch with a bedroll. The CO working R&D radioed them out to their units. Wayne Sr. was waiting out in the corridor by the commissary door. He had known for two days from the laundry list that Wink was on his way there.

Wink stopped in the middle of the corridor at the sight of his pops. He dropped the bedroll to the floor and hugged his father for all of five minutes. It was an emotional moment for them both. Wink felt like he had let his dad down. He was supposed to be the one to make it. "I'm sorry, Pops."

"It's okay, son. It's okay."

Wayne Sr. picked up Wink's bedroll and wrapped his arm around his son's neck, and together they stepped out onto the yard. Wayne Sr. introduced Wink to a few people as they walked the track, catching up on lost time.

Ol' Franko came jogging up. He stopped his workout and gave Wink a long hug for being a stand-up guy. "I want you to always remember something," said Franko. "You are who you really are in a time of crisis." Franko tapped Wink on the shoulder. "You are a man just like your father, and I'm proud of you. I'm going to let you two finish catching up. Come see me after you get settled in." Franko jogged off around the track.

"Well, this is it," Wayne Sr. said, waving his hand around at the compound. People were playing handball, some were jogging, and others played poker, while the majority of the yard watched a tournament basketball game.

"Now let me ask you something," Wayne Sr. said, then stopped.

Wink faced his dad and looked him in the eyes.

"Was it worth it, son?"

"It never is."